The Hired Gun

Book One of Benton Security Services
Christine D. Shuck
Published March 2019

Table of Contents

Blackmail Fail

Danny Witt loosened his tie, undid the top two buttons of his shirt, and let loose a huge breath. He had done it, and now he was going to celebrate. His car, a beat-up hand-me-down, started up, the engine roaring loudly.

"This time next week it'll be a Lexus, by damn!" he said, his foot heavy on the accelerator as he pulled away from the curb and headed out of the city, west towards Denver.

Blackmail was a delicate thing, but Danny had handled it with a light touch, never giving an ultimatum, just reminding his boss of how much he had to lose if the information went public. Dirty deals and fraud. Danny had found the tip of the iceberg and dug in, discovering a laundry list of inflated real estate, payoffs, and irregular cost expenditures. Even a sorry tale of investors swindled out of their money. He had taken his time, realizing the gold mine at his fingertips. Right about now, Danny was sure that his boss was ruing the day Kurgen Real Estate had hired him for the accounting job.

And at a fire sale, by God. That measly $50k a year he made at Kurgen was barely enough to cover expenses, live a little, and pay the minimum on his student loans. Those damned student loans. The college tuition, books, and campus housing had taken up the bulk of the $167k. Sure, he had taken an extra year to finish college after spending most of his first-year guzzling beer at keggers and frat parties. *Hell, that's what college is for, right? Party all night, drink a couple of V8s and sit in the back of class and hope to God the professor doesn't pick on you.*

He had lived off that government-backed loan money. Now it had come due and it cost more than his basic living expenses combined. And that was just the minimum payment!

The briefcase on the front passenger seat included a banded stack of Benjamins that he was going to make use of, living it up while spending a weekend on the slopes with several of his buddies from his alma mater, Denver University.

As he settled in on I-70, he set the cruise control and turned up the volume on the aging radio. *Maybe a Beemer instead of a Lexus. I could handle making some payments, build up my credit.*

The road was clear; he'd gotten a late start, and most of the folks heading out of town for the weekend were well on their way. The cars left on the road were sparse and well-spaced, yet Danny didn't notice the white van following at a discreet distance. His mind was busy tallying the costs for a case of Grey Goose vodka and the huge bag of weed he was planning to splurge on. That would show his frat brothers that he wasn't such a loser after all.

His buddy Zach had started a business during college that mined data for the big-time online retailers and ended up selling the company for millions last year. He had lorded it over them, and given half a chance, he told them over and over how his new company was going to sell for quintuple his investment in a few years.

Jonesy wasn't financially well-off, but he had a goddamn alpaca farm and a baby on the way, way up in some Podunk town in the Colorado mountains. He grew some fine weed on the side since alpacas didn't pay squat. The weed was in better digs than Jonesy and his woman were in. They said they loved living in a yurt.

Yeah, sure they do.

Deep in a stand of trees, well covered and hidden from prying eyes, was a large barn, outfitted with the latest in lights. Jonesy had gotten off to a rocky start, but the week before had seen the biggest harvest yet, four friggin' pounds of Sour Diesel. That asshole was in fucking hippie heaven, a friggin' off-grid paradise on earth.

Then there was Mal. Mal hadn't ever graduated, disappearing halfway through their fourth year, dropping out to travel the world and write a bestseller, by God, that everyone was talking about and reading. Mal had described the book as the biggest pile of monumental horseshit he could have possibly written. But now he was a friggin' millionaire who lived out of hotels and couch-surfed his way through Europe. And, most recently,

Australia and New Zealand, while writing about the folks he met and making an ass-ton of cash. And the load of pussy that dude got put them all to shame. It seemed that, short of being a brooding songwriter, writing a book and looking all melancholy and literate netted you more tail than you could shake a stick at.

Danny shook his head. Until the last few weeks, he had been in a depressive funk, alternating between hating his dad for insisting that he become an accountant *all because I was good at Monopoly at age fucking ten* and himself for letting the old bastard win. But following that trail of money, labyrinthine and hidden as it was, had been like winning the friggin' jackpot. He might be in a "stifling, boring job working for The Man" - as Jonesy had so aptly described it - but he was going to be fucking rich.

"Ten percent of the take, that's all I'm asking for," he said out loud to the empty car, the words lost in the roar as the car hurtled down the highway. His lips moved silently as he ran the numbers again. It would turn his salary into chump change in comparison. *Hell, I could get both a Mercedes and a Lexus. And fuck staying in that cruddy old apartment in Northeast; I'll move to a loft in downtown instead.*

He had copied all the data onto his laptop, and as a backup to the backup, he had also saved it to an SD card and his home computer. He had reassured his boss that the details of the corruption at Kurgen didn't need to be aired. Oh no, he was happy to be included in the Ponzi schemes and more; he even had suggestions on how they could better hide these corrupt transactions so that their financial misdeeds were not only nearly impossible to find, but they could be multiplied exponentially. More money for both of them. He had smiled, charmed his flustered and tense boss, and told him that this wasn't a *bad* thing, it was an *opportunity.*

Danny laughed out loud, the wind carrying it away. *Hell, I was born for this. Dear old Dad had no idea how perfect of a career this would be for me.* His dad had just wanted him out of the house. The teen years, followed by the endless college years of parties and smoking weed and playing video games had been a little too much for the old man. But he was from a different generation, after all, the generation that worked their fingers to the bone instead of making a few clicks on a computer and sitting back to rake in the dough. Dad wasn't a bad guy; he just wasn't very forward-thinking. *Ya gotta make the money work for you, Dad, not sweat all day for a dollar.*

As the hours passed and the radio stations faded into the distance, crackling with static and hiccups of voices, Danny shut the radio off, the mountains slowly rising around him, cutting off cell phone service completely until he reached a plateau of sorts. Ahead in the distance, in the thick darkness, he could see the lights from a car. It was pulled over on the side of the road.

Danny wasn't the type to stop and help. Hell, he couldn't even change a tire. But the sight of the scantily clad, hot-looking chick waving her arms at him had him hitting the brakes. He pulled over, his dented and worn Civic kicking up dust as he rolled to a stop. A friggin' IROC with a flat rear left tire was attractive enough, but the girl, with her skimpy skirt and skin-tight shimmering metallic top, barely left anything to the imagination. The Lycra hugged every tanned curve, and she bounced and smiled at him with kohl-rimmed blue eyes. Her legs were encased in boots with stiletto heels and her dark hair fell in cascades of curls past her shoulders. She walked over to his window.

"Oh my God, *thank you so much* for pulling over!" Her hair spilled over, brushing his side mirror, as a wash of Juicy Couture perfume filled his nose and he became eye-level with her tits. *Those cannot be real.* They were huge and stood out like two missiles. He leaned forward, trying to catch an eyeful of her round ass.

Danny smiled. "Hey there." *Let me just bend you over that hood there.* "Got a flat tire?"

She smiled at him, a pink tongue moistening her lips. "I do! I can't even get a tow truck to come fix it." She waved a cell phone in her left hand. "No service. I can't get a single bar up here! Could you help me?"

Danny nodded, "Uh, sure, let me see if my phone has any service. You never know, sometimes the different providers have a wider reach and all." He powered it on, checked the bars. "Well, shit."

"Maybe if you get out of the car the grade goes up a few feet." She suggested, wiggling her ass a little. Damn, but this girl was *smoking* hot. He stepped out of the car.

How hard could it be to change a tire? I'll bet if I did, she'd let me tap that sweet ass.

A few steps up didn't make a bit of difference. He tried his phone again, getting no love, not one bar of service. By then, bright beams from another vehicle lit the road up.

The headlights were set higher; perhaps it was a truck. He waved his arms and the vehicle slowed, pulling over next to them. Nope, it wasn't a truck, but a plain white van instead. The side door slid open and the dull dome light inside lit up two men, crouching on what looked like a plastic covered floor.

"Hey, would you guys be able to help change this tire?" he asked, walking towards them.

There were two loud pops like the sound of a backfiring car. Danny heard them, but didn't understand why his steps were slowing, faltering, as a bloom of red filled his shirt and searing pain obscured all rational thought. He looked down, his fingers shaking as he pulled them away from his shirt, covered in blood. He didn't understand. His legs buckled beneath him and he crumpled to the ground in a heap, legs twisting underneath, head slamming into the gravel.

He lay there, the sharp gravel digging into his back. He could see the hot chick approach, a dull gray handgun in one hand. She wasn't smiling anymore. She tilted her head, eyes assessing him, saying nothing.

Danny heard shoes crunching on gravel. "Shit, Zella, now there's blood on the ground. We needed this to be a clean hit. You couldn't wait for five more seconds, could you?" One of the men stood over him now, his eyes as cold as the woman's. "You saw the plastic was all laid out, for fuck's sake."

Above Danny, the night sky was filled with stars.

"I didn't like the way he looked at me," she said, her voice barely showing emotion.

One of them was red-hued and seemed bigger than the rest. That had to be Mars.

"Well, how did he look at you Zell?" the second man asked, appearing in Danny's line of sight.

He watched a flash of light fill the sky. He had never seen a shooting star before, but Danny was pretty sure he had just seen one now. He watched it light a path down, down, down before disappearing behind a mountain in the distance.

"Like he wanted to fuck me."

Maybe if he made a wish, it would be granted. And he would wake up and realize this was all a bad dream.

Both men laughed.

"What's so funny?" she asked, narrowing her gaze, her long, slender fingers tapping out a rhythm on the gun.

Coldness was spreading, radiating from his chest, to his arms, creeping up his fingers.

"Zella, everyone wants to fuck you," the other man said. "We just don't wanna get fuckin' murdered afterward." He turned back towards the other man. "What are those damned insects, the ones that bite off their mate's head during sex?"

"Praying mantis."

He snapped his fingers. "Yeah. That. You're a fucking praying mantis, Zella. Or a black widow. It's a wonder you ever get laid."

Zella stared at him impassively. "Whatever. He stared at my tits too long." She aimed the gun at Danny's head and pulled the trigger.

The stars turned to black.

"Damn it, Zella. You clean that shit up. Fuck if there aren't brains to clean up now. That's on you. We weren't supposed to leave any evidence. Hank and I will get the meat." He picked up Danny's legs and motioned for Hank to grab his arms. Together they hauled Danny Witt's corpse into the van and slammed the door shut.

"Heads up." the third man, still in the driver's seat of the van, said, as headlights flashed in the distance.

The first man turned to Hank. "You're up. Inflate the tire, take care of dumping the car, and then catch a ride with Zella."

"'Long as that crazy bitch don't try to waste me too," he muttered, grunting as he straightened up, checking for blood spatter on his clothes.

"I heard that." Zella was rinsing her fingers with some water from her Contigo, having tossed several handfuls of bloody gravel and a piece of skull over the edge of the precipice a few feet away. She smiled at him, her teeth gleaming in the gloom. It was a predatory and dangerous look. "Wanna see my tits?"

The man resisted a shudder even as his dick jumped in his pants at the thought of Zella's pair of perfect tits. If he ever did get to see them it would probably also be the last thing he saw before he died. Zella was like a black widow and far too crazy to mess with. "Nah, I'm good." He avoided looking in her eyes.

She grinned, baring her white teeth. Her incisors looked sharp in the moonlight.

The beams of light sliced through the night; the car was closer now. The van pulled away, a shower of gravel in its wake as it sped up, matching highway speed.

Hank turned to the business of re-inflating the IROC's tire as another car slowed down and stopped. Inside were a young couple, with two kids in the backseat. The wife rolled her window down, a bright smile on her face, "Hi there, need any help?"

"Nah, we got it handled." Hank could see Zella's hand twitching, her fingers busy caressing the handgun she held just behind her slim, muscled back.

The husband leaned forward, ogling the IROC, and Zella.

Hank closed his eyes, *oh buddy, you do not want to do that.*

"You sure?"

"Almost got it. No worries."

"Daddy, Daddy!" a small boy yelled from the back, "Deer's blood on the ground, Daddy! See all the red?"

Zella stepped closer to the car, a predatory smile painted on her face, her even white teeth gleaming. "There was a deer. It ran off."

"Oh Benny, don't look at that!" the kid's mom said. "Poor little deer."

The dad persisted; his eyes focused on Zella's tits. Her hand caressed the gun now tucked in her waistband. "I got a decent jack in the trunk."

Hank stepped forward. It was one thing to waste the target, but a whole family? Zella was itching for another round. "I got it," he said with a little more force. "Almost done."

"You heard the man, Patrick," the woman in the passenger seat said, her mouth pursed in disapproval at how her husband was staring at Zella. "He's got it. Let's go, or we won't get to my sister's until after midnight."

Hank breathed a sigh of relief when the small car, at the urging of the wife, finally pulled away.

Far from Colorado, a phone rang. The room was dark. "What is your status?"

"It's done. I got another guy taking care of the files at his apartment," Hank updated the voice on the other end.

"Excellent." The voice was smooth, emotionless. Hank could hear keys clicking in the background. "Your fee has been paid in full."

"I appreciate it." He listened as the phone line clicked. The boss didn't waste words. He nodded in Zella's direction. "Time to go."

She smiled at him. It made his skin crawl. "I'll drive."

Hank nodded and said nothing. *Next job, I'll be damned if I'm getting stuck with this crazy bitch.* He settled into the car and cinched his seatbelt into place as she accelerated, wheels spinning, engine screaming, onto the dark highway.

Slipshod

"Can I help you?" The pretty strawberry-blond girl at the reception desk was staring at him, a friendly, professional smile on her face.

Alex gulped, winded from his half-jog down the hallway outside. The ticket had specified that one of the techs needed to arrive by 10 a.m. Traffic, snarled and slow around highway construction and blocked lanes, and difficulty finding parking had meant that he was nearly forty-five minutes late.

He gaped at her; she was one of *those* kinds of girls. Her strawberry-blond hair and big blue eyes combined with a floral sheer top over a white cami and shiny gold earrings in her delicate ears. She was pretty. One of those girls who combined beauty with complete unattainability for someone like him. And he reacted to them much like Raj on *Big Bang Theory*, with a wide-eyed silence. Standing there in the office, with its high-end carpet and sleek, spotless furniture, he willed his tongue to work.

"I'm uh," he blinked, "Uh, I'm from..."

I can't even remember the name of the company. What kind of loser can't remember the name of the company they work for?

It was Alex's third week, the training was over, and now he was on his own. Thankfully, the young goddess who had robbed him so effectively of his words was also kind.

"Are you from Nerds R Us?" she asked, smiling brightly. "I've been expecting you. You must be new; where's Ernie?"

Alex stammered. "Uh, yeah, I'm uh, the nerd. I mean, I'm from the Nerds." He closed his eyes, winced, and started again, "Sorry. I'm Alex, from, uh, from Nerds R Us."

The girl smiled again, wider this time, and his pulse began to race.

"I'm Trish." She leaned back and to one side. "Here it is." She placed the machine on the desk and pushed it towards him.

"Oh, right, um, should I stay here or…"

"We have an open office just over there." Trish pointed to a small office within eyesight of the reception desk. "It's, um, not being used at the moment." A look of discomfort crossed her face. Just a flash, before being replaced with a smile again.

Alex picked up the laptop and nodded. "Okay, great, I'll get started on it. Should I just…" He pointed at the office and shrugged, his body language forming a question.

"Yep, just over there. Make yourself at home and let me know if you need anything," Trish chirped. Her phone began to ring and her attention shifted. "Kurgen Real Estate, how can I direct your call?"

The office she had directed him to was small, but it had a great view of the front desk and Trish's shapely legs peeking out of her conservative, yet short, skirt. He sat down, looked at her talking animatedly on the phone, and sighed.

If only the view could be like this every day.

He set the laptop onto the empty desk, plugged it in, and then opened his briefcase and reviewed the ticket.

He was supposed to re-image the drive and delete any business files from the laptop or the cloud. The sign-in screen appeared, the cursor blinking.

"Are you doing okay?" Trish was standing in the doorway, and Alex jumped, his heart hammering in his chest.

"What? Uh, yeah, I'm doing fine. Um, just running some diagnostics." He tried to play it cool, but his words came out fast and ran together.

Face it, dude, there is nothing cool about you. Chicks like this, they don't go out with geeks like you.

"Well, um, would you like the light on?"

Alex realized he was sitting in the dark. No wonder he couldn't find the power strip. He stared at the dark screen of the laptop, back up at Trish, and felt a warmth spread over his cheeks. "I, uh, I mean…"

"It's right here." She reached over and flipped on the light, flooding the room with a bright fluorescent glare.

Alex blinked and blushed even harder. "Uh, thanks."

Trish smiled, her lips curving up in delight. "No problem." She stood there for a moment and then spoke again. "It was so weird. The guy who had this laptop, Danny, he just stopped showing up for work one day." She shrugged. "I mean, this was his office here. The last day he worked, he was walking around like a cat who just ate the cream. Said he had found a 'lucrative opportunity' - whatever that meant - and asked me if I'd go out to dinner with him the next weekend."

Alex swallowed; his mouth was hanging open and he hoped she hadn't noticed. "So, uh, did you?"

"Did I what?"

"Go, uh, go out with him." He stumbled over the words. The sweat was so bad in his hands that they felt damp.

"Oh, gosh, no." She gave him a wide-eyed look. "He was a bit of a perv. He was always staring at me. I'd look over and he'd be staring, and then he would give me this smile that just creeped me out."

Alex nodded and made a mental note not to stare.

At least, don't stare a lot.

"I mean, I didn't tell him *no*, but I really didn't want to tell him *yes*, because, you know..." she said and shrugged again, "...perv vibes."

Alex looked over at a cardboard box filled with personal items and asked, "Is that his stuff?"

"Yeah, he never picked it up. They even tried contacting him and his landlord is looking for him too. He just dropped everything and *left*. It was crazy!" She paused for a moment, leaning out of the small office to look around. "I get so bored sitting at that desk all day. There's no one interesting to talk to."

Alex's face must have betrayed his concern over that.

"I mean," Trish said, looking embarrassed, "I'm sure *you* are interesting. I've just been talking away and not giving you a chance!" She leaned in closer and her perfume, full of floral notes, washed over him. "So, what did happen to Ernie?"

Ernie Ott had been caught in a blackmail scheme with a client and been fired three weeks ago, just as Alex was being hired. On his second day of work, instead of accompanying Ernie on his rounds, he had found himself with Bob, a portly tech with a receding hairline and persistent mournful expression. It had been the longest two weeks of his life working with Bob. By the end of it, Alex had dreaded going to work. It felt like Bob's gloom was infectious.

Meanwhile, the rumors in the small army of IT nerds had spread fast. The client in question had been a well-known call girl with a rather elite clientele. From the mayor, city leaders, and several well-placed businessmen, she had slowly built her clientele. At some point, she had struck up a relationship with Ernie. Whether it was Ernie's idea or hers, the webcam hidden in a potted plant over a period of three months had netted its fair share of indiscretions.

Ernie would then approach the target and give them a memory stick with the videos and stills taken in compromising positions and suggest a sum of money to keep quiet, and a bigger sum of money if they wanted the originals to go away forever. It had been quite effective for the first two, and rather disastrous with the third. Between the man beating Ernie within an inch of his life, placing his Smith & Wesson 9mm in the would-be blackmailer's mouth and suggesting he tell him where the duplicate memory stick was hidden, and then retrieving and destroying the evidence - the jig was up.

The fact that the third target was also a partner in Nerds R Us, silent yet influential due to his mob connections, meant that Ernie was out of a job as well as nursing two black eyes, a broken nose, and two fractured knees. Despite clear evidence to the contrary, he was surprisingly closemouthed to the police who questioned him at length after he was released from the hospital.

Alex couldn't tell Trish any of that. "He uh, I think he moved out of state."

It wasn't a lie. From what he had heard, Ernie hadn't bothered to move out of his ratty efficiency apartment near Twenty-Eighth Street. He had packed what he could carry, hobbled to his car, and left town.

Probably the smartest move he could have made.

"Oh." Trish peeked outside of the office, and then turned back, shrugged. "He was kind of, I don't know, kind of greasy. Like a used car salesman or something." Her intonation was unusual, not with the typical Midwestern twang.

Alex had stopped sweating as much. His pulse, though, showed no signs of slowing down. He was in the presence of something rare, a *nice* pretty girl. *It's like finding a unicorn in space.*

Trish, after another glance outside, walked closer and sat down on the corner of the desk. She was, Alex decided, absolutely perfect. A perfect pink tongue darted out between her lips and Alex's left knee began to jump uncontrollably, the sweaty palms returned and he felt a flush in his cheeks.

"So, tell me about you. How long have you been with Nerds R Us?"

Alex was doing his best to stammer out a response when the doorway was filled with a platinum blonde woman in her early 50s. Perhaps older, it was hard to tell. The woman appeared to be on good terms with plastic surgery. Anything that could be tucked and lifted, had been.

"There you are, Patricia!" Blanche stood there, her lips thin and curving into a false smile, her eyes cold.

Trish flinched at the sound of the woman's voice, and quickly stood. "Ms. Artinian! I'm sorry I left the desk; I was just making sure Alex has everything he needs."

"Alex, is it?" Blanche advanced into the tiny room and Trish skittered around her, heading back to her desk as the phone began to ring.

"Yes, ma'am." He felt a wave of dislike wash over him and tried his best to hide it.

"Well, good, I'm glad you decided to finally make it here." Blanche made a show of examining her watch, eyebrows raised. and face pinched in disapproval. "Standard terminated employee procedure. Wipe the hard drive, reformat it - or whatever it is that you do - and then return it to the front desk." She glanced at her watch again. "How long will it take?"

"Uh, if there aren't any problems, I should be done by noon." He thought of apologizing, but then remembered how Trish had snapped to. If he were a betting man, he would lay down money that Blanche was one of those closet dictators who ruled the office with a fake smile and venom. He had run into a few since starting with Nerds R Us, and they were difficult to deal with. Something in him bristled at the way Trish had jumped when she heard Blanche's voice.

"Excellent." She turned to go, looked around and then asked, "Where's Ernie?"

Alex shrugged and said, "I don't know, ma'am, sorry."

"Hm. Well, let me know if you have any questions." She walked away, towards the reception desk, as Trish hung up the phone. "I'll be out of the office for the rest of the day; forward my calls."

"Yes, Ms. Artinian!" Trish smiled brightly. Alex watched her as Trish's eyes tracked Blanche out of the main set of doors. The girl's shoulders slumped in relief as soon as the elevator doors in the hallway beyond slid shut. She turned, rolled her eyes, and then flashed a dazzling smile at him before walking back over.

"Whew!" She sat back down on the corner of his desk. Alex's pulse began to race again. "She is a beast, let me tell you. Once, I slipped off my heels for just a few minutes and was walking around in my stocking feet. She said it 'wasn't professional' and I swear she *intentionally* stood on my toes in the coffee room with one of those stiletto heels of hers. It *hurt*. I had a bruise for *weeks*."

Alex's cheeks flushed. "Man, that's just, that *sucks*." He bristled at the thought of Trish's tiny feet being crushed under the older woman's pricey pumps. A fantasy of stepping forward and forcing Trish's boss to back off ran pell-mell through his mind. It ended with the pretty girl giving him a kiss in return. The thought of it caused his entire body to react. He hunched over, desperate to hide his sudden erection.

I don't need her thinking I'm a perv.

Trish brightened. "You are so sweet!" She leaned in and tapped his nose with one pink fingernail. "I know some girls go for the bad boys, but I like the sweet ones." She paused, glanced back at the empty office, and swiveled towards him with a smile that was both intimate and exciting. "So, what should we do?"

"Well, I, uh." Alex felt the flush creeping back into his face and the sweat gathering. "I need to work on this laptop here."

"Well, of course you do. But *later*. Everyone, except me of course, is at a team-building event." She pointed at the clock. "Yep, in about five minutes they are going to be locked inside of a room for four hours. It's a mega-event at Escape Room - unless someone drops dead of a heart attack or gets a serious case of claustrophobia, *none* of them will be back until nearly the end of the day, if at all. No one important is going to call, and I can forward the phones to the service and then just write down all the messages and distribute them on Monday like I normally would. I'm always the first one here anyway." She grinned mischievously, brushed her hair back and tucked it behind her ear. "So, what should we do?"

Attraction warred with a healthy dose of fear. He was the new guy, and he couldn't afford to lose this job. But one of the prettiest girls who had ever bothered to talk to him wanted to spend the day with him...how could he say "no" to that?

"Give me twenty minutes. I'll set the reformat to running and cut a couple of corners, but it will get the job done."

Trish clapped her hands together and wiggled with excitement. "Perfect!" She slid off the desk. "I'll go freshen up."

Alex began the process on the laptop, noting first that an SD card had been left in the machine. He popped it out and sat it on top of the open laptop bag. He needed to ask his boss what Kurgen typically did with SD cards; were they to be reviewed before disposal? One of the other techs, Ian, had told Alex about finding porn on an SD card once. He glanced out of the room, but Trish still wasn't back. Should he look at it? He began to reach for it, thought again of the story Ian had told, and decided against it.

It would be just my luck and have something over the top on it and she would walk in at just the wrong moment and think it was mine. No thanks!

He stared at it and said, "Fuck it, I'm not getting in trouble either way." He unzipped a deep pocket and let the small card slide into it. "SD card? What SD card?"

He watched the bar on the machine slowly crawl towards completion. He had already accessed the cloud and wiped the files off it. The notes on the work order had stated that everything important had already been backed up.

Freshening up took all the twenty minutes he had requested, plus some. She disappeared into the ladies' restroom and emerged dressed in tight, hip-hugging blue jeans and a knit top that conformed to her curvy breasts. Her lips were sporting a pale pink with a clear gloss, and her lashes were longer than humanly possible. She smelled divine, the scent of her perfume sliding off her in waves through the air. She walked around the desk and peeked over his shoulder, resting one hand lightly on his arm.

"You ready?"

Alex's leg jiggled under the desk. "Um, sure, where should we go?"

Her lips curved up, shining, pink, and perfect. "Anywhere. Everywhere. Take me somewhere weird and cool."

It was a beautiful Friday afternoon, after all, and Alex slipped his hand into hers and smiled at her. He searched his mind for the best place to take her. "Have you ever been to the hair museum in Independence?"

She blinked and then grinned. "Nope, but it definitely sounds weird and cool. Let's go!" Hand in hand, they exited the building, Trish giggling like a giddy schoolgirl.

The laptop sat on her desk - zipped up and neatly put away, reformatted and ready for the next user. A new employee was starting on Monday.

Anomaly

"Mr. Endon?" The voice at his door was tentative, and Morris tore his gaze away from the stack of contracts he was reviewing with some difficulty.

"Hm, yes?" The girl looked familiar. He'd seen her in the office kitchen the other day fiddling with the coffeemaker.

"I'm Lila, the new data analyst." Her long black hair was pulled back in a neat bun and she was dressed business conservative in a demure silk blouse and gray pencil skirt, something Morris appreciated more and more each day as the Millennials continued to make inroads into the workforce. They brought with them a measure of fashion that seemed completely inappropriate for the office - he still couldn't fathom how golf shirts were considered business casual. Business casual was not wearing a tie, for Christ sake!

"Right, Lila Bu...Ben..."

"Benoit, sir. Lila Benoit."

"Ah yes, Miss Benoit." Morris smiled at the girl and leaned back in his chair. "Please come in."

"I hope I'm not interrupting something important," Lila said as she entered the room, her eyes on the stack of papers on his desk. "I could come back later when you aren't so busy."

He rubbed his eyes. "Frankly, I could use a break. I've been at this for two hours straight. Sit down, sit down."

The girl sat, her long fingers fiddling with the printout in her hand. She nibbled on her lip, obviously ill at ease.

"You started last month, right?"

"Actually, it was in June, Mr. Endon, so almost four months now."

"Please, call me Morris." He smiled at her. "That's right, I was out of the country at the time. You have been reporting to Blanche, isn't that right?"

"Yes sir. And I'm sorry to bother you about this, but Blanche is out of the office and I found an anomaly that, well, it doesn't make sense." She leaned forward and slid the printout onto his desk.

Morris squinted at it; he had accidentally grabbed the wrong pair of glasses as he left the house, picking up his old prescription instead of his newer pair. The letters and numbers remained slightly blurry, but he could still suss out what it was saying.

"A sales report from six months ago?"

"It was in my laptop's files, but it doesn't match any sales report I have seen before. This one lists properties we don't have any record of owning through Kurgen Real Estate. It also shows transactions back and forth between an Oladni Investment Corp, but I don't find any records of such an organization."

Morris kept his reaction neutral. "How odd. I've never heard of this company either; perhaps it was some practice spreadsheet? Maybe something from a training exercise?"

Lila shrugged. "I thought that at first, but then the amounts and dates lined up exactly to a sales report from six months ago, just not the *names*. Everything else matched. And..."

Morris interrupted her, "Well it's obviously not something of ours. As you said, the names of the companies don't match. I fail to see why this is important."

Lila's face betrayed her nervousness. "I guess you're right, sir."

"Please, call me Morris." He tapped the page. "So, this was in your files?"

"Yes, on my laptop. I ran across it when I was preparing data for the upcoming quarterly report. It's just...*odd*."

Morris shrugged, trying his best to appear unconcerned. He could feel sweat beading on his forehead. *Had they turned on the heat?*

"Well, it isn't anything that I recognize. Hell, you could probably delete it and chalk it up as something the technician preparing your computer missed removing. I tell you what." He reached into his desk drawer and rummaged around. "Save it onto this flash drive and drop it on my desk. I'm heading out for lunch and meetings, but I'll look at it later." He handed her the flash drive.

"Thank you, sir, err...*Morris*, I'll do that." Lila looked relieved as she took the flash drive from his outstretched hand. "Sorry to bother you."

"Not at all, Lila, I have an open-door policy around here, and you are more than welcome to stop by if you have any questions or concerns."

He watched the girl leave and the broad smile on Morris's face dropped away.

How was this possible?

He picked up the phone. "Arlene? I need you to look into the records for Ms. Benoit's work laptop. Who had the machine before her?"

Dread formed in a pit in the center of his stomach at her answer. "Let's see, it looks like it was Danny Witt's machine. Wasn't that the accountant that quit and then his family came looking for him?"

Morris forced his voice to sound nonchalant. "Didn't he end up in Tahiti or climbing the Alps or some other ridiculous place?"

Arlene, who was prone to gossip, clucked her tongue and said, "His family insisted he hadn't contacted them, but who knows, you know my niece, well niece by marriage, did something similar. She vanished off the face of the earth for nearly three years before showing up in Detroit, married to some mafioso. It about broke my sister-in-law's heart. Between you and me, the girl always was a bit off. But now he's in prison and she lives in some mansion and is married to someone else with questionable business practices. You just never know."

"Indeed. Thank you, Arlene." He set down the phone and pressed his fingers to his temples, taking several deep breaths in and out. He got up and quietly shut the door to his office before returning to his desk. He picked up his phone and dialed, waited for the familiar voice to answer. "We have a problem but I think I've handled it."

"What kind of problem?" asked the voice on the other end.

"Danny Witt's computer still had one of the files on it. It must not have been reformatted completely. The new girl, the data analyst, found it and brought it into my office today."

"I see."

Morris felt sweat bead along his forehead yet again. "I told her to copy the file onto a flash drive and then delete it from her computer."

"It seems we have been in this place before," the voice said.

"I know, but she doesn't know anything, she just had questions." Morris could feel his anxiety rising.

"She's a data analyst," the voice said, hardening, "she can put two and two together."

"If she hands over the info and wipes it from her computer, it will all be a non-issue."

"We shall see. I'll have Lucifer go through the reports on Benoit's computer and make sure she has done as you asked. If not, then you know what will need to happen."

Morris felt a rivulet of sweat run down the back of his collar. "I'm sure it won't come to that."

God, he really hoped it wouldn't. Witt, he'd had it coming. He'd sauntered in as smug as he could be, looking like the cat that swallowed the canary. He hadn't been smiling in the end.

The line clicked and went dead, and Morris stared at it even as the dial tone sounded through the receiver.

Shit. Please don't let it come to that.

Lila had returned to her desk, a feeling of disquiet lodging lightly in the back of her brain. The document was odd, but Mr. Endon, *Morris, he said to call him Morris*, was undoubtedly right. It didn't match any of the companies and transactions they normally had, so this had to just be some anomaly, some practice spreadsheet from whoever had the laptop before her.

She stared at the document, open on her laptop. There was just something about it she couldn't place, something that bothered her. She stuck the memory stick into a free port and clicked File Save As. The file name, Jackpot, had been the thing that had caught her attention when she had first found the SD card.

God, why didn't I tell Mr. Endon it was on an SD card in the laptop bag? I could have just given that to him instead of the flash drive.

She left the SD card where it was, plugged into the laptop, and typed "odd file" into the file name field and hit Enter. Too late she realized she hadn't saved it to the E drive where the flash drive had appeared when she plugged it in.

"Damn it, where the hell did, I put it now?" she muttered, clicking File Save As again and making sure to choose the E drive this time.

"Talking to yourself again? A sure sign you need to stop working so hard and come have lunch with me at Nara." Kaylee's voice interrupted Lila from her plan to hunt down wherever she had saved the file.

"Oh, I don't know if I should, Kaylee." She stopped long enough to smile at her friend. Kaylee was decked out in a gorgeous pale gray linen suit with Jimmy Choo shoes elevating her diminutive frame by six inches or more.

"Should?" Kaylee shook her head and strode into Lila's office. "Lila, you don't have to work ten hours a day, seven days a week. You are doing fabulous here; Blanche was talking you up the other day and that woman isn't a fan of *anybody*. C'mon, last time you skipped out on lunch at Nara's you *promised* me you would come with me the next time. And that time is now."

"I just need to get this flash drive over to Mr. Endon and..."

Kaylee leaned over the laptop and pointed. "This one right here?"

"Yes, I..." Lila's voice trailed off as Kaylee slipped the flash drive out of the port and grinned at her.

"I'll be right back." Seconds later she reappeared. "It's delivered." She leaned over the desk and Lila was hit with a gentle breeze of Kaylee's perfume, Bulgari Jasmine Noir. "Lila, all work and no play makes for a dull friend. C'mon, their grilled salmon salad is to die for. And you haven't lived until you have tried the spicy coconut curry." She grinned mischievously and lowered her voice. "Blanche won't be in for the rest of the day and neither will Mr. Endon. We could grab a Pomo Cosmo and slip in a little late...no one would notice or care."

"I wish I could Kaylee, I just..."

"Build your own bento box."

"Have a ton of work left before..."

"Crispy smoky tofu roll!"

"Really need to..."

"Come with me to Nara's. I *know*. Now grab your jacket and let's get going before the noon rush hits!"

Lila laughed and acquiesced. When Kaylee set her sights on something, there was no stopping her. "Okay, okay, but I'm sticking to the Nara Cure; there's no alcohol in it."

"Well, I suppose that's acceptable, but only if we split the tempura rumchata cheesecake bites at the end. You have to start living a little, Lila; life is too short for such a Spartan existence!"

Lila rolled her eyes as she reached for her coat. "Right, because a new car and a new apartment isn't enough right now."

"It isn't. Girl, you are in your 20s, no kids, no husband, no commitments. Live a little, will you? We could go by the Plaza this evening and go shopping for shoes. You have to at least visit Aldo and see this gorgeous shipment of boots they just got in."

Lila shook her head. "Not a chance. I've got a one-on-one scheduled with my kickboxing instructor at six. Besides, my wallet couldn't handle a hit from a place on the Plaza, no way."

Kaylee sighed. "Fine. Nara for now, but I'll take you out shopping soon. You need to get out more. How are you ever going to meet anyone if you don't do anything but work and sleep?"

They left the office, bantering back and forth as they went.

That evening, long after the employees of Kurgen Real Estate had left the building, a young girl sporting a piercing in each eyebrow, her lip, nose, and more ran a report. It consolidated the data collected through the keylogger software into a series of data sets that showed her clearly every movement Lila Benoit had made that day. From a quick visit to the Prius dealership website to schedule regular maintenance on her new car, to a handful of Facebook Messenger exchanges with another office worker and obvious friend, Kaylee Stromm, Lucifer paged through every moment of Lila's work day.

She picked up the phone and pressed speed dial. The phone rang twice. "You have an update for me?"

"I do. It looks like she accessed the file in question from an SD card, saved it to her personal Dropbox account, and then placed it on the flash drive. She probably went to lunch then and at 1:52 p.m. she removed the SD card from the drive."

"I see."

"Do you need me to check anything else on this user?"

"No. Thank you, Lucifer." The line went dead.

The girl stared at the phone in her hand, "Okay then." She shrugged and closed the report, turning to the paused game on the other screen. "Let the Battle of Azeroth begin!"

Miles away, Dominic's phone buzzed in his pocket. He handed the waitress a crisp one-hundred-dollar bill, saying, "Keep the change," and slid the phone out of his pocket. "Riehl."

"I have a job for you. It's right up your alley."

Dominic smiled again, nodding to the waitress as he exited the building. He would be back; their saag paneer had been exceptional. "Go on." He reached his car, slid inside it, and closed the door.

"Kansas City, Friday evening, make it look like a burglary or assault turned deadly. Your choice. I'm sending over the basics now." The phone vibrated and he pulled it from his ear so that he could see the picture. He would print it out when he got home. The woman was smoking hot. Dominic grinned; he was going to enjoy this.

"Got it. My standard fee applies." His phone dinged again, this time showing a figure with five zeros behind it.

"I've sent over your retainer. The rest payable after the contract is complete," the voice on the other end of the line said.

"I'll update you then," Dominic answered and the line clicked as the other caller hung up. Dominic tossed his phone into the passenger seat and hummed to himself as he started the car and drove away. It had been more than a month since his last contract and he had been getting antsy. This call had been the perfect end to his evening.

Hitman

Lila's heightened sense of smell may have eliminated the first half-second of surprise, and it certainly saved her life. Such a short amount of time, yet in retrospect, so vital to gaining the upper hand. Dominic Riehl sussed this out hours later, obsessing over how badly he had screwed up while nursing a set of swollen and painful testicles, along with bruised ribs. He would curse himself for a full three days, as he hobbled around the cramped apartment he had rented and listened to the squabbling voices of the tenants above, below, and on all sides through the thin, cheap walls.

If he hadn't indulged in that damned Indian buffet on 75th and Wornall, she wouldn't have turned at just the last millisecond, ensuring that his initial rush towards her was off by just enough. It had to have been the smell of curry that had given him away before he could grab her and stun her with a crack to the jaw. Just another half-second is all he would have needed as he swiftly emerged from the shadows in the poorly lit underground garage.

Lila had found the parking garage in her apartment building slightly creepy. Chalk it up to watching an unhealthy amount of horror movies in her teens, or the news of another body found in a vacant home in the Northland two nights previously, but her spider sense had tingled the second she stepped into the dimly lit expanse of concrete pillars and empty cars. A disastrous blind date set up by her boss Morris had ended in her waiting for some loser that never showed, before she gave up in disgust and ended the night at a late-night movie at the AMC Barrywoods. Just her and her delectable dates - twins by damn - a bag of popcorn and a large box of Junior Mints.

The movie had been creepy and sinister, which would have been great if she were hooked up with a special honey to cuddle up to during the worst scenes. Instead, she had seen the movie with a handful of other pathetic loners, each of them lounging or scrunched in their seats in turn among a sea of empty red leather recliners. She could have just waited for it to come to Redbox and rented it alone.

She pulled into her parking spot, gliding silently into position with her fuel-efficient wunderkind Prius. She noticed that the light near the stairwell door was out again. Why they couldn't use the LED lights, instead of those wattage-sucking losers, Lila couldn't understand. The cheap bulb hadn't lasted more than a month this time. It was dangerously dark in the underground garage and Lila felt a tingle of fear wash over her.

All those damned specters coming around corners. Get a hold of yourself, girl!

She slipped out of her seat, grabbed her purse in her right hand, and closed the door behind her. The remote locked and alarmed it with a quiet chirp. Her heels clicked on the cement floor and Lila felt annoyance all over again. She had dressed up, and for what? Some loser no-show. She hadn't been interested, but Morris had been so insistent. And really, how do you say "no" to your new boss? She was still worried about making a good impression; it had only been four months since she started there, after all.

As she neared the stairwell door, there was an odd odor, something she couldn't quite pinpoint, and then the shadows moved impossibly, coalescing into a man's shape closing in on her. She blinked, delayed for a moment over the impossibility of what she was seeing, a rush of darkness coming straight at her. In the last crucial millisecond, her body reacted and she turned and shifted to one side as a man smelling of curry attempted to tackle her. The mixed martial arts training she had been taking for the past four years came in handy, and so did those endless miles on the treadmill in her apartment building's exercise room, earphones in her ears, music turned up, as she did her best to avoid giving her neighbor in Apartment 1503 any opportunity to ask her out.

Her response, despite being slowed by the stiletto heels she had worn for her "didn't bother to show up or even call" failed date, probably saved her life. Instead of being thrown against the pillar, or being knocked unconscious and choked out from behind, she was now facing her attacker, hands at the ready as he course-corrected and came at her again. He moved fast and powered through her side kick to his groin with a pained grunt, before grabbing her leg and twisting it, pushing her off balance. Lila hit the pillar hard, her right shoulder popped, and the corresponding arm lit up in a bright wash of pain. It felt as if she had touched a live wire, her arm burning and tingling. When she tried to move it, it refused to respond, shocked by the violence done to it. Lila's brain was slow to catch up. Sparring with her instructor or with the other students was one thing, but this was completely different. Her opponent wasn't waiting for her to catch her breath or solicitously inquire as to her well-being.

Riehl's brain and body were still processing the groin hit Lila had scored. Beginner's luck with that kick of hers had cost him his first option on the hit, to make it look like rape. And she sure as hell had made it so he wouldn't get a chance to use the equipment he was so proud of. Having scoped out the patterns of the residents for the past few days, he had figured he had time, or time enough, to have a bit of fun before killing her, thus fulfilling the contract. Instead, his balls were informing his brain that the only thing he would be boning in the next couple of days was an ice pack. It took a conscious effort to ignore the rising tide of pain that was crawling its way up from his balls to his stomach. Hell, he felt the impact of her knee in his throat.

Slamming the woman against the pillar had knocked her breath out of her, and his hands closed on her neck before she could scream. The garage was far from any of the tenant apartments, many floors above, but Riehl wasn't taking any more chances. Lila's left arm slammed into his ribs with a surprising amount of force. There wasn't much to this woman - slender, small-boned - but she had obviously taken some kind of self-defense training. The heel now raking along his instep with brutal sharpness was painful, possibly bloody, but he would be damned if he was going to let his commission get away from him. He tightened his grip. She let out a choked squawk of pain, fingers digging at his, trying her best to break his grip.

One...

"Three seconds, Lila, that's all it takes for a person to lose consciousness when being choked out," Lila's coach had told her. *"If you are ever in a choke situation, get out of it... quick."* She crunched her knee into the man's groin with all her might. His body shuddered in response, but his grip didn't loosen.

Two...

Lila's vision was darkening at the edge, narrowing down to a tunnel...

"What the hell? Hey! You! Get the hell off her!" The voice belonged to a man, someone familiar, but she could see nothing. The hand at her throat shook, broke free at the force of impact, a new body in the mix. Lila flew backward, back against the pillar, cracking her head sharply, scraping skin as she sprawled on the hard cement floor. It was a maelstrom of arms and legs, on the ground, her attacker and someone familiar, someone she knew. It took a moment for her to regroup, and find the top of the pepper spray she kept on her key chain in her purse which lay within reach. Slamming her thumb down hard enough to bruise, the spray shot out, just at the moment her attacker had taken the advantage, and made the mistake of looking down at her.

Riehl snarled curses and fell back, temporarily blinded. So did George, her neighbor from down the hall in Apartment 1503, who had also received a fair share of the spray while being slammed on the rough concrete parking garage floor. George lay there and writhed, caterwauling in a high, shrill voice.

"Oh my God, my eyes, my *eyes*!"

Riehl, realizing his opportunity had elapsed and fighting to see from eyes that were now filled with liquid pulsing fire, had enough sense to get up, stumbling, running, and swearing as he peered, half-blind, out of one half-functional eye. The other felt fully on fire, enough that he was tempted to claw the damned thing out of its socket, if only to end the pain. He disappeared into the depths of the garage, becoming one with the shadows, his footsteps receding.

Lila's throat was constricted, and she could barely speak. Meanwhile, George was screaming loud enough to wake the dead, or at the very least, some of the nearer level of residents. A stream of words issuing from him as well, random thoughts, just... noise...

"Couldn't sleep, thought I heard something, my EYES, oh my God my EYES! Just thought I'd go for a walk, but no, oh God, what if I'm blind? The burning...Jesus..." His nose was bleeding freely as well, but George was too busy pressing his hands against his eyeballs to notice. The blood dribbled over his cream polyester shirt.

George continued to scream while Lila frantically pulled her phone from her purse and dialed 9-1-1. By the time the cars arrived, lights flashing like strobes and weapons at the ready, George had settled down to a pitiful sobbing, and Lila's attacker was long gone. The police had nearly arrested George, thinking *he* was the attacker. Lila had explained for the third time that he had come to her aid, not attacked her.

"Anyone with a beef? A jealous ex-boyfriend perhaps?" The officer asked, his gaze traveling down her long, shapely legs, lingering on the rip in her dress. "Were you on a date with the neighbor, perhaps?" Lila winced as the doctor tried to flex her arm. The shoulder felt as if it were full of hot knives and fire. She caught the cop eying her cleavage; the front of her dress had ripped and a delicate lace bra strap was showing. The sleeve of the dress slipped from her exposed, and rapidly darkening, bruised shoulder.

"George? No, I, no, we aren't dating, he's my neighbor," Lila answered, hissing in pain as the doctor tried again to manipulate her right shoulder.

"Okay, Ms. Benoit, this is going to be a little painful. Just try to relax."

Lila bit back a retort. Why did doctors tell you that and then tell you to relax? She bit back a yelp as the doctor first turned and then gave her arm a short, decisive yank. She felt it pop back into place and rode a red wave of pain. It still hurt like hell, but at least the shoulder was back in the socket where it belonged.

The doctor handed her a prescription bottle. "You are going to be sore for a few days. Especially with those bruised ribs. Make sure to take these with some food and try to avoid driving."

"Thanks, Doc."

The officer muttered something indistinct as the doctor left and asked, "And you don't know anyone who would want to harm you?"

"No."

"Alright then." The officer eased his large bulk up from the small chair at the end of the ER room bed and stood slowly. The woman was a looker and that was for sure. Straight black hair, piercing green eyes, a slim figure, and legs that just didn't stop. Pretty. Her pale skin was bruised, but that just gave her a vulnerable look. The radio on his shoulder squawked and he muttered into it. "Well ma'am, I've got all I need."

"You don't need to do a sketch of the guy or have me look at some photos?" Lila asked.

The officer laughed. When he did, his stomach jiggled. "For a snatch and grab? Sweetheart, you have been watching too much Law and Order. Nah, this guy got the crap kicked out of him and pepper sprayed to hell and back. My bet? He's back at home in the 'hood, washing out his eyes, cradling his balls and thinking that walking the straight and narrow would be a hell of a lot easier than dealing with another babe in high heels schooling him."

"You think it was just a robbery?" Lila felt a sense of unease rise up in her.

"Sure, seems like it. I mean, hell, he probably would have tried for a little more, if you know what I mean. A pretty girl like you, he woulda taken advantage of that." He paused, nonplussed at Lila's reaction. "Why, you got this all figured out as going some other way?" The cop asked, a smug, condescending smile on his face.

"No, I, well, I mean..." Lila's voice petered out. *The way he had grabbed her throat, the look on his face.* She shook her head, which made the room dance and her stomach clench. "I guess not."

The officer smiled. "You got someone to pick you up? Take you home?" His eyes traveled up and down her again, as if he were imagining her without her clothes on. Lila's mouth tasted sour... *ew.*

"Yeah, sure do. Thanks Officer."

"Officer Tom Collier. You can call me Tom." He winked at her and her stomach clenched again. "If you need a ride, you just give me a call."

He handed her a card. She took it and managed not to shudder until after he had turned his back. So *not* her type.

An hour later, her right arm in a sling, her other injuries reviewed and treated, and higher than a kite on pain meds, she slowly eased her way into her friend Kaylee's backseat.

"Oh my God, Lila! What happened?"

She fell asleep halfway through telling the story, slumping in the seat on the short ride back to her high-rise. She barely blinked when Kaylee and her roommate Andy half-walked, half-carried her to her apartment door. As she nodded off in her own bed, Lila was thankful that it was Friday. She had two days to recover before returning to work. No rest for the wicked, or those saddled with student loans.

A Clue

Monday came too soon. Kaylee had called twice, once on Saturday and again on Sunday, to check on her. Lila had reassured her that she was fine and she didn't need anything. If she had relented, Kaylee would have been knocking on her door. All Lila wanted to do was sleep, and the pain meds kept her in a thick haze.

She had curled up in the thick feather-top bed, a new purchase that had arrived the month before, and watched endless episodes on Netflix and napped the entire weekend. It had been a luxury Lila rarely allowed herself - time to recover and rest from her injuries. Her throat, ribs, legs, and arms all had livid bruises from the struggle in the parking garage. She took stock on Sunday night after a long, hot shower, noting that several were turning from a deep black and blue to green and yellow. Her skin was fair, and easily bruised, but she was also fit and active and young. A few more days and they would fade out completely.

On Monday, however, she had to stop taking any pills. She wouldn't have been able to drive or work or even really think if she was all wonked-out on opioids.

Her body was stiff, and her ribs and shoulder hurt like hell. The bruises on her face and neck were still a little shocking, but Lila didn't want to stay in the apartment another day. It felt suffocating, the plain walls devoid of any pictures, a few of the boxes still unpacked.

Besides, she was new at her job. She had done her time straight out of college in a bottom of the barrel intro level marketing position that had made her question why she even bothered with college, especially with those hefty student loan payments. Working for wages barely above the poverty line, with a Bachelor's degree, had been a slap in the face. If it hadn't been for her friend Kaylee who she had run into at a First Friday's event in the Arts District, she would probably still be there.

"There's an opening at Kurgen for a Market Research Analyst," Kaylee had told her after commiserating with Lila's latest tale of woe, the two perched on stools inside of Christopher Elbow Chocolates, sipping coffee while nibbling on the decadent confections. "It's better pay, *and* you would be working with me, so we could lunch together!"

Kaylee was quite obviously making better money, if her Jimmy Choo shoes and handbags were any indication. Kaylee's address had also changed from a ratty apartment south of the city to an upscale loft in the Western Auto building. "They *say* that you need at least four years' experience and a Master's degree, but I've seen the sad line of applications coming through HR and they would snap you up in a heartbeat." She grinned, revealing perfect white teeth, and tapped her long, well-manicured nails on the counter. "Especially with me recommending you." She had leaned in close, washing Lila in the scent of bananas and rum from the Bananas Foster chocolate she had just finished. "Promise me you will go home tonight and email me your resume."

Lila had, of course, sending the resume to Kaylee that evening while the neighbors down the street blasted music that sounded more like a mariachi band and kegger party instead of the festivities for the toddler who was celebrating her second birthday. Lila had watched the older kids playing in the neighborhood from time to time but rarely interacted with them. The neighborhood was relatively quiet, a mix of young families, a couple of old codgers, and plenty of transitory residents, especially in her building. The tiny one-bedroom apartment, complete with shag carpet that had matted in spots into hard, intractable lumps, with windows that rattled and blew in ice-cold air in the winter, and the regular cockroach visitors, was all that she could afford after trying to pay down a hefty student loan balance each month. She poured the rest of her "disposable" income into a decaying Honda Civic and wondered if she would ever be able to afford a new car.

That had been her life four months ago. And now? A modern one-bedroom loft with a view to the west and tons of light that poured in through the tall windows in a secure building in midtown Kansas City, where the scent of the defunct Folgers Coffee plant still infused the air with ghostly whiffs of coffee. After nearly a century of roasting coffee beans before the company gave way and moved into a modern processing facility, the very bricks of the building held the rich scent of coffee.

The Honda Civic had expired, rattling its dying breath on I-70 as she returned from a trip to Lawrence and a show at the Granada two months ago. The payments on the Prius had simply replaced what she was paying to keep the Civic running. The loft space had an option to buy if she wanted it. She was giving it at least a year, and if things continued to go well at Kurgen, she had already decided she would go for it.

Each Saturday morning included a pilgrimage to the lively River Market for breakfast at Beignet's and then shopping for fresh spices and produce with the local market vendors.

Lila was living her dream, finally, and she wasn't about to endanger that by missing any days at work. She would feel better there anyway; there were several accounts that she was working on that were odd - properties that should have sold by now, but had instead lingered on the books for over nine months.

Kurgen Real Estate was a heavy hitter, aggressive, in control of a large part of the real estate market in the Kansas City Metropolitan area, and her job was to make sure that she gave her boss the advice he needed to eradicate dead properties that would glut their portfolio and reduce their profit margin. She had requested the entire files nearly two weeks ago and was still trying to open several puzzling encrypted files, as well as some kind of email correspondence. She would work on that, along with her regular work load, instead of sitting at home feeling sore and sorry for herself.

Morris Endon, her boss, nearly dropped his mug of coffee when he registered her arrival, his eyes widening in shock, his ruddy red face paling at the sight of her. "My God, Lila!" His exclamation brought several other gawkers into the hallway. "Kaylee mentioned you had been mugged. I thought you would still be at home!"

Lila gave a rueful smile, suddenly deeply aware of the dark marks on her face as well as the lurid yellow bruising on her neck. *Perhaps this was a mistake.* "I'm fine, Morris, just a little sore." She forced a light laugh. "Really, there is so much work to do, and sitting at home seemed overkill for an overzealous purse snatcher."

If she hadn't been going stir-crazy at her house, there was also the pesky matter of her neighbor George, who, after returning from his own visit to the ER, had promptly begun haunting the hallway outside of her door. All she wanted was to be left alone, but instead George had come by her apartment no less than six times on Saturday for a variety of reasons. Lila had finally stopped answering the door. She wasn't interested in hearing again about George's insomnia, or how his mother still felt it necessary to buy him underwear and socks, or have to explain why she wasn't interested in dating despite being quite obviously single. Work was a respite from all of that.

Blanche, one of the high-powered sales reps, stared at her bruises in horror. In her early 50s, Blanche had managed to accrue more debt in Botox and plastic surgery than Lila did in student loans, despite making at least triple the earnings. As a result, Blanche looked as if she could be Lila's contemporary, instead of from her parents' generation. "Oh sweetie, you need Vitamin C and K for that bruising! I'll be right back." She zipped away, her diminutive five-foot frame augmented by five-inch stiletto heels. Lila watched her go, consistently amazed that the woman hadn't so much as stumbled wearing those instruments of evil. Lila wore heels, one had to, but she did her best to find the lowest heels possible. The stilettos on Friday had been an exception to the rule and one she would not be repeating any time soon.

She made her excuses, grabbed a cup of coffee from the break room, and escaped to her office in the far corner. It was one of the smaller offices, but it had a view of a corner of the Sprint Center. The walls were a uniform taupe, the same as the rest of the office. The exterior wall was floor to ceiling glass windows. She had opaque, solid walls on each side, and the door and wall to the hallway and cubicles outside were glassed-in as well. Her office had a sleek wood desk, a Herman Miller chair, and silk plant in the corner. She had tried to bring in live plants, but, despite regular watering, they had quickly died. Like her inability to cook, she also seemed to have a black thumb, and any unfortunate plants left in her care immediately returned her attention and love by dramatically wilting and dying.

The office had a couple of extra chairs, and a huge wall of files, but otherwise was rather spartan. Lila sat at her desk, relieved to be in her office away from all the looks of pity or horror. Blanche swished through the door and plunked down a large jar on the corner of the desk. "Here, honey, my plastic surgeon *swears* by this line of supplements. He says it cuts healing time in half and removes bruises overnight. You just help yourself; I'm not lined up for anything until next year, and he hands these things out gratis, so I don't even need to buy them!"

Lila smiled at her co-worker. Blanche was a sweetheart. She had given Lila a welcome basket her first week at Kurgen and taken her out to lunch twice. "Thanks, Blanche, you are so good to me!" Blanche merely waved her fingertips, painted a blood red this week, and dashed out of Lila's office as her cell phone began to sound. She punched a button and Lila could hear her cooing to someone on the other end, probably her granddaughter, a tiny and adorable three-year-old that Blanche had brought by the office one day.

With her cup of coffee in hand, and her computer booting up, she pulled the sheet of paper she had found out of her purse and stared at it. It just didn't make any sense. She wasn't anyone; this had to be a joke. But a joke that just happened to line up with someone who tried to strangle her to death in her parking garage? That seemed a little too coincidental.

She mused, *Occam's Razor, the simplest explanation is often the correct one.* But why? Why would someone be trying to kill her?

"Lila... what the hell?!" A voice at her ear, Kaylee's, made her jump a mile. She had been so absorbed in the slip of paper in front of her that she hadn't even registered her friend's presence.

Kaylee jumped back as well. "Jesus, Lila! What are you doing here today? You had the crap beat out of you and here you are! And what the hell is that thing?" Kaylee grabbed the slip of paper and stared at it, her eyes widening.

"Where did you get this?"

Lila breathed deeply, trying her best to get her breathing under control, her heart pounding from the scare Kaylee had given her. Her friend was dressed to the nines in yet another new designer outfit, her blond hair perfectly coiffed in a haircut reminiscent of the 1920s. Kaylee had a talent for changing her look on a weekly basis. Last week she had looked like one of the actresses on Mad Men, right down to her manicured toes.

"I found it on the ground in my building's parking garage. I wasn't sure what to make of it." The paper was torn, but it had several color photos of her and a general body description, along with Lila's name. It also had something that looked like a price... $30,000...next to her photo, which must have been taken when Lila was just exiting her car. It was a candid shot, with Lila half-facing the camera, caught in the act of turning, her long black hair flying in the wind. For the life of her, Lila could not imagine when it could have been snapped. She certainly hadn't noticed anyone with a camera that close. Could they have used a telephoto lens?

Kaylee sucked in a breath. "Lila, this is bad. I don't care what that cop told you about it just being a snatch and grab. That's bullshit. This is something else, it has to be. Why would that guy have been waiting there for you in the garage? And why you?"

Lila just shrugged. When she had found the piece of paper on the ground, all her senses on high alert, she had grabbed it and then sprinted to her car. Coming here, where there were plenty of people, seemed far safer. "Don't tell anyone, Kaylee. It could just be a joke. It could be nothing. It probably is nothing." Saying it out loud didn't sound any more convincing than it had in her head.

Kaylee looked at Lila, her lips pursed, eyebrows raised, "Right." When Lila's eyes returned to the paper, Kaylee made up her mind. "I know someone and I'm going to give them a call."

"You *know* someone? What does that even mean, Kaylee?"

Kaylee stared at the paper, and a haunted look crossed her face in a brief flash. It was quickly covered up with a glare.

"Look, I'll call them. They are... discreet." She grabbed the crumpled paper and scooted away before Lila could stop her. "I'll be back in a flash."

Lila stared at her friend's retreating back and shook her head. None of this made sense. She was a nobody - she had no family, no money, nothing. She hadn't been the unwitting witness to a murder, and she didn't know anyone with ties to the criminal underground.

Just thinking those words sounds so ridiculously like an episode of Law and Order *gone wrong.* Lila winced at the memory of the police officer laughing at her.

Unless it was a case of mistaken identity. She laughed and shook her head. *Next it will be an alien conspiracy!* It was all crazy and ridiculous. Whoever that guy was, he was gone, run off, and that was that.

Forget It

Ten minutes later, Kaylee was back in Lila's office.

"What's this?" Lila stared at the card Kaylee held out to her.

"You need to call them; they can help you."

"I don't need some damned rent-a-cop, Kaylee," Lila snapped, glaring at her friend, "And I certainly can't afford one."

Kaylee didn't bat an eye. "Good, because they don't do rent-a-cop. Benton Security Services is the real deal. They provide high security, protective detail, and they keep millionaires and witnesses alive while rent-a-cops are busy trying to figure out their asses from their front ends." She smiled at Lila, patted her friend's undamaged hand, and then squeezed it reassuringly. "Trust me on this."

Lila looked doubtful… the bruises on her neck ached and her right arm was in a sling. She had managed to fight off her attacker, but only just. All her years of martial arts training hadn't prepared her for a dark garage and one incredibly fast opponent. If it hadn't been for her neighbor George and his "damned insomnia," as he had put it, she was pretty sure she would have lost that fight, despite getting a handful of solid punches and kicks in, at least one of them to the man's groin. She really hoped he was sitting somewhere hurting like hell and having to ice his balls.

It all happened so damned fast.

"Just call them," Kaylee insisted, handing her the card.

Lila took it from her friend and examined it.

It was on plain white card-stock, with no-frills black type that read Benton Security Services. Lila stared at the card; the feel of the paper was thick, heavy, made for a firm that didn't need to advertise their services, because word of mouth did the job so much better.

"Kaylee, if these guys protect millionaires, they do it for some serious money. Maybe even tens of thousands of dollars. I'm just getting on my feet; I can't afford this."

"Lila, trust me, they can help you and they won't charge you anything. Jack takes on special cases. I've already talked to him and he is interested in yours."

"Jack? You know this guy by his first name? What the hell, Kaylee? How do you know these people?" Lila asked her friend, suddenly intensely curious. Kaylee was petite, with honey-blond hair and big brown eyes. She certainly wasn't the type to need the services of a bodyguard, unless it was to protect her collection of high heels and designer bags. *There is some serious cash going there. What did she know about all of this, anyway?*

Kaylee gave a small, tight smile. "Long story. Maybe I'll even get around to telling you sometime. Meanwhile, would you just call them? Just, call. Seriously, Lila. *Call.*" The look on her face was so full of worry that Lila found herself nodding.

"Okay, okay, I'll call the number."

"Today?"

"Yes, today. Right after I finish this report."

Kaylee gave her a look, one that conveyed her doubt that Lila would make the call. She shook her head and left, calling over her shoulder, "I'll hold you to that, Lila Benoit!"

But Lila couldn't seem to bring herself to call right away after Kaylee left her office. Instead, she placed the card on her desk and did a little research. There was a website listed on the back of the card, and Lila pulled it up on her computer. It was as basic and no frills as the business card. The owner, Jack Benton, was the only name listed on the website. His name seemed familiar and Lila clicked the About tab. There was little information - the company had been started over ten years ago by Benton and it showed a picture of him, well-dressed, professional, with a sprinkling of salt and pepper through his dark hair. He was handsome, *very* handsome.

Lila had seen his face before, but she could not remember where. His posture and demeanor spoke old money to her - he obviously had tailored clothing on but wasn't wearing anything ostentatious - no large diamond cuff links or heavy rings. The watch, half-hidden by his sleeve, looked like a Rolex. Someone that rich didn't have a need to advertise their wealth.

Oh wait, there is his bio.

She clicked on the link and read through it.

There was the connection, and that was why his name seemed familiar. Lila smiled. He was a benefactor for her alma mater and had actually helped pay for most of two years at her college through a scholarship. Lila had run track and played the cello in high school and college. Both of these interests had netted her a respite from the high tuition costs. Jack Benton's name had been on the cello scholarship, as she recalled. The Allison Benton Scholarship, named after his sister, who had been a cello player. Yes, that was it.

It had meant the difference between eating ramen and being able to buy fresh produce and not worry about student loans racking up the equivalent of indentured servitude once she graduated.

Lila's mom hadn't been able to help much, and Lila's dad had died when she was sixteen. They had struggled ever since, so Lila hadn't wanted to ask her mom for help. Her mom had been so proud of her, but Lila had known that she was barely making ends meet, so helping Lila with tuition and expenses was simply not in the cards. As it was, Gina Benoit had been slowly dying for years from terminal cancer. By Lila's last year in college, Gina was in bad shape, and she insisted that Lila stay in school instead of caring for her. "Don't do what I did, Lila. Don't drop out; stay in and get your degree, make something of yourself, or you will spend the rest of your life pushing paper around in some office. It's a meaningless job; you deserve better."

Gina Benoit had even made her death convenient, passing away during the Christmas break. Lila had gone home to be by her mother's side as she took her final breaths. She had buried her, and returned to Georgia Tech in time to start the new semester. Only a few friends from Mom's work, along with their neighbor from across the hall, had attended the funeral with her. Her mother had kept to herself, worked hard, and then returned home to be a mom to Lila. She had been good at it, better than most.

She closed the website, pushed the thick card to one side, and dove into her work. She had three major projects to deal with, plus the odd one; it was time she stopped wasting Kurgen Real Estate's money and time and got to work. As a market research analyst for the firm, her job was to make the data talk - what materials would work best on a job site, how could Kurgen achieve the highest profit in the market, and how could they reduce expenses? She lost herself in the work, and all these questions kept Lila occupied the next few hours. She barely touched the clear clamshell that was delivered to her desk by the secretary, Trish. Even though it contained her favorite veggie sandwich with extra pickles, she kept her nose to the grindstone until well into the afternoon.

Finally, after two more check-ins from Kaylee, who voiced increasing concern, Lila could put it off no longer. She ate a few bites of the sandwich as she tried to figure out how to get out of making a pointless phone call. She couldn't afford their services. And no matter what Kaylee said, nothing came for free in this world. She nibbled her bottom lip and stared at the phone on her desk.

Ugh. Might as well get it over with.

Nervous, her lunch already doing the rumba in her stomach, Lila reached for the phone and dialed the number with her slim, manicured fingers. The phone rang once, twice, before a smooth, calm voice answered, "Benton Security Services, how may I direct your call?"

"I was given your firm's name, I'm... I'm not sure if I need your services or not, but..."

The voice on the other end was crisp and efficient. "Your name, please?"

"Lila Benoit."

"Yes, Ms. Benoit, we have been expecting your call. One moment, please..."

Lila was surprised. "You have? But I..."

There was a series of clicks then, "Hello?"

On the other end was pure Southern drawl, which brought up visions of pecan pie, vanilla ice cream, and a fantasy of all of it between twisted bedsheets. "Ms. Benoit?"

"You can call me Lila." His voice, ye gods, his voice was amazing. She could feel herself blushing; had she just told him he could call her Lila? Why not ask him to whisper some sweet nothings? Or, or, or...

"My name is Shane Ellis." She could hear him smile through the phone. He was probably a toad in real life no one could ever sound that good, that *yummy...* it wasn't possible. She found herself calculating how long it had been since she had broken it off with Todd. Two months? Three? He had been terrible in bed. He had actually asked her to *rate* him once and she had... "We need to meet."

Oh, hell yes! Meet a man that sounded like sex and food all rolled into one? She could see how it would go from there, she closed her eyes, imagining Mr. Sexy Pants Shane Ellis, muscled, molasses dribbled over bare skin, big strong hands, and...

"Ms. Benoit? Are you there?"

Not yet but give me a minute.

"Umm, yes, but..."

Reality interceded. What in the hell was she doing? She didn't have the money for this. Men were never as sexy as they sounded on the phone, and she didn't need this. She didn't need protection, she didn't need Sexy Pecan Pie Shane Ellis whispering sweet nothings in her ear. She needed, she needed, *I need to get laid so bad. Don't care if that is a bad girl thing to say or not, it's the truth.*

"I'm sorry, Mr. Ellis, I - I don't think I need a protective service after all."

"Ms. Benoit, Lila, based on the information given to me, I would suggest that we at least meet to discuss this." He was persistent, she had to give him that. "This hit that was ordered on you, believe me, it is real."

Oh, sure he would say that. In the end, everyone is trying for their piece of the pie, so why would he be any different?

But the reality was, Lila couldn't afford it. She was on track, making all her payments, she was working on reducing that hefty car loan balance by just a little more each month, and life was finally starting to look up. But pay for a protective detail? Those things didn't come cheap. Kaylee had misunderstood, and the whole thing was absurd in any case. The officer's words came back to her; it had been a snatch and grab. Nothing more. She'd just pissed him off by fighting back. That's why he had gone after her throat.

And as for the paper she had found, well, okay, so that didn't jive. *But I'm a nobody. You don't put out a hit on a nobody.*

"Look, just, just, forget it. Really. I'll be fine. I promised my friend I would call, but really, I'm good. I'm sorry for taking up any of your time. You have a nice day." She stabbed her finger down onto the plastic button and hung up the phone.

Brushing her hair away from her bruised face, she straightened her shoulders, despite the pain in her arm. This was ridiculous. She didn't need a bodyguard, and she didn't need protection.

I need to focus on work and stop wasting company time.

Her computer chimed and she saw it was a message from Kaylee.

KayleeS: Did you call?

Lila sighed, and typed back an answer.

LilaBe: Yep, it's all taken care of.

KayleeS: Great! I've got a meeting for the next few hours, good to know you are in good hands!

Lila felt her stomach twist. She hated not telling her friend the entire truth, but honestly, she was too worn out to argue. She had a pile of work, two case studies she needed to dig deep into, and the last thing she needed was to argue with her best friend. Later she would put her foot down and explain that she was fine, and didn't need some overpaid bodyguard.

Shane held the phone to his ear until the dial tone sounded. Lila Benoit had sounded nervous, but not scared. She should have been terrified. The crumpled paper that Kaylee had faxed over was standard in the industry. It had several candid shots in color, along with Lila's basic information. Her address, basic schedule - it was enough for any professional to be able to find their quarry and eliminate the target. Someone had ordered a hit on the petite, raven-haired beauty. Shane didn't know *why* but he was certain of one thing - whether she thought she was in danger or not, Lila Benoit had a price on her head. Her chances of surviving another attack were small and there *would* be others.

He pulled up the sheet on Tor and stared at it. After the failed attempt on Friday, the price on Lila's head had jumped from thirty to fifty grand on the darknet. Whatever this woman had done, or whoever she had pissed off, she was in big trouble. He drummed his fingers on the table. *She's got no idea what is heading her way.* Frowning, he dialed Jack's number.

The phone rang once. "Benton speaking."

"Hey, Boss, Ellis here. She says she doesn't need protection."

There was a pause. "And?"

"I checked the site and the bounty just jumped to fifty."

"Round her up, use that Southern charm if you have to, and take her to the house on the hill. Handle her carefully, but don't take no for an answer."

"Roger that." A dial tone sounded in Shane's ear. Jack Benton didn't waste words or time. Shane stood up from his small yet tidy desk and slid two extra clips into his belt loops and headed out the door.

As the hours passed, and Lila followed up on several leads, her gaze was pulled back to the phone over and over. She would call up the police officer later, show him the paper she had found. There had to be a good explanation for it. And if it was something serious, the cops would do something, protect her, or... *I have work to do right now.*

She dove back into her work, losing herself in the Cahill file, and tried to forget the attack, Kaylee's occasional IMs, and the way Shane Ellis' voice had made her feel. Just thinking about his voice sent a thrill down her spine.

Pecan pie... molasses... mm.

Call Me Shane

Shane watched the woman work. Despite the bandaged arm, she typed at a furious pace, switching between open tabs on her computer, completely absorbed in her work to the exclusion of anything else. He had watched her for nearly an hour now, as the sun slipped slowly behind the horizon and darkness stole across the expanse of steel and glass, removing the harsh glare.

The office was large, meandering, with a mixture of both antique and modern influences - in its furnishings and knickknacks. Outside of Lila's office was a large Oriental wardrobe that was in pristine condition, its lacquer shining despite being hundreds of years old. The company was family-owned and family run. Shane had learned that Mrs. Kurgen spent several months each year traveling the world and collecting treasures. Never satisfied to limit herself to one culture or region, Mrs. Kurgen's collection spanned the world.

He had heard this from the receptionist, Trish, who practically trembled in her seat whenever he smiled at her. She had rattled on for a while about the 15th century artifacts in the west wing, which apparently included a full set of armor worn by a duke or European prince. He had just smiled and nodded as the girl stammered on.

He watched her body and mind struggle to maintain a professional appearance. A few well-placed inquiries and he learned that the real estate firm did not have an internal security system or guards specifically assigned to the floor. The only cameras were in the elevators and a single camera for each main hallway, something easily avoided or short-circuited. In short, the security here sucked.

He waited for most of the staff, including Trish, to leave the office. His questions and research into Lila Benoit had revealed very little about *why* she was being targeted, but volumes about her personality. He couldn't just march in there, sling her over his shoulder, and drive her to the safe house. This had to be finessed. So, he made as if he was leaving, waited out of sight in the men's room in the outer hall, and watched as Trish and the others slowly trickled out, leaving the office empty save for Lila.

"She shows up before everyone else and is still here when we leave," Trish had said. "She's the most dedicated worker here."

He had watched them all leave over the course of a few minutes before 5 p.m., moving with purpose towards the banks of elevators. Lila wasn't one of them. He gave her a full thirty minutes after the last one left before he walked into the office. It was empty, the maze of cubicles quiet, the front desk abandoned.

Shane had also learned from Trish that when Lila had a free moment, she would often walk this floor, gazing at the different pieces. He wondered if she imagined going to those faraway places someday. Shane stood there next to the intricate lacquered cabinet with its depictions of various nature scenes and watched Lila work. The scanned image that her friend Kaylee had sent to his boss - the crumpled and torn note that Lila had found in her parking garage - had given him few clues. Tor had yielded little more. Someone definitely wanted her dead, and they had been watching her for at least a few days. But why? Her record was clean, not even a speeding ticket or fender bender, and she was barely out of college. He shifted his position and continued to watch her.

The fact that she hadn't registered his presence told him a lot about her. She certainly wasn't like the rich bastards he was usually assigned to. He couldn't help but wonder what she had done, or possibly seen, that could have put her in this predicament.

The reality of providing security, especially a one-on-one detail, with high-level armed security, like the services provided at Benton Security Services, was that a solid percentage of clientele were shitty human beings. They weren't victims; they were rich, powerful people who had earned the enmity of others by doing something scurrilous, something that had truly welcomed the price they now found on their heads.

Most of them were folks that made the life he had lived before this look like a walk in the park. Sure, Shane had screwed people over, literally and figuratively, but the rich fucks he was tasked with guarding? They wrote the book on screwing people over.

Shane knew that Jack Benton preferred to avoid those clients and often turned down contracts for the worst of them. But business is business, and Shane had found himself assigned to plenty of cold-hearted, self-absorbed pricks or their spoiled, trust fund babies. After a while, he had gotten a knack for reading people. Hell, he had acquired that before he ever ran into Jack Benton. Watching Lila Benoit now, he could see she was a refreshing change from the usual clientele of half-criminal, egocentric pieces of crap he had been pulling in recently.

The last one he had worked with had been a mob informant that the police weren't sure they could protect, especially not with a mole in their ranks. He had spent three long weeks with the guy. The killing blow had been when the piece of shit broke the code, got online, and they both nearly died. The guy had gone straight to his favorite kiddie porn site, which his old cronies already knew him to frequent. It hadn't taken them long to track his online activity and then the general vicinity of the safe house. Shane had discovered it well before that and relocated him to a new safe house. But not before he punched the perv in the face, breaking his nose.

That was when Jack had stepped in and told him he was reassigned.

No real surprise there.

Less than ten feet away and she hadn't even noticed him. She was alone; the last two office workers had made a beeline for the elevators some twenty minutes ago. He had watched them go, checked in with the boss, and sent a text to Kaylee letting her know he was on location and that Lila was fine. Despite his stare, despite him moving well within her line of sight, still she remained there in her seat, fully absorbed in her work.

Shane shook his head. This woman was definitely different from his usual client. They were nervous as cats, and with good reason; they usually deserved the situation they found themselves in. But her? Not a chance. Still, a little more awareness of her surroundings would be preferable over this. This kind of behavior was what got most people killed.

Hours earlier, when the dial tone had signaled the end of their conversation before it had even truly begun, he had stood there listening to the low drone issue through the receiver. He had stared at it, thought of calling her back, and decided that meeting her in person made more sense. The arrangements had already been made, after all. His assignment had been formally issued from Jack, and Shane had been arranging for the safe house when her call came in.

He stared at her shapely legs, peeking out from the standard pencil skirt, her ankles crossed and tapping a silent beat on the floor, against one leg of her desk chair. She was wearing a charcoal silk blouse that scooped down, just low enough to show a hint of perky breasts. His gaze moved to her neck, which would have been flawless if it hadn't been for the mottling caused by strong, large fingers. The bruises were already fading, and he felt his jaw clench at the thought of her struggling to survive that attack. There was a bruise on her right cheekbone, along with a small cut, and her right arm remained in a sling. It hurt; she winced when she had to move it. And yet, here she was, working harder than anyone else in the office, alone on a Monday evening.

Lila's hair was black, straight, falling just past her shoulders. A few minutes ago, she had gingerly pulled it up in an impromptu bun, twirled it a few times and stuck a pencil in it, wincing in pain as she moved her right arm. She had high cheekbones and was athletic and slim. With her hair up, she reminded him of a librarian he once knew. His lips twitched at the memory of Liv Parker; she had made a difference when few others had.

Lila had been attacked three days ago. The attack had been interrupted by a neighbor within her building, giving her enough time to put some distance between her and her would-be killer. The attack had all the hallmarks of being a planned murder for hire, and the fact that the police hadn't bothered accessing Tor, asking Lila any questions, or even questioned the method of the attack, was puzzling. It hadn't been random.

Perhaps it is because her record is so clean that they didn't bother to investigate. Occam's Razor, and all that. With all things being equal, the simplest answer is usually the right one. A contract hit doesn't make sense.

According to her file, she was single, which Shane found surprising considering her looks. *Who knows,* he mused, *perhaps she's high maintenance. A beautiful woman knows how to twist a man around her little finger. Do they teach pretty girls that maneuver straight out of the cradle?*

Her delicate fingers moved like the wind on the keyboard, typing, pulling up charts and graphs that he could see dimly in the reflection of the glass window behind her now that the sun had slipped behind the buildings and held the world in an orange-hued glow. She was tiring. He could see it in the way her shoulders slumped. That wasn't surprising considering the beating she had taken. And it appeared that she had been hard at work all day. Shane checked his watch, it was almost 7 p.m. and she was still at it.

He didn't trust their isolation to continue. If he was watching, others could be as well. It was time they met.

He cleared his throat.

Lila heard the sound, looked up, and gave a small yip of fear. *Who was this man and how long had he been standing there*? She jumped to her feet, her eyes dark with fear. He watched as she reached into her desk and pulled out a letter opener with her left hand. Her fingers curled around it tightly, her body tense. The office chair drifted away from her, and Shane could see she was preparing to fight or flee.

Shane didn't advance. He didn't want to spook her any more than she already was. "Ms. Benoit? We spoke on the phone earlier today."

Lila took in the man standing in the doorway. He was tall, over six feet, with dark hair and brown, almost black, eyes. A five o'clock shadow covered a strong jaw and he wore a black button-down shirt, tucked into clean, well-fitted jeans, the shirt rolled to the elbows, giving her a tiny glimpse of a tattoo on his upper arm. At first, she was at a loss. Who had she spoken to? Distracted by a hunk appearing in her doorway, she had forgotten, if only for a moment, about that phone call. She stared at him, momentarily unable to speak.

"Ms. Benoit?" He took a step forward. "You called Benton Security Services and we spoke about a protective detail?"

Benton Security Services... he really did look as good in person as he sounded on the phone.

"Oh! You! Pecan pie..." She stopped, looked embarrassed, and shook her head at his puzzled expression. She couldn't seem to concentrate; all she could see was this extreme hotness standing before her. "I mean, I... you..." Trying to *un*-see hotness was apparently too hard for her sex-deprived brain.

And then it hit her.

"Wait a minute, how are you *here*? How did you find me?" And suddenly, she felt a cold wash of fear. She had made a call and now he was here, *here,* at her work. What was he doing here?

Shane, having already crossed the threshold into her office space, sat in the chair farthest from the door. She was nervous... he could see it in her eyes. Lila took a defensive stance, her body twisting and her hands raising into position, ready to strike out and defend herself. *Interesting,* he thought, *she had obviously had some training. Not enough to stop someone with a specific skillset, but still.* He put up his hands.

"I'm not here to hurt you. Your friend Kaylee, she gave us your basic information yesterday. And everything else is online; anyone can find it if they know where to look." He smiled wryly. "She said you would be difficult to convince, that you weren't sure you were in danger." His smile faded. "But you are, whether you are willing to admit it or not. And that is why I am here."

Lila's initial panic faded, and she relaxed slightly as she approached him. She reached out her left hand, which he took and clasped firmly with his. His skin was warm, slightly calloused.

"You can call me Shane."

Atomic Coffee

"You can call me Shane" was standing too close for comfort. *Hell, across the room would probably be too close for comfort,* Lila thought. This close to him, however, just an arm's length away, and she could smell him. He didn't smell of pecan pie and molasses, but he didn't smell bad. It was a clean scent, not cologne or deodorant, just a sexy man smell that reminded her yet again of how long it had been since she had been with someone.

The confining walls of the office galley made him seem even taller than he had in the doorway of her office a few moments ago. She hadn't even noticed the rest of her coworkers leaving the floor, she had been so lost in her work.

"Would you like some coffee?" Lila asked, nervous and hoping to look anywhere else than at his stubbled jaw, sexy lips, lean hips, and muscled forearms. *A man like this, well, he could pick her up, set her against a wall, and...*

"Sure."

His voice was liquid, warm, and she shivered a little in response as she turned away. The coffee maker's light was off, the pot empty and dry upside down in the drain tray. *Well of course it was. The last pot had been made, and consumed, hours ago. I'll have to make a new pot.*

For a moment she paused and considered telling him they were out of luck. But that would mean looking up at his sexy smile and those warm brown eyes and dark hair. She caught herself imagining him walking down the street, random women falling down in front of him, throwing their phone numbers at him, or simply humping his leg like sex-crazed dogs. She stifled a giggle at the last image. No, she couldn't look up, not yet.

The coffee packets were in here somewhere, or had they switched to bulk? Lila couldn't remember the last time she had made coffee. Anytime she offered to, or was even caught doing anything more complicated than operating the microwave, her co-workers looked terrified. Cooking was not her forte, and coffee wasn't either, according to her co-workers who, upon tasting her idea of coffee the first day she had worked there ordered her to never, ever touch the coffeemaker again. It didn't matter what they were doing during their day, if she uttered the words, "There's no coffee, shall I make some?" one of them would jump up and offer.

She sorted through the drawers, locating a bag of coffee, along with creamer and sugar packets.

Shane watched her closely. She appeared nervous, jumpy, but not necessarily as a result of the attack. She avoided looking at him, staring instead at the coffeepot as if it were a great mystery. Her body was stiff, and she maintained as large a distance as she could - a feat in the narrow galley-shaped kitchenette.

He could only deduce it had to do with *him*. He wasn't used to that. Women tended to like him - hell they damn near threw themselves at him - but Lila Benoit seemed to be doing everything she could to keep her distance. And the way she was opening all the drawers in the kitchen told him that she didn't normally make coffee. This suspicion was confirmed as he watched her add nearly triple the coffee he would have used for a full pot, and then overfilled the coffeemaker with water, sending a torrent of water spilling over the side.

"Oh... well, I..." She glanced up at him for a moment, stared at his mouth, paled slightly, and glanced away.

What a perplexing woman.

"I don't make coffee very often; perhaps we should go to Starbucks."

"No." He said it firmly, in a tone that brooked no argument. Lila's hackles raised and she was distracted from her nervous response.

Ugh, he's a chauvinist pig, I knew *he was too good to be true!* "I beg your pardon?"

"I said no. It isn't safe in public spaces."

Shane deftly reached past her, above her head, and pulled out two mugs from an open shelf. One was labeled "Cat Mom" and she could see the script on the other side: "The perfect child has four legs and a tail." He handed Lila a black and white one that read "I work hard so my cat can live a better life."

"Don't be ridiculous!" she sputtered. "I don't need someone to wrap me up in a cocoon and protect me from the world. I can take care of myself."

Shane leaned back, giving her a once-over, his eyes lingering on the bruises, her bandaged right arm. She bristled slightly. "No doubt you can dissuade the casual attacker, wannabe rapist, or garden variety lech."

His eyes moved down her body, cataloging her curves, the tone of her muscles, admiring the shape of her ass and how it fit so perfectly in her pencil skirt. She was fit, obviously kept in shape, and definitely had some basic self-defense moves. She wouldn't have lasted as long as she did down in that dark garage without them. But moves and athleticism notwithstanding, she wasn't going to stop a trained killer.

Lila straightened under his gaze, lifted her chin and eyed him defensively. "I managed pretty well the other day."

He nodded and smiled. "Yes, you did."

Then he moved closer, reached up, placed a warm hand on her neck. Lila shuddered at his touch and he felt himself growing hard in response. Instead of backing off, he used it, stepping even closer, invading her personal space, combining her fear and the desire he saw returned in her eyes to bring his point home.

"Until he had you here." He slid his hand to the same position her would-be killer had used. "You only had three seconds to get out of it. And did you? Or was that when the neighbor showed up?"

It wasn't the work of a trained killer, these bruises, but the man had definitely been hired. A scan of the note scrawled next to her photo flashed in his mind: "Make it look like a burglary or rape gone wrong."

"He would have choked you until you passed out, raped you, murdered you, and left your body there on the cold cement."

Shane had seen plenty of scumbag rap sheets. Rape would have been just one of the guy's list of talents. He'd dug into Tor further on his way here. The guy who had taken the assignment, Dominic Riehl, had done two years in Leavenworth for statutory rape, and another stretch of eight years after that at Farmington Correctional for forcible sodomy and attempted murder. He would have strangled the woman to death if a group of frat guys hadn't been on some bro camping trip and taken that particular trail. Dominic Riehl was bad news, and Shane didn't have to guess at how it was supposed to end; the note said it all. The only question was, why Lila Benoit?

Lila's breath caught at the feel of Shane's hands, however light the touch, on her throat. A hedonistic rush of desire and fear washed over her. *He was so damned strong...just imagining his hands sliding down her, brushing against her breasts, settling on her waist, cupping her ass in his hands, those lips on her mouth.*

His eyes locked onto hers. She was pretty. Usually he found himself attracted to more voluptuous women. A woman like this, with small breasts and a tight ass, were not his usual turn-ons. Despite this, he realized that the softness of her skin had sent all kinds of haywire messages to his libido, and another wave of desire crashed over him. He had thought he had control of this. He let go of her throat and backed up a step, embarrassed by his own response. He was a professional, and this was against The Code, *his* Code. *You don't fuck the clients Ellis. You keep them alive. You do your job.*

Shane forced his attention back to the job. The *job*, the *client*, whose perky breasts and tight ass notwithstanding, needed his protection. The scent of atomic, acrid coffee cut across his senses. "Coffee?"

Lila nodded, broke eye contact, and took a breath. Shane Ellis was a serious hottie, but obviously a misogynist. A well-intentioned, well-muscled, sexual god of a man with a hero complex. He had shown up here, without being asked or encouraged, and was busy telling her, Lila, how she couldn't take care of herself.

If he utters "little woman," I'm kneeing the son-of-a-bitch in the balls and leaving, Lila promised herself. She watched as he poured the acrid coffee into the two mugs. It smelled awful, far too strong, and she wondered if it was possible that the spoons would disintegrate in its intensity. She took the offered cup, topping it to the brim with tiny cups of cream and two packets of sugar. She set it on the counter, carefully stirred the mess, and then took a small sip. *Ugh.*

Shane watched her with something akin to amusement. He took a gulp of his own coffee and regretted it instantly. "This should come with a warning label," he said gruffly, pouring the contents down the drain. "Did all that milk and sugar crap you added make yours any more palatable?"

Lila choked down a second sip. "Um, it's, oh hell." She poured it down the drain, the swirl of creamer chasing the straight black, slipping out of sight into the darkness. "I'm, um, I'm not allowed to make coffee."

"I can't imagine why," Shane commented dryly.

She glanced up and saw him smile briefly. Her body sang in response. He had one of the sexiest smiles she had ever seen. *Hands, hips, right here on the counter. Just bend me over, hike up my skirt from behind, and oh sweet Jesus.* Lila bit down on her lower lip.

His smile dropped. "Ms. Benoit, we need to talk about your protection detail."

Her fantasy fled, and his mouth was all business and no sweet, sexy smile.

"I suppose we would, if I had hired you, Mr. Ellis, but..."

"Call me Shane."

"Shane, then. But I haven't hired you, I doubt I could afford your *services.*" She paused, her words dying on her lips at the look on his face.

Did that sound like she had just called him a prostitute? Oh God, not a prostitute, a gigolo. That's what they call the men. Strong hands, washboard abs, the sex would be... "Athletic." The word just popped out. "I mean..."

His left eyebrow quirked up, confused as she tried to get control of her mouth.

"Word salad, I've uh, got it. The scuffle the other night, I knocked my head, and..." she nodded, shrugging weakly and avoiding his penetrating gaze. "Sorry, word salad."

Oh my GOD, word salad? Really? The man is going to think I'm a complete lunatic!

"Ms. Benoit."

"Call me Lila."

"Lila."

"Word salad." Maybe if she just kept repeating that she would believe it herself.

"Right. Look, Lila, you need my protection. At least until this is looked into further."

"But as I said, I can't afford it, I'm sure I can't." Lila could feel the panic rising right alongside her libido. If this man came one step closer, she was pretty sure she would start humping his well-muscled leg like a dog. He was so hot, so amazingly sexy, and strong, and that voice, that voice. *Pecan pie and molasses, a spot of real whipped cream. Mm, yeah.*

"Lila, I don't handle the books. I don't do negotiations. My boss said this is on the house and I just read the folder, go where I'm told, and keep my clients alive." He eyed her sternly. "And I'm sticking by you until this mess gets sorted out. Understand?"

Lila nodded, managing a small squeak that she hoped sounded like a yes, but didn't.

More of a pathetic whine, really.

If she didn't get control of her response to his uncontrollable sexiness, she was pretty sure she was going to turn to jelly or tear her clothes off, possibly both.

He tilted his head, slightly bewildered, then smiled again, reassuring, almost paternal in nature. "Come on, we need to take you somewhere safe, and I'll explain it on the way to your apartment."

Her legs practically shook off of her body. "My apartment?"

Shane nodded and said, "Yes, your apartment. I'm assuming you will want clothes, toiletries."

Lila shook her head; that wasn't the answer she expected. Although if he had gripped her ass and lifted her up against the kitchen counter...

My mind is never leaving the gutter, is it?

"I need clothes?"

He arched an eyebrow, and she blushed. She could feel the red lighting up her cheeks, her neck, hell, even her ears. "I mean, *why* do I need clothes?"

Oh yeah, great, now I sound like a complete slut, or nudist, or, or...

At the other end of the floor, a muted click of a door closing caught Shane's attention and his mood changed immediately, switching from solicitous and mildly amused to another person entirely. It wasn't just that his entire demeanor changed, but also an almost physical metamorphosis seemed to occur. He felt changed into someone different, capable, and lethal in a period of mere seconds. Beneath his shirt, his muscles flexed as he assumed an alert position.

Lila stared at him and wondered if it were possible to be even more turned on by this handsome "call me Shane" stranger. He reached a hand to his belt, shifting his weight to the balls of feet, alert and listening. His free hand reached out, pulling her close to his side. His lips grazed her ear as he murmured, "Who works here late? Cleaning staff? Co-workers?"

His left hand eased a lethal, gray handgun from a holster she hadn't even noticed until now, his eyes searching for any movement in the corridor outside.

Her heart rate sped up. *Hot man. Danger. It's like something out of a movie. Come with me if you want to live.*

She whispered back, "The cleaning crew comes through later, eleven, maybe? And everyone else went home."

She clutched his arm, close enough to smell him. No cologne, oh no, not Shane Ellis. Instead a clean, almost woodsy scent came from him. He smelled amazing.

The footfalls, noticeable only if one concentrated, were heading past them, towards a bank of offices, Lila's included.

"*Stay here,*" he mouthed to her and her eyes widened. Suddenly it was all feeling very real and not so sexy, just terrifying.

She shook her head at him, but he had already turned away and began to move silently down the hall. In the distance, Lila heard the door to the office open and close again.

Does that mean someone left? Or someone else came in? Who were these guys? And what do they want with me?

Lila's heart began to race, her body shaking. She nearly screamed when Shane reappeared, his hand warm on her arm as he pulled her towards him, his mouth at her ear.

"A second one just came in. We have to go, *now*," he whispered. "Stay close. Follow my lead." And with her arm firmly in his grip, he moved out of the kitchen.

The Stairwell

Lila's breath came in short, panicked gasps.

The last few seconds, a run from the kitchen galley to the stairwell, had been terrifying. As soon as they had emerged from the relative safety of the kitchen walls, a shot had rung out, then another, and another. Shane had gripped her arm harder, painfully, as they dashed from one cubicle area to the next, and his gun firing so close that her ears felt stuffed with cotton, along with a distant ringing. She could hear nothing else, momentarily deafened by the shots.

As they had weaved out of one hallway and into the next, wood had splintered and flown from the lacquered 17th century cabinet outside of her office. The gunshots blasted simultaneously from the far end of the hall, and another shot ricocheted past her ear. The world had tilted on its side, tangling and rolling, as Shane pushed her down with his body and snapped off another burst of gunfire in the shooter's direction. He had dropped like a sack of potatoes. One minute a living, breathing human being, the next, a marionette without strings, limp on the floor, blank eyes staring. Lila swallowed a scream.

Shane had picked her up then. Just one quick yank and she was vertical. She might as well have been weightless.

"Stay with me," he hissed in her ear, a sound she could barely hear. "We need to head for the stairwell."

The second man could disguise his footfalls, but not when he was at a full run. The sound of his feet came at the same time as a flurry of shots, one of them shattering a tall enamel vase on a pedestal just inches from Lila's head. She screamed and hit the floor, the hard concrete below the thin industrial carpet jolting her injured arm painfully.

Shane turned, pivoting on his heel as he fired. Glass shattered, the wall of an office shredding into slivers. He reached down, picked her up by the waist and then shoved Lila into a corner. She winced as she felt a bruise begin to rise on her undamaged arm where her body slammed into the metal edge of a door. Her shoulder took the brunt of the impact and she huddled on the floor, staring at a carpet covered in enamel shards. Each day, on the way to her office in the morning, she would walk this hallway, just so she could enjoy the scenes depicted on the beautiful vase. It was 15th century, from the Ming dynasty, and priceless.

Well, it had *been priceless.*

The shots were deafening - her ears rang and her head ached. With each gunshot, her body jerked in terror, pulling away from the noise, although there was nowhere to go. She was trapped in a corner. She covered her face, curling into a ball, wondering if there was some way to make herself invisible.

Where is Harry Potter's invisibility cloak when it is needed most?

Suddenly, there was silence. Her ears were still ringing, and she felt more than she heard the thud of a second body hitting the floor. She was too frightened to look. If Shane was dead, then the killer was going to put a bullet in her head next. *Why bother looking up and seeing the gun pointed at me? Better to just close my eyes and...* A hand closed on her arm, yanking her upright again, eliciting a sob of terror.

Shane pulled her close and Lila opened her eyes to the view of a black shirt, tight over a muscled chest.

The assassin was on the floor, a spot of red blossoming on his chest. His eyes were open, staring, and Lila watched death take him. The eyes dulled and went blank. Shane had kicked his gun aside as a precaution, scanned for any other intruders, and then pulled her away from the body and on through two sets of doors to the safety of a quiet stairwell. His hand was tight on her wrist, bruising her skin, but Lila didn't complain.

"Oh my God, oh my God, what just happened back there?" She skidded to a stop, her high heels scraping and the sound reverberating off of the cement walls. The handrail dug into her back and the cement wall of the stairwell was ice cold against her. She shook in fear and shock and she barely noticed Shane's hands as he ran them down the front of her. He turned her around effortlessly, checking her back as well.

She gasped as his hands ran over her. "What are you..."

Nothing, no wounds. *Damn, but that had been close.* He breathed a sigh of relief. He'd let himself get distracted, and very nearly gotten them both killed.

"Are you hurt?"

"What?"

She couldn't think, the shock of what had just happened closing in, a dark hand of fear clutching at her heart and throat, squeezing them tight. She felt dizzy. *Can't catch my breath.* She wheezed, struggling to inhale and exhale. Lila closed her eyes. She tried to concentrate on relaxing her throat, her chest.

She hadn't had a panic attack in years. They had come in the aftermath of her father's death, in her mid-teens. It had taken years for her to learn to control them. She had learned guided meditation, was given a prescription for Xanax that she rarely used, and finally found a mixed martial arts instructor who was a firm believer in breath work.

Not even the fight in the garage on Friday had triggered one, but the past few seconds sure had.

His hands paused. "Lila, look at me." He tipped her head up and she opened her eyes reflexively. "Hey. It's okay, I've got you."

She nodded, her eyes wide with panic, her throat and lungs still fighting for air. *There wasn't enough air.*

He set her back against the cool concrete wall, his body close to hers, and he placed a warm hand on her chest. She could feel his warmth, his breath slowing.

"Look at me, Lila. There is only me and you here. Match my breath," he whispered in her ear, "just focus on the breath."

Shane's ears strained for any sounds. They didn't have time for this; there could be more of them out there. He recognized the signs of a panic attack - it wasn't so different from an asthma attack and he had certainly seen his fill of those. He needed her to be able to run, but she couldn't do that if she was in the throes of an attack and he sure couldn't carry her down thirty plus flights of stairs *and* fight any more would-be killers off.

Her body, shaking against his, was distracting him from the job at hand. He could smell a faint whiff of perfume, possibly jasmine, mixed with her natural scent. Desire, so akin to the adrenaline rushing through his body from the shootout, flooded through him again.

What was this woman doing to him?

His hand, resting on her chest between her breasts, itched to move to the left and encompass her breast. He wondered how her nipples looked. The vision of her body, stripped of everything but that black lace bra he had seen tantalizing hints of, and thigh-high stockings, leaned against the stairway railing flitted through his head. He imagined leaning in and slipping his tongue between those red lips, turning her gasps into moans of desire.

The smaller head hardened, straining against the durable denim, eager to turn that "fight or flight" response into a "fuck her senseless."

Damn it, this was his client.

"Just breathe." he whispered, trying to channel calm and ignore the attraction he felt. He willed his dick to go back to sleep and it gleefully ignored him.

The minutes ticked by and gradually her breaths slowed from the ragged gasps to even breaths in and out. The pounding of her heart was no longer a visible thing.

"I'm okay." Her voice was faint.

"You sure?"

"Yeah."

"Okay." He leaned down and pulled one of her shoes off, then the other. He stared up at her, and Lila flushed. It felt *intimate.* "This way you can run easier." He smiled at her. "And far quieter."

He grabbed her left hand. "Come on, we need to leave...*now.*"

"Wait!" She resisted as he pulled her down the stairs, hugging the wall. "Oh my God, we can't just leave them there!"

"Yes, we can. They are dead, both of them," Shane replied tersely. "We need to get out of here, now. Before any more come along and try and kill us."

"*More?!*" Lila squeaked. "But..."

He stopped, his body still close to hers, his breath warm. "Were either of those men the same guy that attacked you in the garage?" He was so close that she could feel him, hard against her. Her body quivered uncontrollably in response.

"No… he was shorter, heavier… but…"

"I don't know why someone wants you dead, Ms. Benoit, but I can guarantee you they are getting pretty insistent. If you want to live, you follow my lead, and do as I say." He was so close and scary with his intense stare, that Lila felt her heart rate speed up even further, jackhammering in her chest, so close. He had killed two men. Men who were trying to kill her, but still.

He began to pull her down the stairs and she resisted. "Wait, my purse, it has my keys and wallet in it. I can't leave it here."

"Shit." He paused, thinking. "Wait here." And with that he vanished through the door, as silently as the two men had. It closed with a soft click.

It couldn't have taken any more than a minute for Shane to return, but it had felt like forever. Lila trembled. She felt exposed, helpless, standing there in the stairwell alone. Every creak, or gust of air, and Lila was convinced someone would appear ready to finish the deed. She jumped when the door opened, biting down on her tongue with an aborted yelp of fear.

Shane smiled and held her purse out to her.

"Thank you." She took it from him and wrestled it onto her uninjured shoulder.

"Come on," he said, "we need to get out of here. Now. Stick to the wall side and avoid the inside railing."

Lila wondered if there were more lurking, just waiting for her or Shane to lean over and look down. A quick head shot, the roar it would make in this echo chamber of a stairwell. She nodded and slid along the wall; her heels tucked securely into her arm sling.

Kurgen Real Estate was located on the 39th floor of a building known as One Kansas City Place. It took a long time to get down thirty-nine flights of stairs. At the bottom of the stairs, Shane stopped abruptly and placed a hand on her shoulder, pushing her firmly against the stairwell wall, out of sight of the door and its sliver of a window. They were at P2, the second level of the parking garage, and had been no other people. No one with bad intentions, or good, had appeared, but it was clear that Shane wasn't taking any chances. He pressed her against the wall and quickly stole a glance through the window.

"Wait here."

He opened the door, the latch clicking quietly in his grasp and the door creaking just enough to start Lila's heart thumping. She couldn't help but imagine hearing the sound of a gunshot and watching Shane collapse to the ground. He peered out, and slowly edged his body out the door. A few seconds later he beckoned to her.

"It's clear. Follow me."

Seconds later they were in his car. He had opened the passenger's side and unceremoniously shoved her in.

"Stay down. Out of sight, until we get out of here." She didn't argue, simply folded her body into the tiny space, still out of breath from running down thirty-nine flights of stairs. He didn't tell her about the dead parking attendant sprawled in the booth, a single black hole between his eyes. A spray of the poor man's blood painted the glass on the far side of the toll booth. Shane drove out of the parking garage and onto the darkened city street outside.

The terrifying events of the past ten minutes, combined with the cold of the car, and of the outside, the temperatures having suddenly dipped into the 30s after sundown, brought on a fit of shivering that no amount of heat from the car vents could abate.

Once they had moved out of the city, and Shane was sure no one was following, he turned down the road, heading for the safe house, and reached over to help Lila out of her cramped position. She had a run in her stockings. He sucked in his breath; she was wearing garters and he caught a flash of them as she struggled out of the footwell and into her seat. She smoothed down her skirt, but not before he had seen a flash of black lace juxtaposed against a smooth white thigh. His dick hardened, then throbbed eagerly in his pants, as randy as a middle-school boy eyeing a cute girl in the seat in front of him. He let out a small groan of discomfort as he calculated how long it would be before he could get to the safe house, explain The Code and what would happen next, and then see her off to bed so he could go to his own and jerk one off.

Although I'd much rather fuck her senseless. Damn, but why didn't I get a fat asshole to protect?

Lila continued to tremble. She stared out at the dark night, "My apartment is off of Broadway, in the other direction." She said it without any real conviction, shell-shocked at the images the last few minutes had given her. She had seen the blood on the glassed-in wall of the parking attendant's booth after all.

Shane reached over, squeezed her left hand, and said, "I'm sorry, but those two guys showing up changes things. It wouldn't be a good idea to go to your apartment right now. I'm taking you somewhere safe." He used his most professional tone, the one he reserved for the rich fucks who paid a hell of a lot of money for him to keep them safe from all the people they had screwed over.

Lila couldn't have screwed anyone over. He didn't know what she had done, or seen, to deserve this, but he was going to protect her. His fingers strayed to the delicate bones in her wrist and he felt his pants tighten in response.

If only he could get back control of his body and do...his...job.

The Code

It didn't take long to reach the safe house, at least, not according to the clock on the dashboard. A mere twelve minutes, which felt more like an hour. The adrenaline rushing through her had slowed, but her mind just kept turning in circles.

Why would anyone want to kill me? I'm nobody!

The black Jeep exited the highway, slipping through the dark fall night, and eventually passing through the seedier part of town. Lila watched the wide streets turn to a narrow, winding road, occupied on both sides by aging, mid-century homes that grew smaller in size. The road dead-ended ahead - the locked gates of what looked to be an industrial plant of some kind looming tall on the horizon.

The Jeep slowed, stopping before it reached the plant, and turned left at a smaller set of locked gates near the bottom of the hill. Shane rolled his window down and keyed in a long code. There was a short pause, and then the gates slid open. Shane put the Jeep in gear and drove through. The gates slowly closed behind them.

Perhaps the dilapidated state of the other homes so nearby was why the house situated high above them at the top of the long, private drive struck Lila as so extraordinary. Built in the low-slung sprawling look of the late '60s, it commanded a view of rolling acres, fortified behind a solid fence, and with a million-dollar view of the Missouri River. Here on the hill, separated by a thick forest of trees from the string of simpler homes below, the views were extraordinary. They turned the corner and the garage door rumbled upwards. Shane eased the Jeep inside, his free hand still resting on the delicate bones of her hand. She hadn't stopped trembling once during the twenty-minute journey.

He pressed a button and the garage door closed, sealing them inside. A light on the door mechanism above shed a weak yellow light over the garage. It was spotless and uncluttered. When Lila didn't move, Shane reached over her, unlatching the door, savoring the feel of her body against his. He paused, his face inches from hers, and saw her pupils expand. Was she afraid? Turned on? Fight or flight response did odd things to a person, and after the experience they had both shared, the answer was probably yes to both questions. He stared at her and strongly considered kissing her. It wouldn't stop there, though, and he knew it.

What in the hell am I doing? She's a client.

It wasn't just him. Not that it made it any better, not that it made it *right*, but he could feel her body respond. The way she held her breath, bit her lip, tightened her fingers against his hand. He forced himself to break eye contact and pull away, to stop his lips from claiming hers and taking what he wanted.

Wordlessly, she exited the vehicle, her stockinged feet soundless on the cold cement floor. She stood there for a moment, the Jeep door open, staring at him as if unsure what would happen next. He shook off the vision of her spread against the warm hood gasping in pleasure and tilted his head towards the door.

"This way; let's get you warmed up."

Hours before he had logged in to the safe house via the secure link on his phone and set the thermostat to seventy-two degrees. With a few more swipes and push of the button, he had also ignited the gas log in the fireplace. He was glad he did. They were greeted with warmth and comfort, and an orange glow emanated from the sunken living room at the end of the hall.

Inside the house, the floors were lined with plush wall-to-wall carpet. Shane led the way down a short hallway, past a luxurious half bath that screamed "I'm from the seventies and proud of it!" It was paneled with a heavy, dark wood on the lower half of the walls and a dark red velvet flocked wallpaper on the upper half.

Shane paused briefly in the front entry, removed his shoes, and placed them neatly by the door before stepping down into the sunken living room and disappearing around the corner. Lila paused to take in the view of rough-hewn beams of the ceiling high above and a wide spiral iron and wood staircase that led to the floor above. A large wrought-iron chandelier also hung from the ceiling above. It was lined with at least thirty dim candelabra bulbs set in wide, faux pillar candles. Their combined glow, however, was bright.

Lila heard the clink of glass, ice, and the low, slow gurgle of liquid. By the time she stepped down into the living room and turned the corner, he was handing her a heavy glass of cut crystal, filled with ice cubes and an amber liquid.

"Here, you look like you need this."

Lila took the glass, her hands brushing his, hers still trembling. She lifted the glass to her lips, took a sip. The alcohol burned her throat, clawing its way down, deep inside her, and warmed her belly. She didn't look at him, but she could feel his gaze just as she had felt his hands glide over her in the stairwell, checking for injuries, for bullet holes. This chain of thought led to the image of the two men, crumpled on the ground, blood blooming from their chests.

Dead, Shane had said, *dead after trying to kill her.*

Shane watched her as she took a second sip, then a third, the trembling slowly fading as liquid courage took its place. He wanted to fuck her. And he struggled with it. This woman, she was doing something to him. He didn't know how or why - she wasn't his type. He loved the loud, brassy women with big tits and asses that could hold up a shelf.

He'd said it to his buddies in college, "More cushion for pushing', man, who wants a scrawny chick when you can go the mile with a real woman?"

But looking at her, he didn't see scrawny, he saw tight. He saw an athletic ride-you-all-night kind of woman. He threaded his fingers through his hair and looked away. He had to get his mind off fucking her.

She's a client, *asshole.*

He stepped away, crossing to the other side of the room, the entrance to the kitchen.

"You need something to eat, and we need to discuss what comes next."

He said it over his shoulder, walking away. She would follow, and she would listen to him now. They all did once the bullets started flying. He crossed the kitchen to the refrigerator and pulled out a package of cheese, some salami, and reached for the crackers in the cabinet next to the fridge.

"There's some fruit there on the table, and some grapes here in the fridge." He reached in and pulled them out.

He arranged it all on a plate, complete with a sharp knife, and then he carried the food over to the table, holding out a chair. She had followed him into the kitchen, her drink empty, save for the half-melted ice cubes. He didn't ask, simply filled the glass with more amber liquid from an expensive cut glass crystal carafe on the table.

"We are safe here, that's the biggest thing to remember." His eyes were dark, fierce, and quite intense.

Lila looked away, first staring at her plate, then out at the lights of the towns across the river. She could see the steady blinking lights of the planes flying in and out of an airport.

He continued, "I expect my clients to abide by The Code while they are under my protection. It's simple, and it will keep you alive."

He ticked off the items one by one on his fingers, watching her as he did.

"Number One, absolutely no contact with the outside. Not your friends, your family, your boss, no one."

He paused, momentarily distracted by the bruises on her throat. *I would happily kill the sonuvabitch who touched her.*

"Number Two, do not leave the safe house without me by your side."

She met his eyes and he was struck by the unusual shade of green. Not unlike jade, but with flecks of brown. He couldn't help wondering what her face would look like mid-orgasm, tilted back, eyes closed, gasping for air as he...

"Shane?" Her voice interrupted his fantasy. He realized he had been silent for far too long. She blinked at him, her mouth a moue of concern.

"Number Three, no unsecured phone calls or internet access. And, most important of all, Number Four, don't withhold information."

Lila stood up and looked away from him out the sliding glass doors to the river and the lights of a town in the distance. Miles away, they could see the planes circling in the sky, descending and ascending, their running lights slowly blinking in a steady, reassuring pattern. She stared out into the distance and drained her glass, nibbling at the tidbits of food on her plate. He refilled her glass.

"Do you have any questions?" His words hung in the air, the alcohol burned in her belly, and Lila shook her head silently. Several moments passed.

"Is this your house?"

"No, it belongs to Benton Security Services, well, to the owner Jack."

"It's huge," she said, her eyes finally moving from staring into the dark night sky, back to meet his. They were such a striking green. Her mouth, a tiny expanse of delicate pink lips, opened enough for the tip of her tongue to moisten them, before darting back to safety.

What he wanted to do to that mouth.

Shane ran his hand through his short-cropped hair. He had to stop thinking about her like that.

He stood up abruptly and turned away. "I'll show you where you will be sleeping." He left the room without a backward glance.

Lila watched him go. A small surge of resentment ran through her. She wasn't used to obedience being something that was expected or taken for granted.

What kind of sexy, pecan pie, sweet molasses misogynist is he, anyway?

Conflicting emotions warred within her. Part of her wanted to stay here, stare at the amazing view, and watch the planes continue to dance in the sky. Another part of her wanted him to walk back into the room, pull her against him, and kiss her ruthlessly. She'd seen the desire in his eyes; he wanted her as much as she wanted him.

I shouldn't follow him like some obedient dog. That will only encourage him to be more of a chauvinistic pig.

For a moment she hesitated and then she couldn't help but wonder.

What does it look like upstairs?

Curiosity won over making a stand. She rose from the table and followed anyway.

The thick pile of the carpet muffled all sound and gave off a feeling of sinking, similar to a sandy beach, with every step. It was everywhere, and Lila followed Shane up wide, circular stairs to the landing above. The wood was heavy and there were large beams of dark, rough-hewn timbers and heavy wrought iron. Shane waited for her to reach him, then turned and opened a door, bowing slightly and motioning for her to proceed him. The door led to a short hallway that opened into a large room with a vaulted ceiling. The dark heavy wood pillars were covered with iron work and it reminded Lila of the inside of a church.

A fireplace with a gas log glowed warm against the far wall. There was a dim lamp in one corner next to a massive four-poster bed. And around another corner, there was a large, pleasantly appointed bathroom complete with a claw foot bathtub. This seemed at odds with the '70s hunting lodge look, but Lila wasn't going to complain - she loved long soaks in a hot bath.

Lila's initial nervousness around Shane had been cured by the liquid courage she had tossed back with the light dinner. The drinks had lit a fire in her belly and loosened her tight, aching muscles. She was no longer shaking, no longer afraid. Instead she could feel all the experiences of the past few hours turning from terror into an intense, hot need.

She stared at the fire, her mind firmly on the man standing behind her.

Southern drawl, pecan pie, whatever, she couldn't help but picture him without his clothes. She would nibble that tattoo, lick her way down his chest, and explore the treasure hidden behind that jean zipper. *Mm...*

His voice brought her back to herself with a start, "I should let you have some time to settle in, update my boss on what happened tonight, and all that."

She turned to face him. He was standing close, too close, and she could feel the heat of his body hanging in the air, warming the layer, an almost visible current of it forming between them. His eyes moved over her, and she caught herself wondering what it would be like to have his hands moving there instead. She felt her breaths coming closer together, heavy, deep, and she took a step closer.

Shane could feel the pull of attraction between them. He stared into her eyes. The alcohol had calmed her, and he could see it in the way she held herself - less stiff and afraid, more languorous, sexy. All it would take was a touch. His hand sliding up her arm, his mouth on hers. He just had to reach out and...

Shane matched her step forward with his own step back, and then another, retreating towards the door. "If you need anything, I'm on the other side of the house, down the hall. In the morning we need to talk."

He put a hand on her uninjured shoulder, keeping her at arm's length. "Someone wants you dead. And we need to figure out why. Otherwise, they will *never* stop."

Lila blinked; the spell broken. Fear flooded her again. *Who was trying to kill her? And why?*

"It has to be a mistake," she said. "I'm no one."

He smiled, white teeth flashing and she melted all over again. "Everyone is someone, Lila." He squeezed her shoulder gently. "Take a bath, get some sleep. Help yourself to whatever clothing you can find in the closet. We will figure this out in the morning."

He turned away from her, walked down the short hall, and closed the door to the suite behind him. His thoughts were whirling in his head, the imperative to call his boss and report the situation warring with an overwhelming impulse to turn around, walk back through that door, and...

Fight or flight, he counseled himself, *she's reacting to everything that just happened to her. And no, it doesn't help that she is smoking hot.*

He had never slept with a client. Never even come close. Of course, it probably helped that most of his clients were pasty-faced white men who owned hedge funds or had seen something they shouldn't. Hell, most of them had done something they shouldn't, and were now running for their lives.

There had been the pair of girls, hollow-eyed, scared. They had also been traumatized, malnourished, and sporting bruises on their arms, necks, and faces. He had looked at them and felt a murderous rage towards whoever had mistreated them. Even when the youngest, a girl of seventeen, had tried to climb into his bed one night, he hadn't been the least interested. The girl needed counseling, patience, and safety - not another man taking advantage of her. He had gently led her back to her room, and the poor kid had looked confused, yet relieved. He had also made sure to lock his door for the next two nights until they were out of his care.

Shane shook his head, realized he had been standing, lost in thought at the top of the stairs, and quickly made his way down and then across to the west wing of the house.

He pulled his phone out of his pocket as it vibrated. "Hey, Boss, sorry I didn't call sooner. The scene was hot, so I had to get her out of there before anyone else showed up."

Jack didn't waste words. "Tell me everything."

Shane described the shootout and the dead guard. "She's not much help. She doesn't seem to know *why* anyone would want to hurt her. My gut says she's telling the truth."

"*Two* hit men?" Jack's voice held surprise. "What the hell has this girl gotten herself into?"

"She's pretty shook. I'll take her life apart piece by piece tomorrow and see if I can get some clarity."

"Yeah, do that. I'll talk to Azule, see if I can get her to dig into Tor further and find out who is sending these guys. Also, Teeny says the police scanner is reporting cops are already on scene. Someone called in hearing gunshots."

"Mine," Shane replied. "Those two men had silencers on their Sig Sauers."

There was a pause and a slow exhale on the other end. "Sig Sauers?"

"Yeah."

"Shit. That means..."

"I know."

"Update me in the morning, Ellis."

"Will do."

Shane's finger was hovering over the End Call button when Jack added, "And Shane?"

"Yeah, Boss?"

"Keep it professional."

"Always, sir." A dial tone sounded in his ear.

I'm always professional. Except for that asshole kiddie porn shithead that I decked. But he had it coming.

Shane stared at his phone, the screen dark and blank. Jack had gotten a look at Lila's file. He was well aware of how smoking hot she was. He sucked in a breath and tried not to think about those stockings and garters peeking out of her rumpled skirt.

No wonder Jack's warning me off her.

Shane tossed the phone onto the nightstand and stripped off his clothes before lying down on top of the covers. He stared at the dark ceiling, brooding, until sleep claimed him.

Crime Scene

Morris Endon stared at the body bag. A few feet away a small yellow photo evidence tag sat next to the shards of a priceless vase. The tall black letters read, "18." He flinched as a bright flash went off from across the room, temporarily blinding him. The detective holding the camera ignored him, focusing on a shell casing next to yet another yellow plastic sign. The flash came again, and then again, as the man took picture after picture, changing angle, moving to the left, kneeling and then standing.

He had been reading *Inman News* on his couch, listening to Tchaikovsky, and sipping from a whiskey highball with ice and ginger ale when the doorbell rang. The deep, rich tone of the Westminster chime had been jarring in the quiet night. The police officer stood at the door, with his cruiser and its indiscreet flashing lights in the driveway behind him. Already he could see his neighbors peeking out of their curtained windows. The HOA bi-annual meeting was next week, he was sure he would be the topic of plenty of idle gossip.

Standing there staring at the officer, Morris suddenly regretted the alcohol. The warm glow of it had spread through his body and engendered a lassitude he found difficult to fight, yet felt necessary to eradicate. Despite his meteoric advancement from the cheap inner-city apartment of his youth to a well-heeled existence in one of the wealthier parts of town, police officers still unnerved him.

It isn't as if he can arrest me for drinking in my own home after all. Or can they?

"Morris Endon?" The officer was young, late 20s at most, and his hand rested lightly on his utility belt, close to his service weapon.

"Yes, what can I do for you, Officer?"

"Sir, I need to ask you to come with me. There's been an incident at Kurgen Real Estate and your presence is required there."

"An *incident*? It's nearly ten o'clock. What sort of incident?"

"A shooting, sir. If you could please come with me."

"Of course." His mind whirling, he wondered if he should call someone. A lawyer? Mr. Kurgen?

What do they want with me? He could feel the panic rising. *I haven't done* anything.

He had slipped on shoes and a coat and locked the heavy, burled walnut front door behind him and followed the officer towards the flashing lights. Morris had contemplated telling the officer he would drive himself but sat in the back seat of the cruiser instead.

He can smell the alcohol on my breath, I'm sure of it.

The ride there had been silent, but quick. There was no traffic this late on a weeknight. Outside a sliver of a moon had risen. It played peek-a-boo in the sky as it repeatedly appeared and disappeared behind the abundant cloud cover. They arrived, and he was taken into the building through the front door, past a coroner's van and the media truck, both parked in the circle drive normally reserved for limousines and taxis.

Morris's eyes tracked back to the body bag. There was blood on the carpet, a deep, red stain that crept to the left and stopped by one corner of the antique lacquered Chinese cabinet. Calling it an incident had been such an understatement. How was he going to explain to Mrs. Kurgen that the irreplaceable antique vase had been shattered? Or the Chinese cabinet shot full of holes?

It wasn't supposed to happen like this. There are rules.

"Sir?" He flinched again. The officer who had escorted him here laid a reassuring hand on his sleeve. "Mr. Endon, if you could come this way, please."

He followed him, away from the body, past the cleaning crew and the detective interviewing them, and two men wearing jackets emblazoned with "CORONER" in yellow on the back.

My office. They are leading me into my *office.*

The detective was in plain clothes, a gold badge clipped to his belt. He stood up when Morris walked in.

"Mr. Endon, I'm Detective Rob Stone. Sorry to roust you out of bed and bring you in here so late." He clasped Morris's hand and gave it a quick, authoritative shake. "Please, sit down."

He sat back down in Morris's new desk chair, motioning for Morris to take a seat normally reserved for visitors. The seats were lower, something that had been quite intentional on Morris's part when setting up the office. It was easier to maintain a psychological advantage that way. He sat down, sinking into the cushioned seat. It was comfortable, but he was sitting lower than he was used to. A thread of resentment ran through him and he struggled to keep it from showing on his face.

"What the hell happened here?" Morris asked, trying to keep his voice even.

There are two god-damned body bags in the office. It wasn't supposed to happen like this.

"We are still trying to figure that out. We have two men dead here in the office, and the parking attendant who serves as security at night has also been killed."

"My God!" Morris didn't have to manufacture that response; he was horrified. How had things gone down like this? "Who would do something like this?"

"Well, like I said, we are working on it. If I were to guess, I'd say that one of these men shot the security guard and then headed up here."

"To what end?" Morris asked, "To steal the collection?"

Perhaps I can steer them in that direction.

The detective shook his head, dissolving Morris's hopes of diverting the police attention. "No, if they had intended theft they wouldn't have been armed with silencers."

Morris blinked at the detective; his face frozen.

Rob leaned back, the chair tilted without a creak of protest, despite the man's girth. "This chair is amazing. I really need to get me one of these."

Morris managed a weak smile, the resentment of being displaced slightly stronger now. "It's new."

"What brand is it?"

"Herman Miller."

"Oh yeah? I've heard about them, but this is real luxury here."

Morris fought to keep his emotions in check. "Yes, the Eames lounge chair is top of the line."

And at over four thousand dollars, it is completely out of your price range.

"Mmhm, I'll say it is," the detective sighed and stared out the window. "Quite the view as well."

Morris felt his face flush. "Detective, is there a reason you had your officer roust me out of my home? Perhaps we could talk furniture choices and skylines when it is daylight out."

The detective smiled and said, "My apologies. I was waiting for a list of office personnel. And we are dusting for fingerprints as well, but I'm sure you can imagine that is quite a task with this size office." He leaned forward, staring intensely into Morris's eyes. "What I'm hoping to understand from you is what two men armed with silencers would have been looking for in a real estate office, and who killed them."

Morris stammered, "I'm sure I don't know." His face flushed and the resentment transformed into fear. They actually considered him a suspect?

I'm not involved. Say it, over and over, until they listen. It wasn't supposed to happen like this.

"You deal in commercial real estate? Or is it residential?"

"It's a mix, actually. Commercial, high-end residential, and corporate clients mainly." Morris answered promptly, relieved that the detective had turned away again. The man stared out at the city's skyline; lights sprinkled the high rises and there were wide swaths of darkness, the closely spaced homes in the distance devoid of light. The city, and most of its inhabitants, peacefully snoozed away.

A silence fell, and the minutes seemed to tick by. His anxiety increased. "I am happy to help with the personnel list if you need any assistance. I don't know everyone; there are a few newer employees that have come on board recently that I am not familiar with..."

His voice petered out and died as Rob stared at him.

"Tell you what," said the detective as he leaned forward, "I'll get that list and talk to you in the morning." He stood up and reached into his back pocket, removing a business card and handing it to Morris. "You could come by the station if you prefer."

Morris was relieved. "Sure, I can do that. What time?"

"Give me a call in the morning when you are up. I imagine you will have a few things to deal with - getting a crime scene cleanup crew in if the techs are done working the scene, insurance claims, and I'll want you to double-check with all your employees. We will get to that last bit tomorrow."

Morris winced at the thought of the blood-soaked carpet. "Right. Will do."

The detective called past him, "Stevens, can you give Mr. Endon a ride back home?"

Morris shook his head as he pulled out his phone. "No need, I'll catch a cab home."

He then stepped gingerly around the crime scene tape and avoided looking at the body bags now being loaded onto gurneys.

It wasn't supposed to happen like this.

Morris did his best to not break into a trot as he reached the outer doors of Kurgen Real Estate and disappeared from the detective's view.

The ride down the elevator was silent as Morris searched on his smartphone for a local Uber to take him home. It was there in moments, and he spent the next ten minutes silently fuming until he found himself relaxing at the sight of his upscale neighborhood.

And really, all they wanted was information; he hadn't done anything wrong. I hadn't been in that office shooting it all to hell.

His heart gave a painful thump at the memory of the priceless vase and antique lacquered cabinet, both destroyed.

Whose bright idea had it been to send those assholes in?

He paid the driver and returned to the warm, welcoming wood tones of his house, relieved and angry at the same time. In his office, he unlocked a small drawer and took out another cell phone and pressed a button on speed dial. It rang twice and went to voice mail.

"I just got hauled down to my office. It looks like a battle zone. What the hell happened there? Call me when you get this; you have some serious fucking explaining to do."

He jabbed at the End Call button and tossed the phone onto the couch in his den. It bounced and then slipped behind a seat cushion. Morris let out a long, ragged breath. Everything had gone so well, for so long, and even the hiccup with Witt had been dealt with quickly and easily. The discrepancies had been fixed, the numbers changed and morphed and slipped into (and out of) different funds until the errors were erased to all but the most practiced eyes. And those eyes could be bribed. How, how in the hell, could this have happened? And how did he make sure it didn't happen again?

His eyes strayed to the cut crystal that housed the whiskey, and the glass, still with a finger of amber liquid waiting inside it, the ice long dissolved. His stomach flip-flopped with nerves. He stood to lose *everything*. The commission would come after him, the one standing in the light, not the others obscured by shadows.

He reached out, grabbed the glass, and swallowed it in one large gulp. It burned, but the alcohol barely touched the fear that was growing in his gut. Had he sold his soul?

Of course, I did. Long ago. There's no going back now.

The heavy gold ring on his right hand caught his attention. The intricately carved black stone on top absorbed the light and hid the small catch on one side. Morris set the glass down, and trailed his finger along the tiny depression on one side, pressing it, and watching as it slid to one side, revealing the primitive shape beneath. The place on his wrist where the tattoo went was smooth, just a slight gleam of white scar.

He had done better than his father. The old man had worn the tattoo proudly his entire life, convinced he had done well, that he was well-placed in the Indalo. He had never even known about the next step up. When they had come to Morris, told him things were about to change, his father had already been in a nursing home for a year, half gone with Alzheimer's. Morris had been eking along, performing infrequent favors, playing the family man, the doting father, and waiting for the chance to truly prove himself.

The degree had been dictated to him years before upon his induction. "You will obtain a degree in finance and apply at Kurgen Real Estate." It had been planned for him, and he had followed the edict, clawing his way to the top of his class, and applied to Kurgen as he was told to do. What followed was a steady climb to the top. The way, no doubt, greased by those in the shadows. They needed a high-level fixer and that is what he did for over fifteen years - through a divorce and an ex-wife who moved away to Oklahoma with his two boys.

In return, he had an enormous house, a discreet high-end call girl who visited once or twice a week, and the boys visited for a month in the summer and alternated Thanksgiving and Christmas. He had everything he could possibly need, and he vacationed in a different tropical destination each year, soaking in sun on pristine beaches and enjoying perfectly manicured golf courses in luxury resorts.

It was a good life. A comfortable one. And Morris Endon could not shake the foreboding certainty that it was all going to crumble down around his ears.

He tipped the carafe into the glass, amber liquid splashing his hand and the silver tray. He ignored it, sucked down the liquid and repeated, once, twice, and finally a third time. The carafe was empty, his glass was empty, and Morris felt the hot rush of it as it hit his bloodstream. He had done everything they asked of him. He was loyal. They would take his years of service into consideration.

Yeah, keep telling yourself that.

Morris sat down at his desk and waited for the sun to rise.

Ten Years

Back in the posh offices of Kurgen Real Estate, Rob had watched Morris leave. There was something the man was hiding. He wasn't sure yet whether it had anything to do with tonight's events, but it was there. He had been doing this job for long enough to have a knack for following his intuition.

He leaned back, the chair tilting without a single creak or groan. He turned to look out at the Kansas City skyline again, his thoughts on the tiny red tattoo he had glimpsed peeking out from under both of the dead men's wristwatches. Both men, both tattooed, the symbol of a man under the canopy of the heavens.

TEN YEARS FELL AWAY, and he was plunged into the memories he had tried so hard to forget. The Indalo, whoever they were, had undoubtedly taken his wife from him, threatened to kill his child, and ended his career at the CIA.

Rob stared at the dark night skyline, but all he saw was a sunny playground in Virginia, less than a month after Claire's death. His memories of that day remained as sharp as if they had happened yesterday.

He had forced himself to get dressed and take their daughter to the playground near the house. It had been two weeks and he was due to return to work. He had made all the arrangements - found the perfect preschool, one that Claire had talked about sending her to, and they had agreed to take her mid-week instead of a Monday. He sat there, watching Maddy run and climb on the jungle gym, his mind still clouded with grief, his heart shattered.

A woman, clad in yoga pants, a T-shirt, and running shoes, the standard attire of a stay-at-home mom, had sat down on the bench next to him.

"They certainly are having fun, aren't they?" she had asked and smiled at him. The children shrieked and ran, several of them engaged in an elaborate game of tag.

"Yes, they sure are." He watched as Maddy's frizzy curls bounced as she slid down a bright blue slide. She was smiling, something that he hadn't seen her do in weeks.

"Let me guess which one is yours. Hmm. Is it that cute little one that's on the monkey bars?" She pointed and he saw a small tattoo peeking from her bangle bracelets. They slid away as she pointed, and he saw it, edged in black, on her right wrist.

"UM NO, THE ONE WITH all of the frizzy curls. I haven't figured out how to wash her hair right," he sighed. "Her mom always handled it." He watched Maddy climb into a tunnel.

"Don't brush it."

"What?"

"Curly hair, don't brush it, just finger comb it while it's wet. It will make all the difference in the world." She smiled.

"I'll try that. Thank you." She nodded, and they sat in silence for a moment. Maddy was still in the tunnel and he straightened, trying to see if she had come out the other end.

"Divorced?"

"What?"

"You said her mom always handled her hair," the woman asked, friendly, her tone relaxed, yet curious. "So, I'm guessing divorce, right? Or she's on a trip?"

Rob blinked and said, "Uh, divorce, yeah." He didn't want another word of condolence. They meant nothing. Just empty words in the face of howling grief.

"Recent?"

"Sure."

"I knew it," she said, her expression sympathetic, "You have that shell-shocked look I normally see on my girlfriends' faces after their husbands leave them for trophy wives."

He managed a weak smile and said nothing. Maddy's frizzy hair disappeared from view as she moved farther into the bright yellow tunnel.

"Kids are wonderful," the woman mused, "Really keep you going when nothing else will, don't you agree?"

Rob thought of the past week. He had spent most of it in pajamas and a bathrobe, the dishes piling up in the sink, staring numbly at the television, Maddy at his side.

"Um, yeah." He stood up. The tunnel had a fork in it. He could see that now, a second entrance and exit that was close to a man-made cave. Had she gone into that?

"I think of them as our little piece of immortality. If we didn't have that, what would we have to show that we were ever here at all?"

"Um, right. I, uh, I don't mean to be rude, but I need to go find where she has gone to. It was nice talking to you." She had murmured something in return, but he had been too far away, all of his alarm bells going off at once.

The first time I take her to a park since losing Claire and I manage to lose sight of her. Nominate me for Father of the Year award.

He had found Maddy sitting at the edge of the rubber matting, near the entrance to the faux cave, tears in her eyes.

"Daddy, I fell and hurt my knee on the rocks there." She pointed a tiny hand at a section of pea gravel.

"It's okay, Pumpkin, I've got you. Here, put your arms around me and I'll carry you." She reached out and encircled his neck with her small arms, leaning her head on his shoulder. He felt her tears wet his shirt and then there was the scrape of paper on the back of his neck.

"What do you have there, Pumpkin?"

"A picture of our house, Daddy; a nice lady gave it to me. She said it was a present for you!"

He took the photograph, staring at it, and Maddy shifted in his arms. "She said you would like it, Daddy."

It was a picture of their house. The car in the drive, and a bouquet of flowers that had been delivered yesterday from an associate who had just returned from vacation and learned of Claire's death. He flipped the photograph over. On the back were two words:

Stop Digging

Rob felt cold fear grip him, washing over him like in an icy wave. It was a hot summer day and a cold sweat formed on his brow, goosebumps on his skin.

"I think of them as our little piece of immortality. If we didn't have that, what would we have to show that we were ever here at all?"

He turned to look back at the bench. The woman was gone. His gaze traveled over the park as he mentally reviewed what she had looked like: brown hair pulled in a ponytail, brown eyes, yoga pants and a T-shirt, the typical look that most of the moms here shared. Skinny, lattes in hand, with their makeup and manicured nails. She had looked like any of them. Nothing stood out, nothing except for that tattoo.

"Daddy? Can we go home now?"

"Maddy, who gave this to you?"

"Some lady."

"What did this lady look like?"

The little girl shrugged. "I dunno. I guess like a mommy. She was in the tunnel. She said you would like it."

"Can you see this lady now?" He turned around slowly; the tunnel was filled with preschoolers. "Can you look, Maddy, and see if you see her?"

The little girl lifted her head up and stared at the children on the playground. Several groups were leaving, even as others settled down at picnic tables to dive into sandwiches and juice cartons.

If Claire had been here, she would have remembered to make a picnic lunch.

He noticed that many of the mothers had claimed the premium shaded spots, staking out their favorite lunch spots as early as possible.

Maddy stared at the playground, her eyes fixing on the kids at the picnic tables. "I'm hungry, Daddy."

"Just look a little bit more, Sweetheart."

A whine had escaped her, "I don't see her Daddy. And I really want some goldfish crackers."

"I know you do, Maddy, but this is important. Do you see the girl who gave you the picture?"

The little girl had begun to cry. "I don't see her. Daddy, I'm *hungry*!"

He had given up, leaving the park, eyes darting as he studied the women he passed intently. His direct gaze unnerved a couple of the mother hens. They had stared at him, and one put a protective hand on her daughter's shoulder, watching him as he broke into a jog. Maddy shrieked with excitement, her hunger forgotten for the moment.

That night, after dinner, she had drawn a picture. It was eerily similar to the mark on the woman's wrist.

"What's this, Sweetheart? Where did you see it?"

"It's pretty, isn't it, Daddy? It was on the lady's hand. The one who gave me the picture for you."

He leaned closer. "On her hand, Sweetheart? Or here, on her wrist?" He pointed to his wrist, and the little girl nodded.

"It was on her wrist." She pushed at his hand. "I need my other crayons, Daddy, I'm gonna make a rainbow now."

"Could I have this picture, Sweetheart?"

She smiled up at him, and his heart broke; she looked so much like Claire. Except for her eyes. Instead of Claire's pale blue, she had warm, chocolate brown ones like his own. "Sure, Daddy, will you put it up on the fridge?"

"I think I'll put it in my office, Pumpkin."

Later that night, Maddy sound asleep in her bedroom, he had stared at the picture.

Two different people, both with the same tattoo. The person who had given Maddy that photograph had done it while she was in the tunnel, nearly thirty feet away from where he was sitting with the woman. It was no coincidence. They were connected. He reached for the bookshelf that rested between his desk and Claire's. She had written fantasy stories for children, and she had been deep in the middle of one when she died. *The Element Encyclopedia of Secret Signs and Symbols* sat on the second shelf down, scraps of paper that marked Claire's research at intervals.

He paged through the book from the beginning, examining the symbols, finally locating the matching symbol a fraction of the way through the thick book.

"Indalo, huh?" His finger followed the text. "It serves as a reminder of the complex belief of man as the microcosm and the Universe as a macrocosm."

He had heard whispers, nothing more than rumors. Hell, that was what most of his existence at work was built on. Follow the whispers, listen, dig deeper. What if this symbol stood for far more than just an ideal? What if it had some very real, very dangerous people attached to it?

He sat back, staring at the image of the Indalo and the words scribbled on the back of the photograph.

Stop Digging

It was all related, he was sure of it. And he was also sure that the last thing he needed was to be involved. That woman had threatened him; more specifically, she had threatened Maddy. And the more he thought about it, the more it felt as if Claire's accident hadn't been an accident at all. Taking a turn too fast, that wasn't Claire's style, not even before Maddy was born. He had jokingly called her Grandma when she was behind the wheel, while she had called him Mario Andretti in return.

His parents were dead. His mom to leukemia when he was ten, his dad and his love of the bottle months before Rob turned twenty-two. Claire had lost her parents to a car crash a year after Rob and Claire's wedding, and both were only children. He was all that Maddy had, and she was the only thing he loved left in the world.

I can't do this job anymore. Not if it means losing Maddy.

The next day he had quit the CIA and put the house on the market. Two days after that, he and Maddy had boarded a plane for Kansas City, leaving Virginia, his life with Claire, and a career as an analyst with the CIA behind him forever. The file he had been compiling, the files and papers he had accumulated over nearly a year of digging, were returned to headquarters. Someone else could research the mysterious group he had found linked to shadowy financial dealings and hired hits across the globe. Someone who didn't have a child to protect. Someone who hadn't lost his wife.

Until tonight, that is. Ten years. It had been ten years since he had lost Claire. And he was as sure then as he was now, that it had been no accident. Someone had deliberately made him a widower, and his child a motherless orphan. Someone had threatened him, and promised to finish destroying what was left of his life if he kept prying. And with a tiny, innocent three-year-old child to protect, who was he to argue?

He had walked away. He had abandoned his investigation and chosen to live. He had fled with the only things that mattered - his life and Maddy's. And here, in the middle of flyover country, he had thought he was safe. Quietly, in a way that would not reveal his curiosity, he had looked up the symbol. The symbol, he learned, was the Indalo and depicted man under either a rainbow or the vault of heaven.

Such a tiny mark. The information he found on it was small. No hint of any shady criminal organization. Just the tattoos, and the warning.

A red Indalo. Just like the black Indalo tattooed on the woman's wrist. She had been part of it, something I had known all along. How do these two men fit into all of this?

And as Rob sat there in an overly expensive armchair, he wondered if he dared to dig deeper. Or should he walk away while he still could?

He reached into his pocket and hit speed dial. It rang twice and she answered.

"Hey, Dad."

"You should be asleep by now."

"Dad, you called me." Her voice held a slightly petulant tone. "What is that term for 'damned if you do, damned if you don't?'"

"An idiom."

"Right. An idiom. So, you call me at almost midnight. If I don't answer, you come home, wake me up, and demand to know why I didn't answer the phone. But if I answer the phone, you ask me why I'm not asleep." She sighed and yawned. "See the problem here?"

Rob chuckled. "I guess you have a point there. But you weren't asleep."

"Nope, I was finishing the book you gave me."

"*Voyage from Yesteryear*? What did you think of it?"

"It was good, but," she paused for a moment, "Do you ever think humans could ever truly get along in a society without government and laws? I mean, *really* get along?"

"You are far too young to be so cynical."

"Whatever, Dad."

"I'll be home soon."

"Okay. G'night." Her phone clicked as she ended the call. He stared at his for a moment. Whatever was going on here, whatever the Indalo were doing here, he was now tasked with finding it out.

How You Find Her

Riehl was fighting. His opponents were falling like dominoes, flying through the air in response to his fists in their abdomens. He snarled, grinning, reaching for a blade on the floor and burying it to the hilt in one man's guts. A quick wrench, left, then right, twisting as he went. Blood flew from his opponent's wounds as the man sagged to the floor, still alive, his arms flailing, a dead man going through the motions until blood loss and shock caught up to him. Riehl felt the bloodlust surge through him.

Only the woman remained. She was petite, slender, tied to the bed, her body writhing in fear. Her eyes pleaded with him, even as he tossed his weapon to one side, slid out of his bloodstained shirt and began to unbuckle his pants. His dick was stiff, throbbing with anticipation and he smiled at her, enjoying the fear that turned to panic as her struggles renewed. That vanilla musk smell he had detected, just before she brought a knee to his balls a few days earlier, made him harder than Chinese algebra. Finally, after tracking her down, after all the days spent cradling his balls and waiting for the pain to subside, he was going to finally get the chance to fuck her.

Everyone else in the building was dead. He had all the time in the world and he planned on making it last for days. The bitch deserved it after what she had done.

"We'll start nice and simple," Riehl said, pushing the zipper down and grinning as she whimpered in front of him. "No one will be here for days. You don't mind, do you?" His tone was conversational. It was a stark contrast to the look of horror in her eyes as he leaned over her, his favorite knife in his hand, slicing the buttons off of her silver-gray blouse, one button at a time. Each button flew in a lazy arc to the right, skittering to the floor and out of sight.

Within seconds her blouse lay open, a lacy bra underneath. He reached up under her skirt and ripped the panties off. This made her whimper in fear as she squirmed, desperate to avoid his touch. He spread her legs, his hands bruising her knees as she fought him every inch of the way and then he thrust into her, hard, and watched as the tears slid down her cheeks.

Just as he was hitting his stride, an insistent and familiar ringing needled into the back of his brain, breaking his concentration, and the world fell away.

Damn it, I was only dreaming.

Beside him, on the battered wood nightstand, his phone buzzed, the green backlit screen flashing as he felt the remnants of his dream scatter. His eyes struggled to focus in the darkened room. Leaning forward put pressure on his swollen balls and he winced in pain, cursing as he reached for the phone.

"What?"

There was a momentary pause on the other end, before the caller asked, "What happened last Friday?"

Fuck.

"I misjudged her." It was the truth.

"You wanted to fuck her. I'm guess it didn't quite go as planned?"

"You could say that."

"The higher-ups are impatient to get this thing squashed. They sent in the Derasmo brothers."

Riehl sucked in a breath. "So, it's been taken care of." The Derasmo brothers were bad news. If they had been sent in, then someone was desperate for resolution. Bringing in the brothers was akin to bringing a nuclear bomb to a knife fight. They didn't do stealthy in and out, with no collateral damage. They did heavy duty, level the building and kill all witnesses, kind of operations.

"The Derasmo brothers are in the morgue."

Against one tiny slip of a woman? "*What?*"

"There's another player in the game."

"Just one? Are you sure? Who is it?" Riehl sat up, biting back a curse; his balls still ached, and one remained swollen and discolored. He stood gingerly, pushed open a curtain, and let in a sliver of light.

"They haven't gotten back to me with that information."

"So, what do you want me to do?"

"Stay put and wait. Sooner or later she will pop up. When she does, track her down and finish the job."

"That's it? What about this other guy? I need intel. I'm not going in there blind, especially not after some asshole good enough to take out the Derasmo brothers."

"You'll get it. And one more thing."

"What?"

"Call the contractor back. He's in a panic after the police rousted him out of bed and took him to the crime scene last night."

Riehl growled, "I don't do customer service. I don't hold their hands and tell them what they want to hear."

"If you hadn't fucked it up in the first place, we wouldn't be having this conversation. The contract would have been completed. So, go kiss his ass. This one's on you."

Riehl cursed as the line clicked and was silent. He held himself back from flinging the phone across the room. "The fucker can wait until I've had something to eat."

It didn't hurt as much as it had yesterday to move. By tomorrow he should be back to normal. He flipped on a light and it blinked for a moment, a low glow, before slowly warming and brightening. The room had a tiny mini-fridge which was stuffed with five boxes of various leftovers. He grabbed one. The smell of curry and tandoori hit him as the box was shifted and opened a small crack.

If he hadn't had the Indian food that night, she would have not had that extra half second of warning. He ate a bite and then tossed it in the trash in disgust.

He dialed the number and let it ring. There was a short pause after the second ring and then, "Morris speaking."

"I was told you needed an update on the situation."

"An *update*? Christ on a crutch, I need more than an update. I need to figure out what to say to the detective in charge of the case. He hauled me in last night and it looked like a goddamn war had erupted. It's on the goddamn news right now!"

Riehl rolled his eyes up, staring at the crack on the wall near the ceiling that traveled the width of his rented room. He had spent three days cradling his balls staring at that crack. The Derasmo brothers worked as a team, and were lethal - Lila Benoit should have been no match for them. So, who the hell was this other player?

Morris was still nattering on, and his voice raised an octave as Dominic said nothing in return and let the man sit and spin himself up into a lather.

"They are asking for a personnel list. They're gonna go down the entire list and talk to her and find out about her being attacked the other night and put two and two together and..."

"Don't include her name on the list," Riehl interrupted.

"What?"

"Leave it off the list and let the police work their way through the office personnel. I'll see that she's taken care of before the police come back to you asking why you forgot her. And if they do, well, tell 'em she was new and you forgot to add her to the list."

There was silence on the other end. Riehl closed his eyes. If he concentrated, he was pretty sure he would hear the wheels of this simpleton's brain turning.

"Do you know where she is?"

"No, but you do."

Morris sputtered, "No, I don't!"

"She has a company phone, right?"

"Uh, well, yes, she should."

"It should have a tracking app in it. Find it and send it to me via the secure email I just texted to you. I'll take it from there and contact you when the job is done."

"Christ. Are you sure this isn't going to blow up in my face? What if she calls the police?"

"What if she does? It will give me her exact location and I'll move on it then."

"This better work. I don't want this blowing back on me. I've worked too hard to get caught up in this bullshit."

Riehl held his tongue. Obviously, Morris Endon had worked hard. He had worked very hard at lining his pockets. But he hadn't covered his tracks well enough, hence the issue at hand.

"I'll wait for the email." His hand pressed the End Call button.

He lay back down in bed, his balls still aching. It set a different tone to life than his dream had. He could only hope he would get a chance to take his time with Lila Benoit. He knew of a place where he wouldn't be disturbed. It wasn't near here, a solid three-hour drive away, in fact. But if he got the chance, he'd take her there. It was remote, at least three miles from the nearest house, and he could take his time, spend days with his prize before he took her on a drive into the canyons and let the animals have her.

It was a natural paradise with bobcat sightings as well as a local wolf population. Disposing of bodies there had never been a problem.

Boxers or Briefs

Lila stared at the door Shane Ellis had closed behind him. The thick carpet had absorbed the sound of his departure, only a small creak on the stairs below betraying his progress away from her door. She stared at the door, willing him to come back and complicate her life further. If he would just pull her up against him, slip his hand up under her skirt, and...

"Oh girl, as if you don't have enough problems!" She shook her head, fighting to get her hormones under control.

She was wide awake and certainly not ready for bed. The bourbon had taken the edge off and her jumpiness had vanished. It had left her with this delicious fire in her belly, one that would easily have been ignited further if hunky "call me Shane" hadn't left so abruptly. How she wished he had stayed, even as she was relieved that he had not. Her bruises from last Friday were still livid and angry against her pale skin.

This summer I really must *get a decent tan. If my skin gets any whiter, I'll look more like a vampire than anything else.*

She stared around her, drinking in the details.

Her curiosity led her to explore the room further. Shane had described the property as a safe house, which brought images of crummy, low-rent motel rooms to mind. Lila may have watched a few too many crime shows; but this room with its plush carpets, heavy ornate furniture, and Victorian-era knickknacks sang a different tune. It was more like staying in a private home, more personal than a bed and breakfast or upper-end hotel room. This house had class.

The room hovered between two distinct eras, however. There was a strong '70s vibe in the rough brown-black timbers that cut across the ceiling. The heavy iron accents and glass sconces added to that. The windows were simple, a crank at each angled the glass outward instead of up, and the molding along the base of the walls was simple, spare. The stonework of the large fireplace, firmly centered on one wall, paired with the rough timbers, iron and glass, gave an almost a church-like feel to the room. She eyed it, and thought briefly of her grandmother, now long-gone, and her attempts to bring Lila with her to Sunday services. Perhaps it was the dour congregation, or the preacher who threatened hellfire and damnation if his parishioners were foolish enough to choose rock music, alcohol, or a host of other Satan-centric activities - after nearly two years of regular church attendance, Lila had begged off. Granny had been going through chemo by then and didn't pursue it. Thankfully, Mom had never been interested, or religiously inclined for that matter, and Lila had been happy to never return.

The other era was positively Victorian, with antiques like the four-poster bed, its headboard carved with cherubs, and delicate, spindle-legged tables scattered through the room among ferns, cloth-bound books, and other bric-a-brac.

There was a built-in dresser in one corner of the room, another sharp trip forward in time to the '70s, accompanied by a large plain mirror. Next to it was the open door to the bathroom. She explored it further, noticing that in addition to the clawfoot bathtub, there was an odd tiled open shower of sorts. It was enormous and large enough for two people, possibly more, as evidenced by the multiple shower heads.

She licked her lips, imagining sharing it with the hot pecan pie and molasses guy who had just left her room. She could still feel the heat of his touch.

"Hell, he's probably some misogynistic prick beneath all that hotness and muscles. No one can look that good and be a nice guy." Lila said out loud to the empty room.

The room didn't answer of course, and suddenly Shane's suggestion of a nice, hot bath, sounded more appealing than anything else she could think of.

She let the water run in the tub until it was hot and steaming. Just stepping into it and slipping underneath the hot water was heaven. The heat melted into the tight muscles of her damaged arm and shoulder and she slid deeper into the water, her entire body immersed up to her earlobes. She loved her modern flat but found herself wishing for a huge bathtub like this. As if she could fit one in the tiny bathroom. It would have been impossible. There was barely room for the tiny shower.

There were three small dark blue glass bottles on the tub tray. The labels were in French, and she smiled as she quickly recognized what each bottle was for. "Shampooing, conditionneur, well those are both obvious. And let's see, sels de bain." She tapped her lip for a moment. "Ah, yes, sels is salts and bain means bath, so that must be bath salts."

She took some time to add the bath salts and relaxed, her hair up and out of the water, her eyes closed as she breathed in the floral scents of raspberry and vanilla. "A safe house, huh? This feels more like a spa."

Steam billowed, creeping along the low ceiling, obscuring the long mirror above the double sink and the window on the opposite side with a thick opaque layer.

Her thoughts turned to Shane. The man was dead sexy. So much for caramel pecan pie being a toad in person. Instead he was ooh la la attractive, confident, and a man of action. If he hadn't been there when those two gunmen came through, she would have been... Lila shuddered.

She hated thinking of it. It was terrifying, and she felt a knot form in her guts. What did they want with her? And why? It had to be a mistake.

She sank lower in the water and willed her mind to think of anything other than the bullets and blood and the fear she had felt. She thought again of Shane, turning away from the fear to the memory of how he had looked at her there in the kitchen, or in the car, or the stairwell. His hands, warm against her, checking to be sure she hadn't been shot or hurt. He'd given her a look that, despite having only a few lovers - Lila could count the men she had gone to bed with on one hand and fingers to spare - she could read clearly. He had been attracted to her, *was* attracted to her.

It had been like some electric current running between them - the lightest touch of his fingertips touching hers when he handed her the glass - she had felt his and her desire meet and sizzle like fire in between them.

He didn't make a move, though. Why? It probably went against that Code of his.

Well, Code or not, it was a shame he hadn't stepped one foot closer. After all she had seen tonight, a man like Shane would have made her forget those terrifying moments in the office. Just the thought of him touching her, the heat of his body...

A sigh escaped her lips at the thought of what it would feel like.

The water rolled slowly through the bathtub, soothing, the heat digging as deep into her muscles as if she were under the competent hands of a masseuse. Lila sighed again, and her left hand slipped down between her legs, fingers stroking the nub of her clit, her mind imagining what it would feel like to have his mouth on her, his tongue licking and teasing her. She closed her eyes and imagined his strong hands sliding along the side of her body, his lips on her neck, seducing her, claiming her body beneath his. Just imagining what he looked like under that tight-fitting shirt was enough to send her over the edge. Lila propped one leg up out of the sudsy water, her finger sliding back and forth, her neck stretched back. The wave of sensation crashed over her, her mouth open in an 'o' of pleasure as her finger danced and wrung out wave after wave of pleasure.

After the waves had subsided and she had slipped into a somnolent state, edging closer and closer toward the dark yet welcoming blanket of sleep, she sat up. Lila poured a generous dollop of the shampoo into her hand, breathing in the heady, clean scent of lemongrass as she lathered her long hair, sliding under the water to rinse the shampoo away. She relaxed every part of her body, letting the hot water dig deep into her sore muscles. It was marvelous, this bath. She stayed, unwilling to leave until she could feel the water beginning to cool.

Lila pulled the plug then and reached for a soft, richly fluffy towel, and wrapped herself in it. Standing on the bathmat, water running in rivulets off her warm, relaxed body, she stared at the clouds of steam that floated through the air, turning, rolling. The heat of the water had turned her muscles to mush and her eyelids were heavy with exhaustion.

Padding out of the bathroom, she walked barefoot, her toes sinking into the plush carpet, and pulled the heavy down comforter back from the bed, then slipped in between the silky bedsheets. The bed was warm, luxurious, and she felt her body sink into it as if she had crawled into a pile of downy comfort. She didn't bother to turn off any of the small lights that dotted the room, her eyes already heavy and her mind slipping into sleep. The day had been full of stress, and within minutes, Lila had fallen deeply into a dream.

The house was silent.

On the opposite side of the house, in the west wing at just past 2 a.m., a red light flashing in the top left corner of his room went unnoticed. Shane was deeply asleep, but the sharp buzz of his cell phone woke him instantly. He sat up, his sight blurred and then cleared as he checked the status of the compound on the app.

A door was open on the property. All vestiges of sleep were gone and his 9mm Ruger was in his hand, his feet in motion the second they hit the thick carpet. No time for clothes; this was a breach, a sliding door off of the kitchen, according to the alert that scrolled on his phone.

He was on high alert, and the dream he had been enjoying mere seconds before was a distant memory as he ran down the dark hallway, down the half flight of stairs, and through the kitchen. The curtains billowed slightly, a cool evening breeze sucking them out to the deck outside the sliding glass door. The deck outside was partially lit by a bright moon playing hide and seek behind dark clouds that slowly rolled across the night sky.

He saw her feet bare on the deck before anything else and immediately lowered his weapon. Lila was clad in nothing but a blanket, her hair dark, and still slightly damp from her bath. She smiled at him, raising her eyebrows as she took in the handgun he held in his right hand. "Don't shoot, I'm unarmed."

"Silent alarm," he explained. "It went off the second you opened the door."

"Sorry about that." Lila pulled the blanket closer to her body. It was unseasonably warm for late fall, but nonetheless there was a nip to the air. "I looked out the window, saw the river and the lights, and just had to take in the view. Is that Parkville, over there?"

Shane stepped closer to her, followed her finger. "Yes, and that's Park University right there and over to the left, that's the airport." She smelled of lemons. It combined with her own unique, sweet vanilla musk scent, and he caught himself leaning closer and reaching for her with his other hand. The dream of her was still lingering in his animal hindbrain - and he suppressed a flash of desire. The things he wanted to do to her, *had* been doing to her in that dream that was so maddeningly interrupted. He placed his free hand on the railing and forced himself to look off into the night sky.

"The view is incredible!" she breathed; her attention absorbed by the stunning skyline. The lights shimmered off the water, the wide river undulating and twisting, the black water occasionally showing a frothy wake as it moved over sandbars, heading inevitably toward the Gulf of Mexico hundreds of miles away.

"When the judge bought it back in 1970, the total acreage was 20 acres, but he sold five of the acres to the city of Kansas City, Kansas so they could build a water treatment plant. It is remote, yet accessible, so it works quite well for our needs," Shane explained.

Lila's eyes were locked on the distant glow of lights from Parkville's pride and joy, Park University, which sat on a hilltop, a collection of turn-of-the-century brick buildings. Even in the middle of the night, the lights clearly lit up the main building.

"Jack Benton, a multi-millionaire who owns a private security firm," Lila said, shivering in her blanket. "There has to be a story behind that."

"Undoubtedly, but it isn't my story to tell."

"But you know it."

"Yes."

Lila laughed softly and said, "A circumspect bodyguard. How interesting."

Shane didn't respond. In his line of work there were many times when silence was the more prudent answer.

Silence followed, interrupted only by the steady low thrum of the plant in the near distance. Lights lit up the plant at intervals and Shane could see a lone security guard making the rounds before disappearing back inside through a side door. They watched a plane take off into the air, lights blinking steadily, as it slowly ascended into the night sky and disappeared into the clouds.

Lila shivered again.

"You're cold. Come on, let me get you inside and get you warmed up." Shane guided her back to the open door, acutely aware that he was rather under-dressed to be outside in late fall wearing only boxer briefs. Lila's eyes traveled over him and he could smell the lemongrass shampoo in her hair as she passed close to him, heading into the house.

"Can I get you a drink?" he asked once they had stepped through the door. It felt wonderful inside after the chilly breeze on the back deck. Shane slid the lock into place.

"Yes, please." Lila stared down the hall into the sunken living room.

"Sit down, I'll get you something."

Chesterfield and Bourbon

The living room Lila stepped into was actually more of a den, fully masculine, complete with hunting trophies. Three rather unfortunate deer heads adorned the dark wood-paneled walls, and an enormous, tufted black leather Chesterfield sofa and chair took up most of the space in front of the fireplace. The plush, high carpet had been abandoned here for a parquet floor and a fur rug in front of the hearth. The thick fur felt luxurious under her feet. Above, the open rafters were a chocolate brown, almost black, rough-hewn and large. The den held that odd mesh of styles - the '70s vibe cluttered with various groupings of Victorian antiques that included an Edison Victrola and large organ with mother-of-pearl buttons, tabs, and pulls. The fireplace emitted a fair amount of heat from the gas logs within, the flame slowly rippling in a lazy cascade of orange, yellow, and occasionally blue.

Lila chose a corner of the immense Chesterfield sofa. The buttons were buried deep in the black leather, and it had a high back and matching arms. It conveyed a feeling of wealth and intimidation all at once and she could clearly imagine men in coattails sitting and puffing on cigars while the delicate ladies of the manse tittered in some small dainty room on the opposite side of the house.

Shane placed a glass in her hand. "Is bourbon alright?" The glass was heavy, cut crystal, and the two ice cubes sloshed seductively in the amber liquid. "Or perhaps you would rather have wine? I could check and see if there is any downstairs."

There was a room below the den, lined in stone, with racks of wine. It was an extensive collection.

Shane had been surprised when Jack had told him to take Lila here. His boss still used this as his own private residence when he was in the area and there were other safe houses that were more modern, less filled with antiques and cut crystal. Nice, but not opulent.

Benton had kept all the odd furniture from the last tenants, two men with a love of everything Victorian who had somehow landed in a 1970s ranch house instead of where their hearts belonged, in Victorian England.

Benton had bought the house, all its contents, and changed little. He said once to Shane that he "liked the cacophony of it all." The wine cellar was one small improvement, and the security cameras and alarms were a big one. No one could come within one-quarter mile of the house without a bevy of alarms being sounded and a host of security cameras recording their every move.

Lila suppressed a shudder at Shane's inquiry. Wine gave her headaches, vodka gave her hangovers, but bourbon or whiskey, when used in moderation, seemed to have zero negative effects on her.

"Bourbon is just fine, thanks."

Shane sat down in the matching Chesterfield chair, swallowed up by the high back and sides. She raised the glass to her lips and let the strong liquor roll past her lips and over her tongue. She didn't drink often. And while she had created a tiny liquor cabinet in her apartment, she had rarely touched it. Only socially, when entertaining, and her social life had been rather hit or miss lately.

The kegger parties in college hadn't really appealed and she hadn't had much in the way of discretionary spending until the last few months, but she had on a few occasions been exposed to quality liquor. Mainly from tiny pilfering of her parents' liquor cabinet where her dad had only stored the really good stuff.

He had told her that there was no point buying cheap liquor. "Your mom is always reminding me that cheap liquor is like buying cheap shoes - neither of them is good for your body. Get the good stuff or don't bother getting anything at all. I guess that means we all need to go barefoot or something like that." Lila's dad had been funny and sweet. She missed him. He believed in quality everything. They didn't have to have the newest, or the most fashionable, but he did want them to have the best that they could afford. Those stolen nips of bourbon, whiskey and more had definitely taught her the difference in taste.

She savored the taste of the bourbon in her glass. This was excellent. It just added to the mystery of Benton Security Services. So far, this whole protection detail was nothing like what she had expected.

Where were the grimy, barren rooms with beige curtains and mustard-yellow walls? There wasn't a grim detective smoking a cigarette and warning her that the bad guys were just waiting for her to step out the door. And this also wasn't the Ritz, with its maddening fusion of '70s wood and beam, and Victorian froufrou.

She stared at Shane, who had settled into the chair, and Lila felt confused and turned on all over again. She tucked her feet deeper into the blanket and tried not to notice the large bulge in his boxer briefs. The rest of his body was bare, smooth skin, muscles prominent but not ridiculous.

Lila couldn't stand those men who spent hours lifting weights until their muscles bulged unnaturally, limiting their movement so that they just lumbered by like a proud stag, flexing their muscles. Who wanted that, really? A guy who couldn't even bend or flex normally? And if she was carrying the metaphor of the deer a little further - those stupid deer got shot. Shane was quick, strong when he needed to be strong, and sexy as hell. That five o'clock shadow, and the chiseled jaw. Her internal dialogue stopped dead as he quirked an eyebrow at her. She had been staring.

"Um, what?" He had spoken, but she hadn't even heard him.

"I talked to my boss," Shane said again. "The men I shot in the hallway there at Kurgen. They were contract killers, Lila." He paused, looked her over, and frowned. "Someone really wants you dead. Got any ideas why?"

"Unless it's for overdue library books, I've got nothing." She shrugged. "I'm nobody, Shane."

"Lila, everyone is..."

She blew out a breath, took a sip of bourbon, and leaned forward, preoccupied with the mystery. "I haven't witnessed a crime or found stolen merchandise, and I'm not into drugs or any illicit activity. I'm a data analyst."

"Okay, tell me more. What do you do for Kurgen in your role as a data analyst?"

"For the most part I simply analyze market trends and then make recommendations - when to buy, when to sell, what markets are up, which are down, that sort of thing."

"So, would you call it marketing?"

"Not really, although marketing is a component. Basically, I'm the translator of data. Information, numbers, statistics. By understanding the data and interpreting it, I help management make better business decisions moving forward."

"That sounds like quite a demanding position."

She shrugged. "I do end up working more hours than I initially thought I would, but it's interesting work and the best job I've ever had. I really enjoy it."

He leaned back, drained his glass, and set it down. "Somehow this has to do with your work."

Lila shook her head. "I just don't see how."

"Occam's Razor. It means..." She put up her hand.

"I know what Occam's Razor means."

"Of course, you do. Look, what else could it be? You're squeaky clean. Believe me, I can smell dirt a mile away and you haven't got any. You've seen something, heard something, maybe just read it. It might be sitting on your desk at this very moment, some piece of a puzzle you stumbled on and didn't even recognize, but it is there."

His words stirred a random memory in her mind.

It might be sitting on your desk at this very moment. It couldn't be that. Surely not.

Lila could feel his eyes on her, assessing her, observing her every reaction. She smiled wryly and took the last sip of bourbon. The fire of it slid down her throat and she could feel it working already, a layer of calm lassitude settling over her. Between that and the fire, her thoughts were slowing, and exhaustion from the past few days seeped into her. Being in pain took energy, fear did too, and her body and mind were conspiring to send her into a warm, fuzzy land surrounded with Egyptian cotton sheets and the slow warmth emanating from the fireplace.

Lila leaned her head back, the high back of the sofa swallowing her up.

"Another bourbon?" Shane's voice was low, and she closed her eyes and shook her head.

Why did he have to sound so damned sexy? Normally a man like that would have her as jumpy as a cat, but now, with the bourbon coursing through her bloodstream and her body and mind exhausted from her injuries, the fear and flight from the office, and the reassuring quiet and isolation of the house she was now in, all she wanted to do was sleep.

Shane watched her. The arch of her neck, her delicate skin still mottled with bruises. The way one delicate breast was half-exposed, peeking out of the blanket. Her legs were drawn up to her chest and angled to the right, exposing a toned, shapely thigh.

He let his gaze travel from her toes all the way to her sleep-tousled hair. He took his time, listening as her breathing slowed and deepened. Shane stood up and plucked the now-empty glass from her hand.

She snapped awake.

He reached out a hand to help her up. "You're done in. Get some rest. We will talk more in the morning."

Lila nodded and made her way up the stairs. Her steps were silent, swallowed up in the plush thickness of the carpet. So were Shane's. It gave her a jolt to realize he was directly behind her, towering over her as she placed her hand on the doorknob and it turned effortlessly. He looked down into her eyes, and reached behind her to push the door open.

He was close, and despite her exhaustion, her heartbeat increased, a sharp desire running through her. She sucked in a breath, and the gap between their two bodies closed as he moved closer, one hand straying to the small of her back.

He bent his head down, his mouth mere inches from hers. "And no more going outside of the house. At least, not without me."

His words were a dash of reality, a splash of ice on her libido. She stiffened and turned away from him, through the door, and closed it with a decisive kick of her foot.

Shane smiled as the door slammed, then shook his head. *Damned if she isn't sexy when she's pissed off.*

The bulge in his underwear hadn't lessened one iota. But he could hear Jack's words echoing in his head, "Keep it professional."

"I'm trying my best, Boss," he muttered under his breath as he descended the stairs and made his way towards the west wing of the house, "But damned if she doesn't have something about her that I can't stop thinking about."

Behind the closed door, Lila stomped to the bed, the sleepy lassitude she had felt in the den gone, replaced by indignation. She slid into the covers, fuming. "Stay in the house. Like I'm an errant child! As if I can't take care of myself!"

The bed, with its silky soft sheets and feather softness, slowly worked its magic. And despite herself, as she drifted off, she couldn't help imagining what it would have been like if instead of speaking, he had kissed her instead. He had wanted to; she was sure of it. She imagined him leaning in, his lips soft yet demanding, his tongue slipping past her teeth. She shivered at the thought of it. A full body-tingling shiver of desire. She closed her eyes and imagined him kissing her breasts, down her stomach, and a tongue touching in the most sensitive spot of all. The fantasy morphed into dreams of hot bodyguards and danger around every turn.

On the far side of the house, Shane sent a quick text to Jack, updating his boss on what little they had discussed. Then Shane lay down in his own bed and spent the rest of the night tossing and turning, his head filled with images of Lila's lithe body in this bed and how it would feel to touch her, kiss her, and slip his way between her legs. He saw the clock click to 2 a.m., 3 a.m., and even 4 a.m. before a deep sleep stole him away shortly before dawn.

Call in Sick

*I*t was her first day of work all over again and Lila followed Blanche into a glassed-in office. It was empty, and she was shocked all over again to realize that it was meant for her, that she wasn't being shunted off to a gray cubicle the farthest from windows and natural light. Instead, the rays of the rising sun reflected off of the building on the opposite side of the street, turning the glass walls into a reflection of the fiery ball pushing its way up on the horizon, round, bulbous clouds slowly marching across the sky. The office was for her.

"Let Human Resources know if you have any specific needs," Blanche said, "And they should have your laptop delivered and up and running by the end of the day."

She had nodded wordlessly, overwhelmed at her change in fortune.

The young man from Nerds R Us had knocked on her door a few minutes later. She had passed him on the way in as he stood at the front desk to talk to the bright-eyed receptionist.

His black polo shirt sported a bright yellow splat on the front left breast, the words Nerds R Us filling it. Below his name badge read Alex M.

"Hi, Miz Benoit? I'm Alex and I'm here to get you up and running on your new computer."

The sun shining in her eyes was bright. It bleached out everything else.

The first bright rays of the sun crawled through the windows and across Lila's covers. She was awake, lying there in the bed, her mind racing. This is how it was for her in the mornings. Often before the sun rose, Lila's brain would turn on and she would know that sleeping in was simply not in the cards. Instead, she would plot out her day, review whatever duties or errands were necessary for the hours ahead, and jump into problem-solving while others were still blearily reaching for their coffee cups.

Today, despite her lack of sleep, was no exception.

The dream still hung in her mind, like gray smoke curling from a chimney... no substance, but still a reality.

Dreams are funny things and Lila usually took hers quite seriously. She had good reason to. A week before her dad had died in a car accident, she had woken up screaming, the image of a huge tractor/trailer bearing down on her as she straddled a bicycle in the middle of I-70. It had been less than a month after earning her driver's license and her mother had dismissed it with, "It is nothing but nerves, dear."

Lila had listened to her mother, smoothed over the image of that enormous tractor trailer, and intentionally changed it to a more positive mental image of her driving a convertible in the summer. On a sunny day in March, a long-haul driver had fallen asleep at the wheel, just long enough to cross the median and crush the compact Smart car Anthony Benoit had so proudly purchased the year before. He had died instantly.

Lila closed her eyes and willed the memories out of her mind. Those empty years after, first in their overly large, quiet house, watching her mother fade, losing her color, her laughter, her ambition. Later in the small apartment they had moved to when the mortgage payments had proved too much for a widowed, grieving mother. Mom had never recovered. They had been high school sweethearts, separated for a decade after high school before reuniting and marrying in a whirlwind romance. They had been inseparable all of Lila's life and losing Dad had hollowed them out, removed the heart and soul of their family.

She pushed the sadness away. She needed to focus on getting the laptop and taking another look at those files. Those files could explain everything. She stretched, pushed the covers aside, and caught a whiff of...bacon? Apparently, she wasn't the only early riser.

A quick review of the closets and built-in dresser revealed basic sweats and T-shirts, all sizes and colors. Lila found a pair of black yoga pants and a zip-front gray sweatshirt, both of which had plenty of room on her lean frame, and slipped them on. They would do for now, until she could get back to her apartment and change.

By now, the delectable smell of bacon and fresh coffee had drifted fully into her room and her stomach had responded, growling. Lila walked out onto the landing, then down the carpeted stairs barefoot, finding her way to the kitchen with ease, guided by her nose and grumbling stomach.

Shane was dressed in black jeans and a black T-shirt, his back to her as she entered the kitchen. His jaw was stubbled with a five o'clock shadow. She swallowed down a squirmy feeling of desire and nerves. He was good-looking, dead sexy, and she was all alone with him in this enormous house.

Beside him was a plate filled with bacon and he was apparently cooking the entire dozen eggs.

"Where is the army?" she asked, reaching for the bacon. He smacked her hand. "Hey!"

"Not yet," he said, "wait for the eggs. Have some coffee." He didn't even make eye contact and she was amused and annoyed at the same time.

"Good morning to you too!" she said, and poured the rich black coffee from the glass French press into a waiting coffee mug. A man who cooked, what a novel concept. Her dad had been completely hopeless, and Todd, the few times she had stayed over, was even worse. He had kept microwaveable bacon in his cupboards, rows of it. She shook her head, remembering it, *absolutely disgusting.*

"Cream? Sugar?" Shane asked, jolting her out of her memories of Todd, bad sex, and even worse eating experiences. He pointed to the small sugar dish. "There's creamer in the fridge."

Lila sat at the long dining room table, the mug steaming, warming her hands. The sun's rays lit up the eastern set of sliding glass doors and she would have been blinded in the bright light if it hadn't been for the thick curtains. Shane's work at the stove yielded two large plates, one of bacon and one of scrambled eggs, both heaped high. He handed her a plate and a fork, and then helped himself after she had taken what she wanted.

"So, where's everyone else?" Lila asked, gesturing towards the food left on the plate.

Shane quirked an eyebrow. "I have a high metabolism."

He wasn't kidding. He ate every scrap on his plate, before returning for more, stopping only once to offer one last chance at the food before he finished it off. Lila watched, fascinated, until the last bite was consumed. She had never seen anyone eat so much food in one sitting.

"I need to get to work," Lila said, breaking the silence that had gathered between them.

Shane shook his head. "No. You need to call in sick."

"What? I can't call in sick, I don't *want* to call in sick!"

Shane leaned back in his chair, tossed down the last of the coffee in his mug, and regarded her steadily. "Last night someone tried to kill you."

Lila snapped, "Yes, I do remember that, I was there."

Shane raised an eyebrow. "I can't protect you in a public place. You need to stay here until we can get to the bottom of things."

"I can't just stay home from work. I can't, I'm *new*. I *need* this job." Not just that, but she needed to look at her laptop. Somehow it was connected with her dream, she was sure of it.

"No can do. Besides, no one in your office will be at work today. I checked in and they still have it roped off while they process the scene. The only place you are going is to the police station to make a statement, and that's *when* they contact you."

Lila thought of the men dead on the floor. The priceless art, the possible finger of blame that might be directed at her. She had been there. They would dust the cups in the sink and find her fingerprints, and, and...

And what? Know you worked there? Big deal. They had bodies to deal with.

The eggs and bacon suddenly turned in her stomach. The memory of blood staining the carpet amid shards of the priceless vase was burned into her brain.

Can I even go back there after that?

Still, his attitude rankled at her. He wasn't asking her; he was *telling* her what she would do. And that didn't sit well with her, not at all.

She tried a different tack. "Look, I need to be at work, or at the very least *working*, and that requires my laptop."

"And your laptop is at the office."

"Yes, well..." She blinked, remembering suddenly. "Hold on, I've got one at home that has all of the same files and access to the rest on the cloud. Would that be easier to pick up?"

He nodded. "Yeah, that could work. Let me make a couple of calls and I'll see if I can't get it for you."

"And what am I supposed to do until then?" She sounded bitchy; she knew she did. She hated the feeling that the entire world was out doing something and she had to stay hidden. *I didn't do anything wrong, so why is this happening to me?*

He stood up, gathered her empty plate, and turned to the sink. "I'm sure you will think of something. Stay inside, though. I need to talk to my boss and get some updates and by noon we should have a plan of action."

Lila swallowed back a biting remark. Her life had been turned upside down in the past few days. The hearty breakfast she had eaten sat heavy in her stomach. A week ago, her life had been perfect. *Well, nearly perfect.* And now it felt like a train going off the tracks. She sighed and stood up.

"I'll wash, you dry." She shooed him away from the sink and plunged her hands into the soapy water. It was, after all, an excuse to do *something*.

She tried again after the dishes were done and the kitchen back to the way it had looked last night, neat as a pin, everything in its place. "Look, I just need to get there and pick up the laptop." She reached out and touched his hand. Men liked that, at least, that's what Kaylee said worked for her, and from what Lila could tell, Kaylee ruled half of the floor on just a smile and a light touch of her hand. She mustered a bright smile. "You could come with me."

He slowly looked at her hand resting on his and moved his eyes up. She forgot to breathe as they crept up her, a slow crawl of desire coupled with danger, a threat of the rules changing. She had changed them; she had crossed the line.

When he pulled his hand away, it didn't feel like rejection. She wasn't an overly sensitive girl who hung meaning on every word or movement from a man. She was, however, relieved. Once she had touched him, felt his heat, stepped into his personal space and broken that unspoken rule, she had been unable to let go. *Third rail.* Like the trains in the tunnels that flew along, electricity humming, hugging that third rail that enabled the connection and through which one could feel a raw, surging power. Touching him felt like it must feel to stand on the third rail and make a connection guaranteed to light your hair on fire and scorch your shoes. She stepped back as their connection broke, feeling the electricity between them snap and release.

"I'll go and you will stay. This isn't a negotiation." He said it in a cool way that dumped metaphorical ice all over her raging hormones.

Now *that* was rejection, or at the very least a smack-down that made her bristle with indignation before turning away. She hated that he was right. This man had saved her life, the least she could do would be to stay on the property for now. He would bring the laptop and then she could see if her dream had been the clue that she needed to solve this mystery. A cold wave washed over her, dampening her indignation further as she remembered the night before.

After all, he's right, someone is *trying to kill me.*

Shane strode away from her, trying desperately to ignore the growing bulge in his jeans. As he headed down the hall, phone in hand, he shook his head, trying to desperately to rip the fantasy of what he wanted to do to her from his mind. *Fucking the client is not allowed, Ellis. Yeah? Tell your dick that.*

He jabbed at the phone in his hand and Jack answered a few seconds later. "Talk to me."

"She's gung-ho about going to work. More specifically, she needs her laptop. She mentioned she also has data backups at home, on her home laptop." Shane answered.

"I'll have Lou retrieve the laptop from her apartment. If we go directly to the company and someone is dirty, they will know she has help. I'd like to keep her invisible and them in the dark for as long as possible," Jack said. "Meet me at the usual place at 10 a.m. sharp."

"Will do." Shane snapped the phone shut and checked his watch. It was nearly nine. He had time for a shower and a quick shave.

Suspicions

Rob sipped the coffee, curling his lip at the saccharine sweet aftertaste. "Ugh."

"Buck up, Dad, it's better for you than sugar." Madeleine slid past him and reached into the fridge.

"A couple of teaspoons of sugar can't hurt," he answered. "And what's with this inky black color? Are we out of creamer already? I thought I got some last Friday."

She shuffled containers around. "I threw it out."

"Why would you do that, Squirt?"

She emerged; a small stack of containers balanced in her hands as she toed the door closed. "Do you realize we never eat leftovers? And then they fill up the fridge and block the yogurt and produce bins."

"It's still good."

"Yeah? This one has green fur growing on top."

She deposited the containers into the sink and he could see a green creeping mass on top of the white rice in one, the other streaked with orange was a mystery he wasn't interested in solving.

"And that 'couple of teaspoons per cup' adds up to a lot when you drink twelve cups in a day. Ms. Watts says you need to watch your triglycerides as well, so I tossed the creamer and we are both going to get used to drinking it black."

"Oh, for crying out loud, that health teacher is out of her mind." Rob glared at his daughter. "I'll eat what I want."

She stared at him, her eyes big, looking just like Claire would when she was determined to win an argument through whatever means necessary. Rob had to wonder if it was something Maddy remembered or if it was just ingrained in her feminine psyche.

"Dad, all I have is you. If you drop dead of a heart attack, what happens to *me*?" She looked vulnerable and scared, and even though he knew she was manipulating him as only one possessing such formidable feminine wiles could, his resistance melted.

"Fine," Rob mumbled, and sipped his stevia-laced coffee, his shoulders sagging in defeat. He never could muster a defense to that kind of argument. It was pointless to try. Maddy smiled and kissed him on the cheek.

"I have to leave early. I'm meeting Julia at her house; she needs help with her spelling practice. We're entering the spelling bee and I promised her we would practice before school."

"I should drive you."

Maddy rolled her eyes. "Dad, she's at the corner. You can watch me walk there, okay?"

"You have the pepper spray, right? And your phone?"

"Yes, Dad, of course I do." She rolled her eyes, reached up and hugged him. The past year had seen a growth spurt and his daughter had shot up two, maybe three inches. The top of her head reached his shoulder. She had nearly passed her mother's height and she still had a few years of growing left to go. Her strawberry-blond hair had darkened to a fiery red and it was shoulder length and a mass of ringlets.

He hugged her back.

Maddy was a beauty. Rob sighed. *Just like her mother.*

"Did you sign up yet, Dad?"

"Sign up for what?"

"The link I sent you, Meet Your Match."

Rob groaned.

"Dad, you *promised*."

"I promised I'd think about it. And I did."

"And?"

"And I have time before you go off to college. Plenty of time. Five years' worth of time, girl. Stop playing matchmaker."

"Look, Dad, you need to find someone before you get any older."

He choked on his coffee, liquid spraying from his lips. "Christ."

"See what I mean, Dad? Hand-eye coordination is one of the first things to go." She grinned. "Besides, I'm seeing some white hairs in that goatee."

"Believe me, girl, they are all thanks to you," he growled, dabbing at the coffee that had dribbled onto his shirt.

Her lips tickled his cheek. "Gotta go. Love you!" She was out the door, the storm door banging closed behind her.

He really needed to fix that door spring so that it didn't make such a racket. He took another gulp of coffee, his lip curling in disgust. Its saccharine-sweet taste was disgusting. He stood up and poured the rest down the sink.

His spine popped and his left side spasmed. He'd pulled his back out last year while clearing some brush in the yard and it hadn't felt right since. *Christ, I am getting old.* He shook his head and headed to the bathroom. As he brushed his teeth and ran a comb through his hair, he remembered Claire plucking at a white hair that had sprung out of his chest.

"Can't have you turning into a silverback quite yet, now can I?" She had pulled it out, root and all. It had hurt like hell. In the decade since, that one silver hair had been joined by a sprinkling, and in the past year, a cascade of others.

"Time and tide wait for no man." He leaned in closer, peering at the streak of white among the still mostly dark hairs. He kept it trimmed neatly; Claire had liked it that way.

Rob sighed, staring at his reflection. If he could ask her, he knew what she would say. Hell, she *had* said it.

"Life is too short. Grieve, but get over it. Face it, my love, we humans are better suited to relationships than not."

But meeting someone else, all the delicate dances that come from learning how to live with someone else, to anticipate their moods, their needs, and finding a way to balance being a father to Maddie while sharing time with someone new?

He had gone to the site and been run through its paces. Answering the questions on the personality quiz had been challenging and frustrating. Was this really how people did it these days? Answer some quasi-scientific questions and get connected with your future mate? It had to be bullshit. A computer algorithm couldn't tell him who he was supposed to love. Yet he had kept returning to it.

I'll try it out and do a test run. Hell, it could be fun.

He left the bathroom and headed down to the basement where he had built a small office and kept everything under lock and key. He was a homicide investigator, after all, and Maddie didn't need to see how base and cruel humans could be with each other.

Rob sat down at his desk and opened an email from work and stared at the tattooed image of the Indalo on each of the dead men's wrists. There was no mistaking it, the symbol was simple, rudimentary, and exactly like the tattoo he had seen ten years ago. He reached into a box, rifled through its contents until he found Maddie's crude drawing, now a decade old. A memory flashed through his mind of the day before their trip to the playground, when he had called Milo and Steve at the CIA. The case they had been working on, spearheaded by Rob, had languished in the weeks after Claire's death. He had conferenced them in, told him he would be returning to work in two days. It was time to take the bull by the horns and get back to work, he had told them.

The next day had been their trip to the playground and the run-in with that woman, the not-so-veiled threat of the two women with the photograph and the note. Was it the phone call to his co-workers that had triggered the message to be sent? Had they bugged his house there in Virginia? Had he gotten too close to figuring out who they were? Rob searched decade-old memories, trying to remember details of the case he had investigated.

He hadn't called Steve or Milo again, just left them to be targeted in his stead. He took a deep breath in and released it slowly. *I'm no fucking hero, am I? I just took care of me and mine and said fuck off to the rest.*

But now, here in Kansas City, in flyover country, where politics, shady financial deals, and hired hits were unheard of - here is where the Indalo had popped back up.

"Indalo."

Just saying the word gave it substance. This wasn't something he could run from. If they were here, then they were everywhere, or damn near. He shook his head and stifled a rueful smile at the thought of running away with Maddie to some lone mountaintop with sheep and mountain goats. She would *not* be down for that. The girl was connected at the hip to her iPhone. So much so that he had banned devices at the dinner table and at the movies. How could she watch a movie while texting on the phone, anyway?

His hand reached for his phone and then stopped. *Could they still be listening?* The question sent his mind spinning. He wouldn't have been hard to track, after all. He stood up from his desk. For the first time in nearly ten years he felt afraid, unsafe even, in his own house.

His cell phone buzzed. Maddie's face flashed on the screen, red hair, curls, and her beautiful brown eyes.

"Everything okay, Sweetheart?"

"Everything's great, Dad. I forgot to tell you it was a half day and it turns out that Julia's mom is taking her to Coco Key after school today and they invited me. Can I go?"

"Sure. Do you want to come back here and get your swimsuit?"

"Nah, mine's here from the last time we went swimming. We were planning on dinner and a movie after, is that okay too?" He smiled, even if she couldn't see it.

"Sure. Be home by ten?"

"Will do. Thanks, Dad. I love you!"

"Love you too, Maddie."

His shift didn't start until 6 p.m. tonight, so he would have the house to himself for a few hours. And that was convenient; he didn't need an excuse to get Maddie out of the house while he swept for bugs. But first, he needed some supplies and to visit someone he knew could help. He grabbed his keys and headed out the door.

A short drive to Historic Northeast and Rob parked his car in front of a nondescript brick building and got out, locking the door.

"Hey there, handsome, looking for a date?" The voice was effeminate, and a prominent set of breasts protruded from the top of a skintight dress, but the Adam's apple was a dead giveaway that not all was as it appeared.

Rob said nothing, just flashed his badge as he walked on past. The effect on the male prostitute was immediate. He said nothing, just spun on his high heels and disappeared around the corner in two seconds flat. Rob suppressed a smile and entered the building, a small buzzer sounding as he walked through the doorway into the brightly lit shop.

"Robbie!" The grizzled older man stood up and walked over, clapping him on the shoulder, "I haven't seen you in nine tomorrows, where have you been? And how is that beautiful little girl of yours doing?"

"Hi, Ben, good to see you." He hugged the older man. "You've lost weight, old man."

"Eh, the fuckin' cancer came back." He shrugged. "They keep tellin' me I got six months, tops. Hell, I've been hearing that for four years now, but the last few weeks have been vexing."

Rob stared at him, a long look that took in the dark circles under his eyes, the pale, unhealthy sheen to Ben's complexion, and the way his clothes hung from him.

"Shit, Ben, I'm so sorry."

Ben shrugged. "Eh, c'est la vie. I've lived a great life, Robbie, traveled the world and loved a woman long after she left me for greener pastures. I've seen plenty and lived more than most. Sometimes it's just your time, y'know?"

Rob nodded. "Yeah, I do."

Ben clapped him on the shoulder again and grinned at him. "How old is Maddie now?"

Rob shook his head and groaned. "Thirteen going on twenty-one. The girl is starting to turn heads."

"Time to get that shotgun primed with rock salt, Robbie. Put the fear of God in any of those hormonal teenage boys that come sniffing around."

Rob laughed and said, "I'm working on it. Believe me, I'm working on it!"

"So, what brought you my way today? I can see you have something on your mind." Ben might be dying, but he was as astute as ever.

"Let's say I think that someone's listening in."

"House or work?"

"My home."

Ben nodded and was still, his face thoughtful. "That would be odd, considering you are a homicide detective. Unless you are thinking it's mafia-level."

"I wasn't always a homicide detective, Ben."

"I'm aware. Hell, you still carry yourself like a company man. It's spooked some of my customers over the years."

Rob and Ben had met over eight years ago after a spike of murders in Historic Northeast had played out along Independence Avenue. The older man's background with the police, he was once a homicide investigator like

Rob, and his keen eye for noticing when things were off, had helped collar a man targeting prostitutes on the Avenue.

The older man didn't play games, he didn't ask questions he had no place asking, but he also saw far more than he let on. He'd known what Rob was, and said nothing.

"I need to find out if someone is watching or listening."

Ben nodded. "I've got what you need, but it would be a good idea for you to bring any laptops or other devices in and have my techie look at them. Be able to tell if there is any keylogging software installed."

"I'll bring mine in on Saturday if that's okay. As for that kiddo of mine, I'm pretty sure she's attached at the hip to it. It might require surgery. If the operation is a success, I'll bring hers in as well."

Ben snorted, "Tell me about it. That's the way all the kids are these days. Give me a couple of minutes and I'll get you set up."

Rob nodded and examined the wares in a new glass case Ben had installed since the last time he had visited the shop. "Hey Ben, add one of those onto my order, please." He pointed to an object in the case. "You never know when that might come in handy."

"Sure thing, Robbie."

A few minutes later, his purchases bagged and paid for, he hugged the older man. "Let me know if you need anything, Ben, anything at all."

"Hug that beautiful girl of yours, Robbie. And stay safe."

Rob nodded. "See you on Saturday."

Re-Open the Case

Rob walked into the house. It was time to get answers, one way or the other. He pulled out the detector and began moving through each room of the house. By the time he had reached the third room, he was so angry he couldn't trust himself to speak. His home, his sanctuary, had been defiled. And for how long?

Had they listened to every conversation he and Maddie had ever had in this house? Listened as she grew from a tiny little girl missing her mom to the teenager with a full bevy of friends and middle school crushes?

The times he had spoken to Claire, out loud, missing her so bad it took his breath away, telling her about their child, how Maddie had learned to ride a bike, how she had read from her first book one night, just days before starting kindergarten. And all the moments in between.

He had thought it was all private, that he and Maddie were safe here, but he had been wrong. So wrong. There was nothing safe or private about this place.

Rob felt lightheaded, his heart rate skyrocketing as he stared at the red x's he had drawn on the walls. He dug into the sheetrock with his knife, feeling the difference when the tip of it found the bug. He pulled it out of the wall, seething, and carried it into the garage. He ground it into a mass of plastic shards under his foot on the bare cement floor and returned to the house. One by one, he dug them out of walls, found them in light fixtures, and the undersides of furniture. One by one, he carried them to the garage and ground them under his shoe. In all, he found fifteen, two in Maddie's room. The fury he felt at that, at his child being watched by these bastards, ran through him, a river of ice and fear.

And who could he trust? Was there anyone he could go to, talk to, and be sure of?

What did these people, this shadow organization, want? They had taken Claire from him; he was sure of it. They had threatened him, threatened to hurt his little girl, and that was more than he could bear. Maddie was all that he had left. Finding the bugs had proven to him one thing; they had *not* gone away and they never would. No more running. It was time for him to become the hunter instead of the prey.

But first he had some spackling to do. Maddie didn't need to know about this and he would do whatever he had to do to keep her safe.

Later that afternoon, Milo Barnaby picked up the phone and answered it, distracted, his attention on the report in front of him.

"Milo Barnaby."

"Milo, Rob Stone here."

"Stone? Rob *Stone*? Damn man, it's been years! How are you?"

"I'm doing well enough. And you? How's Diana?"

"We split three years ago," Milo sighed. "She traded up for silver hair, a Porsche, and a house in the Hamptons. I get a visit with Gus when they go out of town and a month in the summer. She told me her mother always said she had married beneath her. So much for happily ever after, right?"

Rob whistled, "Damn. I'm sorry to hear that."

"Hell, that's all right. I'm dating a twenty-something intern now. She's a knockout. Natural tits that defy gravity with nipples that'll put your eye out. It's a hell of a way to go blind, but still."

Rob laughed.

Milo dropped his voice, "Now what's going on with you, man? If you are calling me, something has gotta be up. All I get is some goddamn Christmas card every year. You never call and I'm thinking there's a real good reason for that. You got my spider senses a'tingling."

Rob smiled. Milo had always been good at reading people and he still was.

"I tried Steve first, but couldn't find him in the directory. Has he moved on to greener pastures?"

"Shit. No." Milo paused and he closed his office door. "You hadn't heard? He died maybe six months after you left. Lung cancer, extremely aggressive. It was a few weeks between diagnosis and then hospice. A few weeks after that and he was gone."

"Lung cancer? Steve never smoked a day in his life."

"Eh, it's like breast cancer in men. No one ever thinks a man can get breast cancer, but goddamn, they sure as hell can."

"He wasn't exposed to anything?" Rob asked, rocked at the thought of a world without Steve in it. How had he not heard? And then he remembered that his cards never had a return address. A small idiosyncrasy, one that made no sense since he was easily tracked here to Kansas City if anyone had been so inclined.

Milo practically guffawed, "Seriously? We're *analysts*, Rob."

"Milo, I've got to ask about the investigation we were working on, the one right before I left."

Milo's easygoing demeanor changed, and his tone became guarded. "Stone, you know the rules. You aren't with the agency and we *cannot* discuss this."

"Hear me out, Milo. The file I had been compiling, the files and papers I had accumulated over nearly a year of digging, were returned to the agency. They threatened me, Milo. They probably killed Claire and then they threatened to do the same to Maddie. When they sent me a photo of our house from the day before, sent it *using my child* with a note to stop digging, I did what I had to do."

Rob sighed and leaned back against the park bench. The air had a nip to it and his knees were aching. An early snow was in the forecast. Home wasn't an option right now, not until he was sure he had found all the bugs.

"I did what I had to do to protect her, and myself. I thought it would be over if I walked away, if I cut all ties. But I just did a sweep of my home and found monitoring devices - in my office, the kitchen, my bedroom, even my kid's bedroom, for fuck's sake. If you closed the case, re-open it, because after a decade, these bastards are not only watching me, but *they are here*."

"Jesus, Rob." Milo fell silent, but Rob could hear a drawer opening and papers rustling. "Fuck this smoke-free workplace bullshit." The click of a lighter and the steady drag of a cigarette came over the line faintly. "Are you sure it isn't something from your line of work now?"

"I'm a homicide detective, Milo, I don't work for the Company anymore. I deal with shootings and assaults and burglaries gone wrong, nothing more."

"Shit, Rob, I wish I knew what to tell you." Milo sighed. "You aren't missing a thing not being here; even the higher-ups are pussy-whipped and I've been handed bullshit assignments while the real issues get locked down. That's what Steve would have told you before he died. The higher-ups shut the investigation down. No reason given. Steve was all set to fight it and then his health took a swan dive. And we all know you two were the smart ones. I wasn't gonna rock the fucking boat, not with Gus going into that nice private school in Avalon. I had bills to pay and a marriage on the rocks."

"I hear you, man. But, Milo, do you have anything, anything at all that could help? Any of your files, or even Steve's, that I could..."

"Jesus, Stone! No! I got nothing. And even if I did, I would *not* give it to you. Not for love, or money, or a night with the woman of my dreams. Gus is lined up with an early acceptance to Georgetown and I just passed the twenty-year mark here. Don't try and take back channels or this shit will blow up in your face harder than Tailhook did for the Navy back in ninety-one."

A cold drizzle was beginning to fall. Rob felt a hot anger swell up inside him. Milo wouldn't, hell, he *couldn't* help him.

How long had those bastards been listening?

He had become complacent, let his guard down, and allowed himself to be frightened off in the first place. More than ever, he was convinced. The Indalo, for lack of a better name and description, were the bogeyman under the bed. Claire's death, that note telling him to abandon his investigation, and now even Milo and Steve had been pulled into this. Rob didn't buy lung cancer, not for a minute. Inhalation of enough polonium 210 would certainly manifest as a particularly aggressive lung cancer. Steve had led too healthy a life to explain this away so easily.

"Stone? You still there?" Milo's voice crackled in his ear.

"Yeah, yeah. Look, I'm sorry, man. You are absolutely right and I shouldn't have pushed you. I gotta go, so..."

"Don't worry about it." Milo's voice had returned to its natural friendly tone. "I'll just pretend this never happened. Try not to let ten years go by before you call again. Y'hear me?"

"Will do. Thanks, Milo, you take care."

"You too, buddy."

One thousand miles away in his small office in Virginia, Milo set the phone back in its cradle and stared at it. "Shit." He lit another cigarette; fairly certain he wouldn't have anyone poking their head in through the door. He needed to get one of those ionizers and stick it under his desk. His hands shook until the nicotine mellow hit. He chain-smoked three cigarettes in a row before getting up the nerve to pick up the phone again. This time it was a small flip phone hidden in an inner suit pocket. He pressed a button and waited until he heard a voice on the other line.

"I just heard from Rob Stone. He was asking me to re-open the investigation."

He ground out the last of the cigarette butt into an old takeout box and then stuffed the box into the trash. "Yeah, I know. I told him I couldn't help him. But Stone does what he thinks is right and to hell with the consequences."

He listened and nodded. "Yeah, he knows about those too. Look, I want out. I don't know anything, and I'm not interested in pointing any fingers, I just want *out*, got it?"

He waited, listening to the voice on the other end. "Yeah, you do that."

Milo ended the call and stared at the phone in his hand.

He'd damn near sold his soul - all so that his life would go on as usual. In return, his marriage had failed and his son barely spoke to him. And the twenty-something tail he'd been chasing had been quickly losing interest after realizing he was up to his eyeballs in debt.

A sick feeling of dread began to form in his stomach. They would never let him walk away. Folks like this, they never did.

Fuck it.

He stood up and strode over to the bookshelf where Diana's last gift to him resided. A soldered, heavy Steampunk masterpiece of gears and cast-iron parts from long-demolished engines. It was heavy in his hand. He returned to the desk and brought it down hard on the burner phone, a grim smile on his lips as the plastic crunched.

No more. To hell with the consequences.

Signal Lost

"Indalo." The word, spoken aloud in the target's house, had triggered a report, and the report had pinged Lucifer's email with a red flag alert. A moment later, her phone buzzed and played the first notes from The Imperial March.

It woke her up and she lay there in the half light of morning, the heavy blanket of sleep still fogging her mind and wondered why the hell she was awake. She had been online until 3 a.m., her armies victorious, surrounded by a sea of dead trolls before she lay down her flaming sword and retreated to the comfort of her bed. It was far too early to be woken by anything, much less an alert. *God, I have to work. And at this ungodly hour of the morning?*

She groaned and blearily reached for the phone among a menagerie of objects that crowded the bedside table. Annabelle flopped over and groaned, stretching in the bed beside her.

The lip balm skittered off the table and rolled across the cement floor. The bottle of aspirin made more of a clatter and Annabelle whoofed in alarm, rolled to a standing position, and shook. Her collar and tags jingled. She jumped off the bed and walked, her toenails clicking on the floor, to stand by the back door.

"So much for sleeping," Lucifer muttered in disgust, still unable to find the phone in the gloom. Annabelle whined quietly at the door. "Yeah, yeah, I'm coming." The dog, once wakened, would not stop until she was let out to do her business.

She stumbled out of bed and let the dog out. The sun was bright and she retreated from it, shutting the door firmly behind Annabelle, and cursed as the door caught and dragged across the top of her bare foot. "Shit! Ow!" Lucifer limped back to her bed and cradled her foot while Annabelle barked outside, intent on chasing squirrels, no doubt.

"It is too early for this crap," she growled and lifted the covers, searching for her phone. It clattered to the floor; she reached for it and banged her half-shaven scalp into the sharp metal corner of the bed frame. "Fuck!" She rocked on her heels, clutching her head, and then lurched to the other side of the room where a bank of computers and monitors hummed. As she sat in her chair, the movement jarred the desk and the hum changed, monitors blinked on, and the room brightened, lit by the multiple screens before her.

She set her phone down and ran her fingers along the keys, reaching over to click the mouse. *It's easier to read on a screen anyway.*

Her fingers flew over the keyboard and she sucked in a breath as her eyes took in the information on the screen. "Shit, that is not possible." She whistled, "Shit, shit, *shit.*"

She grabbed her phone and rapidly typed a message.

RE: Subject RS

The lights are out but the power is still on. Call me.

-L-

She checked the connections, made sure there weren't any power outages reported, and double-checked her reports. Then, with nothing left to do but wait for a call, she opened up World of Warcraft and plunged in. Two hours later, surrounded on all sides by trolls, she groaned when the phone rang. Her hand hovered over it.

It rang twice, then a third, before she answered, "This had better be the six-foot-tall, hung like Michael Fassbender cabana boy I ordered from Guilty Pleasures."

"Sorry to disappoint."

"I'm guessing you want an update."

"Yes."

Lucifer leaned back in her chair and rubbed at her scalp. It still hurt where she had banged it against the bed. "All of them are offline."

"Offline as in…?"

"From the little information I have, I would say that he found them and disabled them. They didn't go off all at the same time. That would have been a power or connectivity issue since they piggy-back on his Wi-Fi signal. Instead, they went off at irregular intervals over a space of two hours. I'd say he used a locator and then dug 'em out one by one. No matter how it happened, he got them all. We no longer have eyes or ears in the house."

"I see." There was a small pause. "I want you to look through the past two weeks of data and see if you see any patterns."

"Already on it. Also, he used a trigger word, about an hour before the first device was deactivated."

"A trigger word?"

"Yeah, the voice recognition software notifies us if certain words are used. And he used one. *The* trigger word." Her voice dropped to a whisper, "*Indalo*."

The voice on the other end said nothing, just a hiss of displeasure.

Lucifer gulped and continued, "Anyway, I'll keep you updated if anything comes up. So far, nothing much out of the ordinary. Just the typical tween bullshit coming from the daughter and all the old man does is go to work, come home, and Netflix binges in between tailgating from his home all the Chiefs games. Oh yeah, and two more things."

"Go on."

"He joined a dating website last week."

"Very interesting." There was a short pause. "A dating site, you say?"

"Yeah, Meet Your Match; it's a local company."

"What was the other thing?"

"He tried calling a Steve Hardison in Yorktown, Virginia. But there wasn't anyone by that name listed in the directory."

The caller's voice changed, sounded almost concerned, "I see." There was a long pause. "You still can monitor the website searches and log keystrokes, right?"

Lucifer allowed herself a smug smile. "Yep, there's no way they find that; I buried it with a rootkit virus. It sends me hourly updates and then scrubs the evidence of the updates."

"Keep me updated on any internet searches as well."

"Parameters?"

"You'll know. He's looking into *us*."

"Got it."

"Thank you, Lucifer. Your hard work continues to be a boon to all of us." And with that the line went dead.

Lucifer grinned like a Cheshire cat. The boss didn't hand out compliments very often and that made them like gold, especially to the likes of her. She understood better than many just how low she was in the organization, and how inconsequential. Her Indalo tat was red, the color of blood, and if she got out more, she would have had to fend off curious looky-loo's who usually wanted to know why a sweet little girl like her had marked her skin with some heathen-looking icon.

That would be especially true at home in Highfill, Arkansas, where everyone not only knew everyone else, but were related somehow. Returning last year after five years away in glitzy L.A. had been a shock to Lucy's system, and to the gentler denizens of Highfill. Her once luxurious shoulder-length locks of blond hair had been transformed into a jet black, ragged, chopped rat's nest, with one side buzzcut so short she could see her scalp had pimples. Well, at least no one would be calling her that "cute little Eastman girl" anymore.

She clicked on the feed one more time looking for cameras and bugs. Nothing. She went down the list. Damned if he hadn't gotten every single one of them. The Indalo had been watching Rob Stone long before Lucy Lucifer Eastman was recruited five years ago. So, what had tripped the mark up? What made him suspect he was being watched? And how the hell did a Podunk cop in flyover country know how to find not one, but *all* of the bugs in the house? Those were questions Lucifer would have asked, if there was anyone who would have told her. But the nature of what she did, and the people she did it for, did not encourage those lines of questions.

"Well, at least I've got the keystroke and activity tracking," she mused. "That should yield something." She would dig in and see what she could find. The customized virus she had created for the Android phones Stone and his daughter carried, similar to Ghost Ctrl but better, continued to provide her with a stream of useful information.

A whine and a short bark at the door informed her that Annabelle wanted back in. To hell with the World of Warcraft, she had work to do.

Broken Code

The property was massive, some fifteen acres in total. The trees that lined its borders were in the height of their fall colors - the leaves alternating between yellow, orange, and a fiery sunset-red. The day was clear and sunny, but there was a cold chill that the sun had not yet chased away. On the ground lay a fine layer of fallen leaves.

Lila walked through the open field, noting a pair of horses in the distance. The smell of woodsmoke was heavy in the air. Despite the faint sounds of the highway in the distance, it felt as if she was alone in the middle of nowhere. From the north along the border of the property farthest from her, hidden by the trees and skirting the edge of the river, she could hear the steady clickety-clack of a train. The air was crisp, clean, and she stopped by the small orchard at the edge of the field and selected two rust-red and yellow-striped apples from one of the trees. The branches were heavy with them and she could see from the high grass that it had been a long time since the orchard was tended.

Two horses now hung their heads over a fence, their eyes on her and the apples in her hands and nickered. Lila grinned. Her mom and dad had taken her to a farm when she was small, visiting a distant cousin, and there had been two horses there in a corral attached to a barn. She had fed them apples and even gotten a chance to ride one, her legs stretched over the wide body, her feet dangling miles away from the stirrups. The horse had been old, gentle, and slow. She remembered how the coarse hairs of its mane had felt, that and the velvet smoothness of its nose as it had taken the apple from her outstretched hand with such delicate care.

Shane had left an hour or more ago, saying little, except to remind her to not leave the house. But it was such a beautiful sunny day, and winter was just around the corner. To stay inside would be such a waste. She was safe here and no one knew where they were, so what could a short little walk hurt? She would stay on the property, which seemed rather vast, and keep to the grounds.

She headed across the field towards the horses and they tossed their heads and nickered louder as she approached, their eyes firmly on the treats she held in her hand.

"Hello, you gorgeous beasts. Would you each like an apple?" One horse was a soft brown, with white on its lower legs that reminded her of lace, the other was mottled with tan and white patches all over. They nudged her hands with their velvet noses, snuffling softly, clearly interested in the apples inside. She smiled and held her hands open. The fruit disappeared in seconds, velvety lips and strong teeth gently removing them from her hands and crunching down on the sweet treats.

Lila ran her fingers lightly over their soft muzzles, sighing at the velvety richness. The tan horse snorted and pulled away, her hooves dancing on the ground, but the brown one held still, light chuffing noises issuing from his throat. He leaned further over his side of the fence, his nostrils flaring as he sniffed her, looking for more apples.

She loved the feel of his soft hide and the earthy smell he gave off. It brought to mind one of her earliest dreams as a girl. She trailed her fingers along the side of his face and leaned closer. "Do you know what I dreamed about when I was little? Having a horse just like you. I wanted to live on a farm, raise chickens, and sheep and ride horses all day." She laughed. "So how in the hell did I end up in an office job, anyway?"

Lila sighed and leaned against the horse. He chuffed again, his massive flank expanding with each breath. She shuddered as memories of the night before suddenly shot to the surface. Blood pooling on the carpet, eyes wide, staring at her vacantly from the floor. Why was this happening to her? What had she done to deserve it?

The horse tossed his head then, stomping his hooves, and Lila pulled back from him. "Done with me now that the treats are all gone, eh? Well, okay then, I think I'll check out the pond while you go hang out with your friend. I'll bring you more apples later if I can!"

The horse wheeled around, tossing his mane, and took off at a trot. Lila watched him go and then turned to the east where a creek and small pond cut through the property. It was mostly hidden by the trees, but now that the leaves were falling it was easier to see. The pond was not very large, but apparently it was deep enough for a boat. A small aluminum one was out of the water and leaning against a tree. She made her way down the path. Frost glistened here and there in the thick shade untouched by the sun. It was strange to stand out here and realize that, just a few miles away, there was a city filled with people, sirens, and traffic. Here it seemed impossible, an oasis of nature flanked on all sides by trees. The clickety-clack of the train faded into the distance. Even the water treatment plant was silent and, except for a sprinkling of cars, deserted.

She heard the crunch of gravel before she saw the car. Shane was back. She waved and his expression suddenly changed. The car stopped abruptly at the base of the drive and he emerged striding towards her.

Uh oh, he looks pissed.

"Miss Benoit, *what* are you doing out here?"

Ooh boy, he really was *pissed.*

"I was just..."

His anger seemed to stretch his legs and he closed the distance between them in two more strides. He reached for her wrist; his hand hot against her skin. "Get in the car now, please, Miss Benoit."

He had an iron grip and she fought the urge to rip her hand from his. "Let go of me this instant."

He was standing inches from her and she could feel his anger. *All because I went for a walk?* She stared up at him, her eyes snapping, angry enough to match his sharp edges and roughness. *I'll be damned if he's going to manhandle me!*

His nostrils flared, his jaw was set, but his hands released her wrist gently, taking a deep breath before he spoke again, "My apologies, Miss Benoit. It is not safe outside of the house. I need for you to please get in the car and accompany me inside."

His measured tones were contradicted by the pulse jumping at his neck. *How very interesting.* She nodded, tried to calm herself as well, and led the way to the car, which was still idling at the foot of the drive.

Sitting next to him in the Jeep brought back memories of the evening before. And the anger left her, replaced by the ever-present question. *Why would anyone want to kill me?* Which immediately caused her to blurt, "My laptop? Did you get it?"

A quick shake of the head shot down all of her hopes of understanding *why* this was happening. "Your apartment had been tossed. The laptop was missing."

"Tossed? Oh God, I need to go there, who knows what else might be missing!"

"It wasn't a robbery, Lila, although they certainly wanted to leave that impression. All of your electronics, iPad, Kindle, and laptop - everything that might have the information on it was missing." He shifted out of park and drove up the hill, pressing the button to open the garage door.

"If we can get my laptop from work..."

They drove into the garage and Shane killed the engine and pressed the garage door button again. It slid down, quietly plunging them into darkness. "We can't get to it right now."

Jack had reached out to Kaylee Stromm, Lila's friend who worked in the office, and asked her to try to retrieve it, but the office was closed for the day. The host of insurance inspectors and a cleanup crew would need to fix the place up first. There was plenty of work to be done spackling over the bullet holes in the walls and replacing the bloodstained carpet. Whether the laptop was in the hands of the police or the company, no one knew for sure.

"Damn it!" Lila felt like screaming or hitting something. "I hate this!" Her fingers curled into hard fists. "Someone is trying really hard to kill me and for what, and why? And I'm stuck here, where I can't even go outside without you turning into some damn knuckle-dragging caveman and yanking me back inside by my hair."

Shane felt a smile tugging at the corners of his mouth. "I didn't touch your hair. I'm far more circumspect than that."

"Circumspect? What kind of bodyguard are you, Shane Ellis?" She laughed ruefully. "I'm sorry, the knuckle-dragging comment was rude and inaccurate."

Shane laughed in return and held his knuckles up as if examining them closely. "I dunno, there might be some callouses from dragging them while I chase around angry women." He paused. "Look, I can't get you your laptop, but I can help you deal with it in a constructive way."

"How's that?" she asked, her curiosity piqued, and that familiar surge of attraction she felt when she was near him quietly began to build.

"Well, first, how do you feel about guns?"

"How do I *feel* about them?" She arched a delicate eyebrow at him.

"Have you ever handled one?"

"Are we speaking in metaphors here?"

He laughed then. "C'mon, let me show you the basement." He slid out of the driver's seat, tilted his head at her, and smiled. Lila felt her insides heat up. *Does this man have any idea how sexy he is?*

She slipped out of the passenger seat and followed him out of the garage, inside and past the half bath, and down a set of stairs she had seen him use the night before. A half flight down and there was a door directly on the right. A long hallway stretched in front of them.

"Right down here," he said, "and watch your head on the last step." She passed under it easily and turned in time to see him duck. "I guess you aren't six foot two."

"Try five foot one." she shrugged. "It has its advantages, but it sucks when I need to change a lightbulb." She turned away from him and assessed the room, "So definitely not metaphorically speaking."

He admired her chutzpah. She had held her own against an attacker in an underground garage, then been shot at by two highly paid assassins. Many would have lost it, hell, he'd seen grown men shivering and crying under similar circumstances, but Lila had spunk. Spunk would only get her so far, however.

"No matter how you feel about firearms, knowing how to use one, and how one can be used against you, is important." He walked over to the area Benton had set up as a firing range and unlocked the cabinet door. "Have you ever held a pistol?"

"No, my parents were both children of hippies. I'd probably have to dig into a third, possibly fourth generation before I found anyone in my family tree who was familiar with any weaponry." She smiled at him and he felt a surge of attraction in response. "I'm not anti-gun, I've just never had the opportunity."

"I'll give you a rundown of the different parts, and then we will fire off some test rounds and let you have a little practice on a target." He leaned towards her and placed large noise-canceling protective gear over her ears.

She nodded and moved closer to him, too close, as he detailed the different parts of the weapon, disassembled and reassembled it in front of her, and reviewed the basics. "Never aim it at anything you don't intend to shoot," he cautioned. "Slide this back to load a round in the chamber, keep your knees and elbows slightly bent, and line the sights up."

His lips brushed her hair and Shane felt the slightest quiver in response, her musky vanilla scent intoxicating in his nose. His voice dropped lower, quieter, and he hovered behind her, trying to focus on the task at hand.

"When you are ready, pull the trigger back gently."

She stood still, her knees slightly bent, her elbows as well, and she stared down the sights, aiming for the center of a simple black outline on white paper at the far end of the firing range. She tried to focus on the target, and not on the man so close to her that she could feel his body heat. The target hung there, waiting for her. There was an explosive bang and concussive recoil of the gun in her hand as she pulled the trigger. The target fluttered slightly.

Nothing.

"You missed, but that's okay. Try again."

Her hands shook a little as she raised the weapon up and squinted down the sight line. She squeezed the trigger again.

A hole appeared in the target. "Nice shot. Center mass. You did good, Miss Benoit."

"Lila."

"I'm sorry?"

"Call me Lila. Every time you call me Miss Benoit, I imagine a seventy-five-year-old librarian with a bad attitude and intolerance for noisy patrons."

He laughed. "I've known some pretty sexy librarians."

"Were they seventy-five?"

He grinned and stepped closer, his hand on her waist. "No, a fair sight younger."

"And here I was imagining you with a cougar." His eyebrow quirked up and he smiled, slow and sexy, and her insides turned to jelly. He was close, too close, and she resisted the urge to grab his shirt in her fist, wrap her legs around him, and kiss him in a dirty, uninhibited way. He looked at her, standing that close, and studied her face, a half-smile on his lips.

He nodded at the gun still in her hands. "Go ahead and empty the magazine. Keep aiming for the center of the chest and take the shots nice and slow."

Two shots went wild, but the rest remained tightly packed center mass on the target.

"Excellent, you're a natural."

"So, I shouldn't aim for the head?"

"No, a shot to the chest is both easier since you have more to aim at, and just as deadly."

"Got it."

His hand slid over hers, warm, hot even, and plucked the weapon from her hand. "How did it feel?" He was standing so close. Her fingers tingled where he had touched them.

"To shoot a gun?" She shrugged. "It's heavier than I thought it would be. It's quite a bit of recoil for something so small. Loud as well." She paused, her green eyes assessing him. "I guess, when it comes down to it, I'd use one if I had to, but I don't particularly feel comfortable with it."

"You have a healthy amount of respect for a deadly weapon. There's nothing wrong with that." He disassembled the weapon with ease and efficiency and began cleaning it. "I figured you wouldn't mind killing time and learning something new. You never know when knowing your way around a firearm could save your life. Even if you never have to pull the trigger."

"I didn't mind at all. Thank you for that." All the hairs on her arm felt as if they were filled with electricity. He was so close that she could feel his body heat. His gaze dropped to her lips, and Lila leaned closer, just as her stomach took that moment to complain, loudly, about its lack of food. Lila felt her skin heat up, her face blushing in embarrassment.

Shane chuckled, "I think we had better rustle something up in the kitchen."

"Indeed."

Reaching Out

Rob scratched his head and looked at the list of employees that Morris Endon had sent over yesterday morning. "Someone's missing."

"Talking to yourself again, Stone?" Max asked, two coffees and a small bag from Donut King clutched in his hands. "Christ, take this damned thing. They made 'em nuclear today. I think the coffee is eating through the Styrofoam. I'm pretty sure my fingerprints have been melted off."

Rob reached up and took one of the cups. "Piping hot, just the way God intended." He waved the printout at Max. "You're late, Peisker, I've handled all of the paperwork."

"Huh, sounds like I was right on time."

They both laughed and Max pointed to the printout. "Whatcha got there?"

"A list of employees at Kurgen Real Estate. There was a total of twelve offices and work stations, but there's only ten names on this list," Rob answered, staring at the list again.

"So, they have a couple of extra workstations for visitors or they're down a couple of staff members."

Rob shook his head. "Nah, I did a schematic of the office, based on my memory of the layout and the crime scene photos." He pointed to the board. "This office here, it had personal belongings, a couple of pictures of family, and also one of what looks like Kaylee Stromm, who *is* listed on the personnel list but works in this office right here." He pointed to the far side of the diagram. "So possibly a friend?"

"So why isn't this person on the list?" Max asked, leaning back in his chair and taking a large bite of an enormous glazed donut. He leaned forward again and shoved the bag in Rob's direction.

"Perhaps their new, perhaps Morris Endon left this person off the list on purpose. I asked him to come in to the station, but he put me off, said he's got his hands full with dealing with the mess at the office."

"You think he might be hiding something?"

Rob reached into the bag and pulled out a twin to the giant donut Max was quickly making disappear. "He seemed nervous, had a hard time maintaining eye contact, definitely set off my bullshit meter when he asked if the art collection was intact. It might have made sense, but I kind of got the feeling he didn't give a shit about the collection. Nothing concrete, but yeah, something about him was fishy."

"Sounds like it's time to pay him a visit." Max tried sipping at his coffee and jerked it away just as quickly, wincing. "I'll leave my coffee here; it's still too damned hot to drink."

The drive to the exclusive enclave of upscale homes was a short one. Tucked into a hill off Highway 169, close to the shopping center at Briarcliff, which housed the well-stocked, if more expensive Green Acres Market, was a small, exclusive housing development.

The lawns were neat, perfectly manicured, and the cars, when visible, cost more than either detective made in a year.

"Damn, what the missus wouldn't give to live in a place like this," Max commented from the passenger seat. "She's been on me to put the house up for sale and move to one of those goddamn HOA communities. I keep telling her horror stories and she tells me crap like that doesn't happen to police officers." He groaned, "All those ticky-tacky boxes that all look alike, nothing out of place, the same beige fucking paint in each one. Who the hell *wants* that?"

Rob snorted, "Good luck with that, Peisker, that woman has got your balls in a vise grip. You'll be living in HOA land in two shakes of a lamb's tail." He slowed the car, "And here we are. Shit, all he's missing is a moat and guard dogs."

The house was impressive, stone walls and large leaded glass windows gave off an old-world vibe on a house that couldn't be more than five years old. The copper guttering had already aged into a soft rich green patina and the large, over-sized front door was made of a thick, hand-hewn dark wood that looked one of a kind.

Real estate really pays well.

They parked in the large circle drive and walked to the front door. It had a large wrought-iron knocker which seemed connected to a doorbell system. The solid thunk of the knocker was followed by a loud gong that echoed inside of the house.

Morris Endon opened the door a few seconds later and Rob caught a look of dismay on his face at the sight of the two detectives, one that vanished almost instantaneously and was replaced with a look of pleasant surprise. "Detective Stone, I didn't expect a visit this morning; I'm actually running a bit behind."

He made a show of staring at his watch, a platinum and gold Rolex if Rob didn't miss a guess. "Perhaps I can spare a few minutes. Please come in, come in." He ushered them inside and gestured towards the living room. It was austere, filled with tasteful white couches and chairs. "Please, have a seat."

"Nice place you have here," Max commented, his eyes on a large painting on the west wall.

"What? Oh, thank you, yes, I love the community, I really do. Very peaceful." He checked his watch again. "So, what can I do for you, Detectives?"

"Well, we wanted to give you an update on the investigation and double check the personnel list you provided us with," Rob replied. He leaned forward and passed the printout to Morris. "We've contacted everyone on that list and interviewed them, and no one seems to know anything about a reason why those men would be there in the office at that time or who might have killed them."

Morris gave a smug smile. "Well, obviously it was a robbery then. Perhaps they shot each other squabbling over the priceless artifacts."

"Perhaps, but the angles are all wrong. That, and the men had silencers. Robbers often carry weapons, but silencers?" Rob pointed to the printout and continued, "Could you look again at that list and tell me if you might have missed anyone, left them off of it by accident? Possibly someone new to the department?"

Morris looked disgruntled. "Well, sure, but then I really need to go. I'm meeting with the owners of the company to brief them on the current status of re-opening the office on Monday." He stared at the list, then frowned slightly. "I think there might be a new girl. She's in the southwest office. A Lila-something. I'm sorry, she's new and I must have forgotten her entirely."

Max spoke up, "That would make sense. A Kaylee Stromm, one of the sales managers, mentioned her friend Lila. I thought you had interviewed her, Stone."

"Nope, sure didn't." Rob stared at Morris as he said that, watching the man's face intently.

"Say, does this community have an HOA?" Max asked, standing up and looking out of the massive picture window that gave a stunning view of the golf course behind the house.

"Uh, yes, of course," Morris stammered, frowning at the change in questions. His eyes slid away from Rob's.

"My wife keeps on me to find us a house in an HOA community," Max mused, staring out of the window. "She says the houses don't just keep their value but appreciate over time."

"Most HOA communities hold that as a core value," Morris said, warming to the topic. "It is a significant factor for people who see their home as an investment." He glanced at his watch. "I hate to cut this short, Detectives, but I really must be leaving."

Rob stood up, held out his hand. "Thank you, Mr. Endon, we will be in touch if we have any other questions."

The man gave him a limp, rather sweaty, hurried squeeze back. "Of course, Detective, any time, any time at all."

The door closed behind them, then opened just as quickly. "I remembered the girl's name. Lila Benoit," Morris said. "She's our new data analyst. Market trends, property values, that kind of thing."

Rob jotted the name down in his notebook. "Benoit, got it. Thanks again, Mr. Endon."

As they drove away, Rob gnawed on his lip.

"What's your read on Morris Endon, Stone?"

"He's lying. He left Lila Benoit's name off that list on purpose."

Max nodded, staring at the upscale homes they passed. "Yeah. But why?"

"I'm not sure. To buy time, maybe?"

"You think he's the one pulling the strings here?"

"I'm not sure, but I want to talk to Lila Benoit. Now. See if you can pull up her info."

Max nodded and pulled the laptop open, typing the data into the police computer. "Got her. She lives off Broadway Street, in the old Folgers Coffee building."

"Hell, that's just a few minutes south of here. Let's go check it out."

They headed down Highway 169, passing the Downtown Airport and crossing the Broadway Bridge. The old brick building was one of a string of historic buildings in the area, their all-brick or stone exteriors holding their turn-of-the-century age well.

"Looks like the parking is for passholders only. No guard. We'll have to park on the street." Rob pulled over a block later and parked. They caught a break; there was no front lobby and the doors were well-secured, but a resident leaving held the door for them to enter when Rob flashed his badge.

"She's on the third floor, number thirty-eight," Max commented as they entered the elevator.

The door, when they reached it, was ajar. "Shit," Rob said, drawing his Glock. He entered slowly; Max close behind.

The main room was a fair size, with tall ceilings. The door to the bedroom and the one bathroom beyond that was also open. It was clear that the loft had been trashed. Someone had emptied every drawer, every cabinet, and gone through Lila Benoit's life with a fine-toothed comb. A desk near the tall windows overlooking Broadway Street below had drawers open or on the floor. The top of it, slightly dusty, showed a clear rectangular laptop-shaped space where there was no dust.

"Clear. And cleared out. Looks like her laptop is gone. And whoever went through this place was clearly looking for something." Rob holstered his weapon and Max followed suit.

"Whatcha thinking now?" Max asked as he slowly evaluated the scene.

"I'm thinking Morris Endon ordered a hit on Lila Benoit. I'm thinking those men were there for her. And wherever she is, if she is still alive, she's being hunted."

"Jesus, Stone. This isn't the CIA. We live in flyover country." Max shook his head.

"Yeah? Got something better for me?"

"Not really. But *damn*." Max stepped to avoid a pile of papers strewn across the hardwood floor. "So, you think they tossed the place looking for something. Not just her, but something she has?"

"Yeah. And then there's the..." Rob stopped; he wasn't ready to explain the Indalo to Peisker. If his partner thought he was paranoid now, wait until he told him about the mysterious shadow organization, he suspected was following him.

"The what?" Max asked.

"Nothing. Half-assed thought that just vanished clear out of my head." Rob stared at the scene before him. "We need to talk to Kaylee Stromm and find out what she knows. Also, we need to dig into this Lila Benoit. Who is she and why is she being hunted?"

Kaylee Stromm lived in a cute little house in Brookside. She ushered them into a tiny living room filled with warm colors and tasteful furniture. "Can I get you anything? Coffee, tea, or water?"

"I'll take water, that would be great," Max answered, smiling at her.

Rob shook his head. "Nothing for me, thanks, though."

A moment later, she sat down on the gray modern couch. "How can I help you, Detectives?"

"You are friends with Lila Benoit, is that correct?" Rob asked.

The girl's warm brown eyes showed concern. "Yes, I am, we were in college together, and I helped get her the job there at Kurgen this past summer."

Rob scribbled in his notepad. "We didn't have her on our initial list of employees."

Kaylee frowned. "Well, that's strange."

"Perhaps it was just a mistake. But we went by her apartment and it looks like someone has trashed it. Have you seen or talked to Miss Benoit since work on Monday?"

The girl looked apprehensive. "No, I haven't."

"That seems odd considering the circumstances."

"She's safe." The girl looked down at her hands. "And that's all I can really say about it."

Both detectives stared at her. Rob spoke first, "Do you know where your friend is, Miss Stromm?"

"I do not." She said it firmly, looking up, her eyes showing firm resolve. "You will need to speak with Jack Benton, of Benton Security Services, for further information on that."

"Miss Stromm, what are you saying?"

"I'm saying that someone tried to kill Lila. Not once, but twice. First last Friday, in her parking garage, and again on Monday at Kurgen."

"And why would someone try to kill your friend, Miss Stromm?" Rob asked, his heart rate increasing.

"I have no idea, Detective. But she found something, in her parking garage a few days after the attack. A piece of paper that indicated that someone had put out a hit on her. I told her to call Benton Security Services."

"And how do you know about Benton Security Services, Miss Stromm? What is it they do?"

"Jack Benton is a personal friend. And they do what you think they do; they keep people alive."

Rob sat back. His mind was spinning. None of this made sense. Paid assassins, a data analyst barely out of college and now under protection of some bodyguard service, and a well-known real estate firm. Not to mention the assassins were Indalo. *Here.* The name Benton was familiar as well. A street in the area was named Benton, but there was something else, something in the back of his brain. *Benton. Benton. Jack Benton.*

"We need to speak to Lila, Miss Stromm."

Kaylee nodded. "Yes, I'm sure you do. She stood up. "One moment." She walked out of the room and Rob turned to Max.

The other detective's mouth was hanging open. "What the hell kind of crazy case have we got here, Stone?" He shook his head. "This just keeps getting bigger and bigger. I feel like I've stepped into the Twilight Zone."

Kaylee returned and handed a card to Rob. "Here is Jack's direct line."

"Thank you, Miss Stromm." Rob took the card from her and paused. "How is it that you are friends with Mr. Benton?"

She smiled. "Please don't take this the wrong way, but, that's really none of your business, Detective."

They left the tiny house silently, the door closing firmly behind them.

Max whistled. "Two dead assassins, pretty girl in Gucci with a secret past, hits ordered on a data analyst still wet behind the ears from college, a lying manager, and a tossed apartment. This feels like the beginning of a damned action movie. Next thing you know there will be missing nuclear launch codes and the missing data analyst will have to save the world."

"We need to call this Jack Benton character and get access to Lila Benoit. Maybe then things will be a little clearer."

Closer

The mood between them kept changing, and Lila wasn't sure how to feel about it. She had been so mad at him earlier, indignant at the way he manhandled her outside on the grounds. And then he showed her how to handle a weapon and she had felt everything from scared to thrilled as she aimed it at the target and pulled the trigger.

There had been a moment between them when she was sure he was attracted to her. A moment ruined by her traitorous stomach as it growled like it hadn't been fed in weeks. Her cheeks flushed, embarrassed, and she took the steps up to the main level at a jog, the thick carpet swallowing up any sound.

"Do you like Vietnamese food?" Lila asked as Shane headed for the kitchen. "There's the Vietnam Cafe, and we could get it delivered through Uber Eats."

"No deliveries, no leaving the property."

Lila bristled. He was so annoying when he said it like that and she remembered how he had marched her back to the car and insisted she stay inside.

"Oh, is that against The Code?" she asked, her voice betraying her irritation.

Shane had his head deep in the refrigerator. He took it out, met her eyes, and smiled. "Exactly."

Smug jerk.

The man was infuriating. He was also extremely good-looking.

He continued to paw through the fridge, pulling out produce and setting it on the counter.

"What are you doing?" Lila asked, her curiosity outweighing her irritation.

He closed the fridge and pulled the elastic off the broccoli. "I'm going to cook dinner." He reached into a drawer on the left and took out a chef's knife, deftly slicing one end off of an onion from the basket on the counter, peeling the skin off, and beginning to dice away.

Lila blinked. "A bodyguard who also cooks?"

He shrugged. "It comes in handy. Everyone needs to eat." He set a pan on the stove and turned on the burner underneath it, drizzling oil into the pan before returning to chopping vegetables. He pointed to a cabinet behind Lila and said, "Grab me the pressure cooker in that cabinet there, will you?"

"This one here?" She reached inside, pulling out a large, heavy contraption. A cord dangled from it.

"Yeah, there's a plug on the wall next to the cabinet. Just plug it in there."

Lila followed his directions, adding rice and water into the pot and seating the lid in place before pressing the Start button. "So, it just cooks the rice in there, without you having to do anything?" she asked, staring at the pressure cooker as it began to steam, building up pressure.

"Yup. It'll be done in around ten minutes. Just in time." He added the diced onions to the pan and they sizzled. "We have some chicken I can slice up and add to the stir fry if you like."

"Sure." Lila stared, entranced by his efficiency. Stir fry was something she had only had in restaurants. Her mother had managed basic foods, and Lila never really learned much past reheat and toast.

Shane looked up at one point, tilted his head at her. "What?"

"Nothing."

He shrugged and continued to add ingredients. Carrots came next, followed by celery and seasonings. A small bottle of sesame oil yielded a rich smell that permeated the kitchen and Lila's stomach rumbled again, reminding her that she hadn't eaten since early that morning.

He pointed with his free hand. "Could you hand me the fish sauce? You'll find it in that cabinet up there."

"Fish... sauce..." That sounded horrific, but the smell of the food cooking was making her salivate and her stomach rumble fiercely. She would leave it in his capable hands. She retrieved the bottle and handed it to him.

"Thanks." He uncapped it and poured it deftly onto the browning pieces of chicken.

Behind her, the pressure cooker beeped, indicating it was done. "Could you press Cancel?"

She pressed the button and turned back. "What now?"

He mixed the vegetables and the meat together, drizzling another thick brown sauce onto them. Steam billowed from the pressure cooker and the smell of rice joined with the stir fry.

"The dishes are in the cabinet closest to the table," he replied.

Lila retrieved two plates and searched until she found the silverware drawer, retrieving two forks.

Seconds later, they sat at the table, plates of steaming stir fry and rice in front of them. Shane's plate was heaped with twice as much as hers. As it was, she wasn't sure she would be able to eat all of her plate, despite her hunger. She dug in, closing her eyes at the tang of the ginger, the sweet, salty taste of the teriyaki, and the crisp vegetables.

Cooking had always felt a little bit magic to her. How did a person manage to add a little of this, a little of that, and come up with complex flavors that worked? Every time she tried to be adventurous it ended in unpalatable, over-seasoned, salty disasters. She couldn't even brew a pot of coffee without turning it into nuclear waste.

There was a piece of chicken in the next bite and she closed her eyes, a wash of culinary bliss flowing from her mouth down to her stomach.

"Oh, my word, this is *so* good. Seriously, how did you learn to cook like this?" she asked, rolling her eyes, taking another bite. It was a huge mound of food. But it was amazing, so full of flavor, that she was determined to eat every single bite. She scooted her chair in closer, digging into the food.

Shane shrugged. "It was just my mom and me growing up. She taught me to cook and when she got too sick to take care of herself, it came in handy."

"Is she still...?"

"Alive? No. She passed away when I was 21, almost ten years ago now, of congestive heart failure." He shoveled a forkful into his mouth.

"I lost my mom too," Lila said. "Well, both my parents. My dad in a car accident right after I turned sixteen and my mom one semester before graduation. She had breast cancer. I was closer to my dad, but we grew really close after he died. I really miss her."

"It never goes away," Shane said, "Missing them, that is. My mom was great, a real rock, she kept me in line and didn't let me get away with any of the typical teenage bullshit. I got into some trouble after she was gone, but if it hadn't been for her, I think I would be a very different person."

"How long have you done this bodyguard thing? What were you in school for?" Lila asked, as she slipped another bite of the stir fry into her mouth. Shane could see a small smear of sauce on her chin.

"Nearly six years now. And I had wanted to be a doctor at one point."

She raised her eyebrows. "A *doctor*? Seriously?"

Shane grinned. "Hey, don't sound so shocked." He shrugged and said, "When my mom got sick, I dropped out to take care of her and lived on the student loans. Fell behind, couldn't go back, and then I met Jack."

She leaned back and regarded him. "The way you said that, that you 'met Jack'... there's something more to that, isn't there?"

She was intuitive, he had to give her that. No one had ever asked him these questions before and he hesitated, unsure of how to answer.

"Isn't there always?"

"Does that mean you aren't going to tell me?" she asked. She pushed aside her plate, decimated, with only a few bites of food remaining.

"Quid pro quo. What do you need the laptop for?"

Lila smiled at Shane's parry, and then the smile dropped away. "I think I found a file I shouldn't have. It's the only thing that makes sense."

"Tell me about the file."

"Uh-uh, you first. Tell me about meeting your boss."

"I broke into his house and was planning on stealing from him."

"*What*?!"

He smiled. "So, tell me about the file."

"It's a list of transactions with a company I've never heard of Ol...Olad...something," She answered. "Did he catch you in the act?"

"Yes, but I also saved his life. My partner was going to shoot him and I stopped him."

Lila's eyes were round in shock. "Oh my God. Did you go to jail?"

Shane gave her a slight shake of the head. "Why do you think this file is out of the ordinary?"

"Fine, fine. Because it was identical to another sales report, same dates and amounts, but with companies we have done business with."

"So, what, fraud?"

"Oh no, you don't. Tell me what happened next."

"I disabled my partner, restrained him, and then ran like hell. Tried to disappear." He had finished his plate as well and pushed it away, sliding his chair out from the table. "So... fraud?"

"Fraud, or something else. I didn't look at the whole document. It was large and on this SD card in a pocket of the bag that came with my work laptop." She leaned forward. "So... what happened next?"

"Benton found me. And against all good advice to the contrary, he offered me a job." Shane stared back at her. "Who else knows about this file?"

And that is when it hit her. "Oh shit." She closed her eyes, remembering Morris Endon's face, the odd way he had reacted when she first came into his office over a week ago. "Only one person," she whispered. "My boss, Morris Endon."

He set it up. He ignored me completely until I showed him that file and then I would see him every day. He was watching me, watching my every movement, and he's the one who set up the blind date with the guy who never showed up.

"Except he *did* show up. In my parking garage three hours later." She stood up abruptly. "I think I need a drink."

Shane followed her. "I think I missed something there. Did you say your boss was in the parking garage?"

She made a beeline for the liquor cabinet, locating the scotch easily in its cut crystal flask. She poured two fingers into a glass and sucked it down. Poured another two fingers and swallowed it as well and reached for the bottle, exhaling, her heart racing.

"Woah there, tell me what you are thinking." Shane plucked the bottle out of her hand, set a second glass down, and deftly poured more of the scotch into her glass and his.

"Morris Endon, my boss and the president of Kurgen Real Estate, he set me up on a blind date last Friday. Except the guy never showed up," she practically spat. "Because it was all bullshit; he had a guy waiting there in my parking garage. He was there to kill me." She shuddered. "Mr. Endon was the only one who knew anything about the file, the only one I had shown it to. I didn't even *know* anything and he wanted me dead." She put the glass to her lips and swallowed it in one gulp, giving another small shudder as she did.

Lila reached for the bottle, intercepting Shane's hand, her fingers shaking. He caught her hand, held it, and she felt a surge of desire run through her body. He was warm, hot even, standing so close. He smelled good, no cologne, just a down-to-earth manly smell that made her insides twist and turn. He was attracted to her, she was sure of it, and at the moment, the scotch was turning fear into a loose, swirling pool of want. How she wanted to feel safe, cared for... wanted.

Shane breathed in her scent, a musky vanilla, the scotch on her breath. She was upset, scared, and he wanted to pull her against him, tell her it was going to be alright, and slide his hands underneath her shirt, touch her bare skin, taste that sweet spot behind the ear, and...

They stood there for a minute. It might have been an hour, a day, a lifetime. Neither of them moving, neither of them breathing, both fighting to find a space to exist, to separate themselves from desire and fear and attraction. Shane was the one who broke the spell, lifting the bottle out of her hands.

"Take it easy on the scotch; it bites back."

Right on cue, the alcohol hit her bloodstream and she swayed, suddenly enveloped in its influence, the euphoria hitting and pushing her in a haze to turn away and sit down heavily in the embrace of the tall Chesterfield armchair. It swallowed her up and she looked like a small child as she tucked her legs up underneath her and stared off into the distance.

Shane poured more scotch into the two glasses, set the bottle down and brought Lila's glass to her, settling himself on the couch. "It's a lot to take in," he said, gazing at her steadily. "You are safe here, and once we get access to the laptop; we can take a look at the file and turn it in to the police. It will all work out."

She shivered, not from the cold - it was toasty warm in the den, and a fire crackled merrily in the hearth - but from fear. *How had her dream job turned into a nightmare? And was the file truly responsible? Was Morris Endon really a bad guy, someone who had ordered her murder? It didn't seem possible.*

"He looks like a nice guy, I mean, he was *nice* to me."

"Looks, and actions, can be deceiving." Shane sipped at the scotch and watched Lila closely.

She tipped the glass back and drained it, swallowing the scotch in a gulp, her eyes troubled. "So, it would seem."

"Perhaps we have it all wrong. We might be linking two separate events that have nothing to do with each other." He leaned forward. "Let's look at this another way. Was the laptop new or did someone else have it before you did?"

Lila shrugged. "I'm pretty sure it was someone else's, but who I don't know. I'm sure there are records there in the office. Perhaps Kaylee, no, never mind. I don't want Kaylee involved in this. I would never forgive myself if anyone else got hurt, especially Kaylee."

"Have you known her long?" Shane asked.

"We were roommates in college together. We've been close friends ever since. She helped get me the job at Kurgen." She shook her head, sat up abruptly. "Look, can we, I don't know, can we not talk about this anymore? Could we just do something? Turn on some music, maybe. I saw there was a pool table in the other room."

Shane watched her steadily. She was struggling with it all, and really who could blame her? There wasn't much that could be accomplished at this point. Jack would call with an update and to check in later, and it would do her good to take her mind off things.

He stood up, offered her a hand, and smiled. "I should warn you; I play a mean game of pool."

Stay

It had been a while since he played pool regularly. Years, in fact. And Shane was dismayed to realize he had lost his knack for it.

They had taken their glasses with them into the large game room where a competition-length table sat. Perhaps that was the problem, he was used to playing on bar-length tables. And Lila played better than any woman he had ever played against. He had just four shots to get it right before she took control of the table and ran it, dropping balls into the pockets with precision.

"I think I'm being played," he said dryly and shook his head.

She laughed. "Beginner's luck."

He could see she was teasing him. "Right. Or you hustle pool at night as a side gig."

Lila giggled. "Hardly. But Kaylee and I did get pretty good. It was how we blew off steam during finals. The studying would get to be too much and we would go down to the student commons. I had to be good at it; I only had a couple of dollars to spend and it had to last me all night."

"Necessity is the mother of invention. Another game, then. And take it easier on me; I don't know if I can afford this."

That earned him another laugh and he racked the balls and let her break. That game was better, or at least less of an annihilation. It ended with just one of his balls on the table, instead of four. "Believe it or not, I used to play pool for extra side money."

"I believe it, you are good. I'm just better." She grinned at his indignant look. "Another game?"

"Of course, but hold on." He walked over to the stereo in the corner and selected songs from the display. Benton had a significant collection of music. "We have everything from classical to hip-hop, heavy metal to elevator music." He gave Lila a once-over. "I'm going to take a guess and say that you might enjoy Marian Hill, and some Phantogram, along with some other alternative rock."

He pressed a button and the first notes of "Blackout Days" started playing. Lila stared at him. "How did you do that?"

He shrugged. "Actually, I had no idea what you would like. I was just hoping we liked the same music."

For the next two hours they played pool, listened to music, and laughed. It was what Lila needed. Her fear slid away and she found herself flirting with Shane as they danced, played pool, and raided the freezer for ice cream. Outside, a light rain began to fall, the darkness around the isolated house nearly complete. Only the lights from Parkville, miles away across the river, shone blearily through the drops of rain pelting against the windows.

It was almost ten when Lila yawned. Her jaw popped and she grinned sheepishly at Shane. The effects of the scotch had worn off and now she was tired, worn out from worry and uncertainty through and through.

Shane lifted an eyebrow and she shrugged as she said, "My dad used to tease me when I was a kid that, as soon as the sun went down, I started yawning and was ready for bed. He said that I had to have been a chicken in my former life."

"Do chickens go to bed when the sun goes down?" he asked, an amused look on his face.

"They sure do. My dad said that they were the only creature with any common sense. I don't know if I would take it that far - chickens are pretty stupid - but as soon as the sun goes down, so do they. And me too, apparently!"

"Well, you've had a rough couple of days, it's understandable."

"Is it?" She looked embarrassed, self-conscious.

"Of course. Take a hot bath, relax, and I'll talk to Jack about contacting the police in the morning and seeing what we can find with that SD card."

Lila nodded, paused, and then reached out to Shane, her hand on his shoulder. "Thank you," she said softly. She looked as if she wanted to say more, but instead she turned away and walked up the stairs silently without looking back.

He could still feel the warmth of her hand on his shoulder, a memory of her touch lingering there. He was relieved when she walked away. The swirl of attraction he felt towards her had intensified with her touch. He wanted to slide his hand around her waist, to the small of her back, run his mouth along her neck, and...

Get a hold of yourself, Ellis. She's a client.

He watched her walk away, disappearing up the stairs, a tantalizing fantasy and someone he had no business getting close to. Shane gathered the dishes and walked into the kitchen. A few dishes to wash and then he would call Jack and update him. He stared at the dishwasher, shrugged, and turned the water on. *It's easier to wash them up right now.* He wiped down the countertops while waiting for the water to heat and was just about to begin when he heard Lila scream.

Adrenaline fueled his dash up the stairs as he took them two at a time, his Glock unholstered and a round in the chamber, safety off. He burst through the door and nearly knocked Lila to the ground as they intersected in the small hallway that opened into the large bedroom.

"It's a bat. It scared the hell out of me when it swooped through the room." Her face was bright red. "I didn't mean to scream; it just flew past me and I couldn't help myself!" Behind her, Shane could see the bat zip from one side of the room to the other and back again, even more frightened than Lila had been by the presence of two humans.

Shane realized he had Lila folded in his arms, smashed against his chest and that their lips were inches apart. He tried not to laugh, but he couldn't help it. A small chuckle escaped and Lila, looking first embarrassed and then amused as well, laughed right alongside him. The bat continued to swoop back and forth in the room.

"We can't hurt it," Lila said, "we just need to find a way to get it out of the house." He stared at her. Most of the women he knew were terrified of all manner of creatures.

"What?" she said defensively, "It just... *startled* me, that's all. I'm not scared of it and I don't want to see it hurt. I just want it to leave."

Shane couldn't help but admire her. Lila had spunk, and a kind heart. "I'll open a window and see if we can convince our little friend to leave." He opened the window, slipped an unused towel off the towel bar in the bathroom, and slowly moved towards the bat. It had stopped wheeling about back and forth and settled in a corner of the room, probably hoping they would forget it was there, hiding its face against the wall. When in flight, its wingspan was nearly two feet in width. On the wall, however, crouched there, its wings folded in tight, it was scarcely bigger than a large mouse. Shane closed in; the towel bunched in his hands.

"Careful! Don't hurt it, it's so beautiful and the poor thing is probably terrified!" Lila cautioned; her eyes fixed on the tiny creature.

"I'm doing my best," Shane murmured and gently wrapped the creature in the towel. A low buzz came from it, a sound that they could both feel in their bones, off the auditory register for humans, only slightly within their range. He felt the tiny body within the folds of the towel and gently maneuvered it so that it came away from the wall and was wrapped in the towel, unable to move, but also unhurt. The buzzing increased.

He turned it back towards them and Lila gasped and leaned in close. "Oh, hello you! You poor dear, I hope we haven't frightened you too much." Her hand rested on Shane's arm, and her face was less than a foot away from the creature. There was no fear on her face, only fascination. Shane watched her, his attraction to her growing.

Beautiful. Sexy. Smart. Strong. Likes animals. He ticked off Lila's good qualities in his mind, running through scenarios that were completely inappropriate. *She's a* client, *damn it.*

"We had better let this little guy go. The rain has stopped and he should be able to find a better place to hang out than in here."

"You're right. I love seeing wildlife. Especially in the city." Lila shrugged. "Even though it is certainly more like the country out here." She followed closely as Shane walked towards the open window, reached both hands outside, and gently released the bat from its bonds. It sat there for a moment, sure that its freedom was a mistake, an impossibility, and when Lila shifted at Shane's side it darted away, disappearing into the darkness.

Shane stared out into the night, a small smile on his face. "That was amazing." He closed the window and turned towards Lila. They were inches apart.

This woman is a client. Jack will have my ass.

She smiled at him. A small, sexy smile that turned him on and made his jeans uncomfortably tight.

Her hand on his arm. "Stay."

Heat and desire swirled between them. He stepped closer and she closed the gap between them, her left hand setting his hand on her hip, leaning up to run her soft lips against the stubble that lined his face and neck. He smelled *divine*. She had read once that individuals who smell good to the opposite sex are the best possible breeding partner - the best genetic choice one can make. Her mind registered this analytically, but her mouth was too busy reaching up to take the tip of his earlobe in her mouth. "Stay... with... me." She breathed softly in his ear. She felt him shudder in response. *Now look who is trembling...*

His reaction was instant. She felt his hands reach around to encircle her waist, closing the few inches between them as he pulled her up, her feet leaving the plush carpet below. Her legs wrapped around him and he held her tight against him. She could already feel his erection pressing into her lower belly. Desire danced through her, knowing he was turned on, feeling the heat of him so close to her.

Shane growled, a small rumble of lust crawling up from the back of his throat. He leaned down and claimed her mouth with his own and moved his fingers down under her waistband, hooking into her panties, then sliding in from one side, dipping into her depths.

Her neck arched back, breaking from his hot lips and gasping sharply as his fingers slid into her, forcing a low moan from her throat.

Lila's left hand moved feverishly over his body, kneading his shirt, resting on his neck, sliding her fingers into his hair. He liked the feel of it. She wasn't tentative, girlish or shy. Instead, she was woman who knew what she wanted, and didn't play mind games. Shane dealt in facts, actionable movements and in real life and death.

His mouth moved over hers again. Shane felt her moan into his mouth as his hands probed, rubbing, teasing. His erection increased, throbbing now in his jeans, feeling how hot and wet she was for him. She gasped as his tongue slipped into her open mouth, his thumb moving against her clitoris, his tongue thrusting deep, tasting its sweet freshness, and behind it, the heat of the bourbon. Who needed a bed? He was ready to fuck her here, in the middle of the room.

At that moment, just as his fingers were easing open his fly, his other arm encircling her and having settled for the moment on pressing her lithe, hot body against a nearby pillar with enough force to make the wrought iron and glass sconces rattle, his back pocket began to vibrate. The boss was calling.

"Fuck..."

Ignore That

"Ignore that." Lila's voice was husky, wanton, and a delicate hand pulled on his shirtsleeve.

Shane groaned, pulling away from her as he reached into his back pocket. "I wish I could, darlin'...but..." The phone pulsed; his dick was pulsing as well, but only one was going to get any satisfaction. "I've got to answer this."

He pressed Accept on the phone, sliding away from Lila, turning towards the door, his voice professional, clipped. "Ellis here." A small pause then, "Hey boss... yeah... okay... yeah... will do." He pressed End and slipped the phone back in his jeans.

He stared at her.

Lila was leaning against the pillar, clothing askew, a black lace bra exposed. His gaze traveled down to that warm, hot center of temptation. She was returning his gaze, and her hot sexy tongue dipped out and licked a corner of her lips.

Shit.

He should have walked away.

He should have told her that a police detective wanted to talk to her like Jack had asked him to do. So, they could get to the bottom of this mystery and stop whoever wanted Lila Benoit dead.

He should never have touched her in the first place.

She wasn't his kind of woman.

Two steps, that was all it took for Shane to return to her. She had a smile on her lips until he growled, pressing her against the pillar, rattling the iron and glass sconces as he matched his mouth to hers, seeking that quick, delectable tongue with his own. His hands roamed over her, pulling at her shirt, demanding all of her, in motion, prowling over her body.

She wrapped her long, athletic legs around his waist, her left hand fighting with the buttons on his shirt, eager to see the skin and muscle hidden beneath. Her injured right arm was tucked against her and nearly forgotten except for an occasional twinge of pain when his body connected with hers. The pain was almost pleasurable, and she was lost in a heady swirl of lust. One of his hands was neatly cupping her left buttock, the thumb traveling between her legs, straining to reach her hot, wet clit. His tongue was assaulting her mouth, sending waves of passion through her.

Pulling her tight against him, he could feel her heat as she squirmed deliciously against him, and he thought briefly of the bed in the opposite corner. *Later.* Her hand was moving frantically now, dipping down to his belly, pulling insistently at his jeans, fucking his mouth with her sexy pink tongue. Here was a woman who knew what she wanted and didn't hold back.

Shane unbuttoned his jeans, slid the zipper down, and eased the denim away from his almost painful erection. They slid down to pool at his ankles. He kicked them off, continuing to unbutton the last buttons on her blouse as he did so, determined to view the hot, hard nubs he could feel straining against the t-shirt.

Lila had unbuttoned his shirt, and was pushing it off his shoulders with her uninjured hand, while grinding her pelvis against his. Her panties, a ridiculous and insubstantial little strip of lace firmly clasped between two fingers, barely made a sound as he tore them from her body. Lila let out a lustful moan as Shane's kisses moved off her mouth, trailing a tongue along the curve of her jaw, then down her long, thin neck, stopping for a moment to savor the hint of salt on her skin. He lowered her gently to the ground, her bare feet digging into the rich carpet pile, as his mouth moved over her. The stubble on his chin, and his teeth gently nipping, set her skin on fire.

Lila weaved her fingers through his hair and sucked in a breath of pleasure as his mouth continued to travel down her body, zeroing in on her breasts. He pulled the shirt off of her, tossing it on the floor before circling back to hook one of the delicate lace bra straps off of her shoulder roughly, exposing a small, pert breast. He cupped her breasts, teasing them with a rough, calloused hand, then leaning in for a taste. They tasted amazing. He had been with his fair share of women, and the tits were always his weakness, the more the merrier. Lila's were small, perky little things. He doubted she had more than a B cup, but they tasted like nothing he had ever experienced with any other woman. There was this delicate vanilla musk scent and taste to them, and he took one small, taut nipple in his mouth, and sucked hard enough for her to tighten her fingers in his hair, pulling hard in response to his attentions, moaning. His dick throbbed as he fastened his mouth on the other breast, rolling the nipple with his tongue before lightly nibbling it with his teeth. Lila clenched her left fist in his hair, pressing her body against his.

Outside the wind had picked up, and regular pings on the window indicated that rain was moving in. The windows rattled, as did the iron and glass sconces on the pillar, as Shane and Lila moved, shifted, and twisted, their bodies hot with passion.

His hands slid back down her body, returning to swirl and probe between her legs, into her slick folds, moving in, out, and around. Shane used two fingers to enter her, thrusting up to his knuckles into her as she moaned, her hips gyrating in time with his thrusting fingers.

Lila's body felt as if it had been torn open and filled with liquid fire, full of lust and wantonness. It had been months, *months*, and this man obviously knew how to give pleasure to a woman. Shane was such a far cry from her last boyfriend, who at the moment she was having a ridiculously hard time remembering the name of, especially now that Shane had slipped most of his hand into her, while biting her nipple lightly. Lila felt as if it was all one-way; she wasn't even sure what to do with her left hand, and the injured right hand was desperate to join the fray, wrenched shoulder or not. His mouth on her nipple, hot, alternately flicking it with his tongue and then nibbling it with his teeth, was threatening to bring her to orgasm there and then. His hand worked between her thighs, a finger now probing her ass, adding a new dimension to her desire.

Just as she was about to beg him to fuck her, he moved again, sliding further down her body. He looked up at her then, seeing her half-lidded eyes, heavy with desire, her lace bra askew, with the straps off her shoulders. He lifted her then, pushing her hard against the pillar, spreading her legs and pushing his mouth deep between her legs, licking her, nibbling, his tongue pressing in until it felt the hard, erect nub of her clitoris. He began with the letter "A."

Lila's hips bucked as his tongue found home. What man had ever done this to her? None, not a one. From the fumbled backseat adventures of her first boyfriend in high school, to a handful of men in between, Lila was unused to this level of attention. She fell into it, felt every thrust of his tongue against her clit and his hands on her skin, honey and gold and pecan pie all rolled into these moments of ecstasy. Shane reached "H" when Lila shuddered, crying out wordlessly, her hips rocking back and forth, hot slickness spreading. He didn't stop.

Lila couldn't help but wonder if it was possible to pass out from such an intense orgasm. She was seeing stars, and even after she came, he kept going. Like some goddamn Energizer bunny. She wanted to argue with him, or do something in return, but feeling his hands roaming over her, his mouth and tongue flicking against her most sensitive parts, it was addictive.

Ecstasy, like liquid gold, flowed through her. She was close to a second orgasm, her entire body pliant under his capable hands, his mouth. But she wanted more than that, she wanted to feel him inside her, feel and hear his own pleasure as he fucked her. She tugged on him, pulling him back up her body. He moved up, his hands cupping her breasts, thumbs stroking the tips, his breath hot on her neck. His dick pressed against her belly, and she reached down to stroke it, feeling its velvety smoothness. It throbbed in her hand as she continued to stroke it, gently squeezing, rubbing, and her mouth moved to his neck, to his ear, "I want to feel you inside me...*now*."

He growled, low in his throat, thick with lust and heat. It took only a second for him to guide his dick to her wet, hot opening and thrust into her willing folds. Lila gasped with pleasure. The second thrust took him balls-deep, filling her depths, causing her to cry out a single wordless scream of abandon as he followed it with thrust after thrust. Her slender back dug into the pillar, the metal and glass rattled emphatically, his mouth sucked and pulled on a tender earlobe and she tensed her long, slim legs around him as he fucked her. His hands cupped her buttocks, lifting her off the carpet, thrusting into her body with a quick intensity, slowly building in speed. Her moans increased with each thrust, both of them building in anticipation, thrusting again and again.

The sensation of heat, her moans of ecstasy, and finally the rush of the orgasm sent fireworks rocketing behind his closed eyes. Lila tightened her legs, her legs rubbing against his hips, and exploded, a star on fire, right along with him.

Butt Dial

They rocked there in place. She had closed her eyes, her mouth open, riding the wave. He had never seen a woman come like she had. Such abandon. Just feeling her body shudder made him hard all over again and her eyes shot open in surprise, meeting his. This time, this time he would take his time. He could feel his erection swelling, responding to the waves of orgasm that continued to shake her lithe frame. He shifted his hands, taking her uninjured hand and pinning it to the pillar and reaching the other up to rub her nipple.

Sweat beaded both of their bodies, and he could feel the lust building inside of him again. He thrust once, deep inside of her, before a voice stopped him in his tracks.

The owner of the voice spoke... from the vicinity of Shane's jeans just a foot away. "I believe that is one of the more innovative questioning tactics I have heard of, Ellis," Jack Benton, Shane's employer and the owner of Benton Security Services remarked dryly. "Give me a call back when you have... well, when you have a moment." There was a click and a beep as the call ended.

Lila gasped, her eyes widening, and Shane slid out of her hot body, cursing quietly.

"Do you think he…" Lila asked, pulling her bra back in place, self-conscious.

"Oh yeah," Shane answered, tight-lipped. "I, uh, I need to talk to my boss. And you should probably get some sleep."

"Sleep?" Lila stared at him, unsure of what came next, but she was certain that sleep was not on the list. She watched Shane gather his clothes, dressing hurriedly.

"Yeah, we will talk more in the morning." He didn't look at her as he left, and Shane could feel her stare hot on his back as he slipped out the door. The door clicked closed behind him and he dressed in the hallway, his fingers and lips still holding her musky vanilla scent. He dug the phone out of his jeans and stared at it for a moment, wishing he didn't have to call Jack Benton back, and split between the desire to go back inside the bedroom and fuck Lila Benoit late into the night, or somehow completely undo the last half hour of his life.

Shane had never, *ever* slept with a client before. *Technically speaking, you haven't* slept *with her, just fucked her senseless,* he couldn't help thinking. It helped that most of his clients were fat, rich assholes. There had been a small handful of female clients, even a couple that he had found quite appealing, but that wasn't the job. The job was to keep the client alive, not put his dick in her. What the hell had he been thinking? What was wrong with him? Just thinking of her sexy body against his woke his dick up again. It jerked in his pants, hopeful as only a penis or a five-year-old with an entire bag of candy hidden in his room can be. He growled in frustration and dialed Jack's number, walking down the steps to the main floor of the rambling house, up another half flight and down the hall to the security office.

Shane sat down in front of the array of monitors that showed real-time views of all angles of the rambling property and waited for his boss to answer. Jack Benton answered on the second ring. "I trust you are in a less compromising position, Ellis?"

Shane could feel his face flush red. "Sorry about that, sir, it won't happen again."

Jack chuckled. "No, it won't; your next client will weigh 300 pounds and be on the outs with organized crime. He will also have a wife and kids, all of which will hate him and you in turn. And just to really make your day, I'm planning on sticking you in butt-fuck nowhere with spotty cell service and no internet or cable TV."

Shane winced. "Understood, sir."

"Can I trust that your attention is fully on the job at hand?" Jack asked.

Shane's spine straightened instinctively. Jack Benton couldn't see him, but that didn't matter. "You can, sir," he responded decisively.

There was a moment's silence and Shane felt a cold sweat building. This wasn't just any job. This was a good job, and a fucking great boss, and he had just fucked it up completely by boning a smoking hot client. A *client*. Jesus Christ, he had fucked a client. *You don't fuck the clients, Shane, you keep them alive.* The silence was killing him. Just as he was sure Jack would fire his sorry ass and worse, Jack broke his silence.

"So, the dead men. Definitely both contract killers."

Shane shook his head; no matter that Jack Benton couldn't see him. "It makes zero sense. She's young, no ties to organized crime, an orphan with no drama."

"Something she might have seen?" Benton asked.

"Nothing she can think of. There is a file on her laptop at work that she mentioned. Something she thinks might be important. She mentioned an SD card as well," Shane answered.

"I'll see if I can get access to the laptop."

Shane could hear the pipes running. "She's in the shower now; I can talk to her afterwards."

"Give her the night to rest up. Tackle this in the morning and report to me then."

"Will do, sir." Shane sat back in his chair. It made no sense. Lila wasn't a criminal, and she hadn't been at the real estate firm for more than a few months. Before that, she had worked a series of dead-end jobs to get through college and beyond. Her last digs had been in an aging apartment building in a high-crime section of the city. Perhaps she had seen something there? He would ask her in the morning.

The monitors showed an ever-changing array of images of the grounds and house. Most of them focused on the border of the property and the outside of the house, but every room was monitored as well. Shane watched as, after nearly half an hour of water running through the pipes, Lila emerged from the bathroom, naked, hair dripping, tendrils of water still making their way down her slender back. She had removed her shoulder sling and her right shoulder and arm were a series of livid, dark bruises. The cameras were in black and white, but there was no mistaking the bruising. It was a wonder she could even use the arm.

Seeing her there, naked, her long, shapely legs and perky nipples, as she made her way to the bed, made him hard all over again. He reached into his pants, adjusting everything in what were suddenly rather tight quarters. His dick pulsed, calming only when she slipped under the covers, her body hidden from his sight.

He closed his eyes, shook his head, her scent in his nose, on his lips. He would be damned lucky if Jack Benton ever trusted him with a client again. His dick calmed, relaxing, and Shane yawned. It had been a long day, an eventful evening, and it was high time he got some shut-eye.

Date Night

"Dad, for crying out loud, you cannot wear that on your date."

Rob tugged at the collar of his shirt and then glanced at Maddie perched on the side of his bed. "Why not, kiddo? This is one of my nicer golf shirts."

"Because, it practically screams *cop*." Maddie slid off the bed and threw open his closet door. "You need one that isn't so in your face. Something that doesn't promise to arrest her if she has more than one drink and doesn't call a cab to take her home." She pulled out a short-sleeved Hawaiian print shirt and said, "How about this one?"

He stared at it. It had been a gag gift from the department head two Christmases ago. It was a bright, flamboyant red and had a large gold-colored tiki on the front guzzling an enormous drink.

"Seriously?"

"What?" Her mouth was twitching as she tried to suppress a smile and failed. "It's cute and you look good in red."

"I'm not wearing that."

"Okay, fine. Wear the black shirt and don't forget to show her your taser."

Rob sighed. "You're killing me, kid."

"Just try it on."

"Not a chance."

"You are being incredibly recalcitrant, Dad."

"Recalcitrant, eh?" He grinned at her.

"And that's not a good thing."

Rob suppressed a snort at the serious look on Maddie's face. "All right, I'll try the shirt on, but I think it looks ridiculous." He slipped off the golf shirt and Maddie bounced up and down as she handed him the red shirt. It was silky, and the fabric felt cool against his skin.

"Huh," he said, cocking his head to one side as he contemplated his reflection, "That isn't half bad."

"Told you!" Maddie crowed, giggling. It was moments like this Rob wished would last forever. Maddie was growing up so fast, but at the moment, she was as excited for him as she would have been to go to the movies or miniature golf just a few short years ago, before her friends had taken priority in her day-to-day existence.

Not that I have anything to complain about with Maddie's friends. She had good friends, kids who were respectful and kind. Her friend Amanda down the street was one of the best. Her parents had instilled in her early a need for service and she had quickly roped Maddie into it as well. The girls volunteered at a soup kitchen twice a week and also helped an elderly neighbor by walking her dog.

"Aren't you going over to Amanda's tonight?"

"Yes, but I wanted to make sure you were ready for your date first, Dad. I mean, obviously, you *needed* me!" She bounced once more on his bed and then headed back to the closet.

"What now?"

"Shoes," Maddie answered, her voice muffled as she rummaged inside of the space.

"I was just going to..."

"Uh, uh, Dad, those are cop shoes." She emerged with cowboy boots in her hands.

"Oh hell no."

"Dad." Maddie's face had taken on a long-suffering expression, "You will look great in these. This patch of gold here, it matches your shirt."

"I'm not sure what look you are going for Mad, but I doubt that me looking like a cowboy visiting Hawaii is in the date night playbook."

"Dad, trust me. You don't want to look like..."

"Like a cop. Right. Got it." He sighed. "Fine, give me the boots. What the hell, the first date is usually awkward and uncomfortable anyway. I might as well send her as many mixed messages as possible. I'm a cowboy. I'm not a cop. I'm a devout worshipper of an angry Hawaiian tiki god." He pulled the boots on, one at a time and stared at his reflection in the mirror. A relic of Claire's, he had hauled it halfway across the country when they moved from

Virginia. Eventually, it would go to Maddie. It had been in Claire's family for generations and the glass was old, wavy, and the paint that covered the ornate carved wood, was chipped. Claire had painted it white, but, beneath, it had once been a particularly awful shade of pink.

"I look stupid."

"You look retro with a flair of je ne sais quoi."

"Jenny say who?"

Maddie giggled. "Je ne sais quoi. It means that which cannot be understood or explained."

"That doesn't sound good at all."

"Dad, it means you are mysterious, perhaps even Avant Garde, which is a lot better than your clothes screaming *cop* when you walk in the door."

"Says you." He turned and peered at himself sideways. At least he didn't have a gut like most of the men in his department.

"Says me." She gave him a bear hug. "You look great. Any woman who can't see that doesn't deserve to date you."

He hugged her in return. "If she's mean, I'll call you and you can come beat her up." Maddie giggled and snuggled against him. He glanced over at the clock on the wall. "Oh hell, I've got to get our laptops over to Ben for updates before I meet my date. I need to hit the road, or else I'll get caught in traffic and be late."

"And I need a ride to the soup kitchen on Paseo. I'm meeting Amanda and her mom there. Do you mind if I sleep over at Amanda's tonight?"

"If it's okay with her mom, sure. But make sure first."

"Thanks, Dad, I'll call her now." She jumped off the bed and was dialing the phone before she ever left the room.

Rob suppressed a grimace as he watched her disappear down the hall. He had checked the house every morning and every night of the last three days for additional listening devices. Tonight, was the first time they would both be out of the house and he had to wonder if anyone would try and access the house and reinstall any bugs while he was gone. Probably not. They knew he knew. The question was, what would the Indalo do about it?

He had agreed to this date only because he wanted more than anything to maintain the facade of normalcy for Maddie. The move halfway across the country, that had been for her. Claire had loved visiting Kansas City when they were first together, childless, and fancy free. She had especially loved the Nelson-Atkins and burgeoning arts scene in the Crossroads.

Here, in flyover country, Maddie could have a normal childhood and grow up in a safe neighborhood. At least, that was what he had thought it was. He hadn't imagined they were watching. In the past few days, one question kept rolling through his head; *When had the bugs been planted*? He was working on getting those answers, but meanwhile it had to be business as usual.

Ben had promised to help make sure that Rob and Maddie's laptops were not being monitored. Rob had simply told Maddie that the bios needed updating. She hadn't questioned it, but of course, if it had been her phone, she would have questioned it more. She knew how those updates worked.

The traffic on I-70 heading into the city was congested. Plenty of people heading to the stadium for a Chiefs game and the rest heading for dinner or the bars in Power & Light. It slowed to a crawl before the stadium exit and then picked back up again. The Chiefs had begun the season strong, and plenty of folks were hoping for a Super Bowl win this year.

Independence Avenue was crowded as well, although with a far different crowd. Sure, some were hitting the various restaurants, grocery stores, and the Dollar General. Others were shopping for drugs or sex. The sun's rays had disappeared behind the skyline, and the rapidly darkening sky was alight with the deep pinks, reds, and oranges of the sunset.

"Shall we play 'I Spy,' Dad?" Maddie joked. An inside, rather off-color joke to be sure. He had taught her how to spot prostitutes and drug dealers last summer and they had made a game of it.

"I'd say 'yes' but there are far too many of them," Rob commented dryly as they passed what had to be the fourth prostitute in as many blocks.

A handful of blocks were passed in silence before he slowed and pulled the car over in front of Ben's shop. "Come in with me; I don't want you waiting out here alone."

She nodded. "Fine with me."

The front light was off, and the door was locked, but Rob could see Ben inside along with a young man. He knocked on the glass and Ben smiled and unlocked the door for them. "Madeline! You have sprouted on us, I see. How are you?"

Maddie grinned. "Hi, Uncle Ben!" She wrapped her arms around him and gave him an exuberant hug. "Dad said he needed to come by and have you handle some updates on the computer, and I am volunteering at a soup kitchen on Paseo so I came with." She drew back and looked at him, her face worried. "You are super-skinny, Uncle Ben. Why don't you come by for dinner at the kitchen? We are making a beef stew!"

Ben laughed, pulling back and patting her hand. "I might just do that."

The young man studied them; his thin, angular frame remained hunched over a computer and his dark eyes looked over Rob with suspicion. Ben motioned to him. "Liam, come here and meet Rob Stone and his daughter Maddie. Two of the best people you could ever know."

Liam unfolded himself from his seat and Rob realized he was looking *up* at the boy. He didn't look much older than Maddie, but he was over six foot in height.

"Hi," the boy said, obviously uncomfortable. Rob nodded and Maddie smiled at him, an open sunny smile that made the boy's mouth twitch up in return.

"Son, could you go downstairs and get that bag of software we talked about?" Ben asked Liam and the boy nodded and slunk away silently. Ben waited until he had disappeared through the door that led to the back room and down into the basement. "He's been staying with me for the past six months. His father's in prison, his mother's a drug addict, and I found him sleeping in the basement in late spring. He'd been there for months, going in and out through a window."

"I see," Rob said. "I could make some calls for you, see about getting Family Services to help him out."

Ben scoffed. "Family Services? Hell, might as well send him to Juvie right now with first-class tickets to prison after. He's better off here with me. I got him enrolled at Northeast High School and they didn't even bat an eye when I said he was my nephew. He's been getting straight As and working for me here in the shop. Besides, it's nice having someone around."

Rob knew how much Ben had lost - not just a wife, but also his young daughter, victims of a hit and run nearly twenty years earlier. He had worked for a time as a consultant for the CIA specializing in spy hardware and software before moving to Kansas City and opening his own store.

Rob nodded. "Say no more, my friend. And let me know if you need my help, for anything; you know you just have to ask."

Ben clapped Rob on the arm. "You know I will, Stone."

"I brought in the laptops so you could, um, update the BIOS for me," Rob said, stealing a glance at Maddie. She had wandered over to one of the display cases.

Ben followed his gaze and slowly nodded. "Right. I can have them back in your hands by Saturday, if that works for you."

"That'll be great. Thanks, Ben." He set down his card on top of the laptops. "Here, give me a call when you know more."

The boy returned, a stack of CDs in his hands. His eyes were glued to Maddie and he set down the software and walked over to her, murmuring something Rob couldn't hear but it made Maddie giggle. She whispered something back and Rob's hackles rose. He didn't know this boy and Maddie was thirteen, for Christ sake. *Time to start cleaning that shotgun and priming it with rock salt.*

He cleared his throat and the boy flinched away from Maddie, his flirtatious grin disappearing from his face. Rob tried to not bristle as the boy slunk past and back to his work station behind the main counter, astutely avoiding eye contact with Rob.

"Time to go, Maddie. I'm sure Amanda and her mom will be wondering where we are by now."

"Okay, Dad. Bye, Uncle Ben. Bye, Liam!" she chirped and headed for the door.

Liam managed a half-audible "Bye!" before glancing at Rob and then ducking his head down to his work. Rob could feel the boy's eyes follow him and Maddie out the door.

The drive back down Independence yielded less than half of the prostitutes. They had been replaced by lean, twitchy men on various street corners. The sunset was gone and the dark had descended fully, broken only by the streetlamps and headlights of passing cars. "I hate how early it gets dark," Maddie sighed. "It makes it feel so late. But it isn't even five thirty yet."

The parking lot was well-lit, and Rob insisted on going inside with Maddie. The neighborhood could be rough, but he knew that the people who ran the soup kitchen and Maddie and her friend were in good hands.

He walked her to the door, verified that she would be spending the night at Amanda's, and hugged and kissed his daughter.

"Remember to smile, okay, Dad?"

"Will do, kiddo, will do."

"Have fun, Dad, and use protection!"

"Christ, Maddie." Rob shook his head, feeling his ears heat up with embarrassment. He couldn't meet Amanda's mother's eyes. "I'll see you tomorrow."

It was a short drive to the Power & Light district and barely a hop and a skip away from the grisly crime scene he had dealt with on Monday night. He looked up at One Kansas City Place, noting that the floor was dark. It had taken them most of Tuesday to process the crime scene. After that, it was held unchanged for the insurance adjuster and then a specialized crime scene cleanup crew would go through. One last run-through with new carpet, and the office would be back in business and open by next Monday. He had finished interviewing the last of the employees on the list that Morris Endon had provided and none of them had been in the office that evening. He needed to compare notes with his partner Max, who had handled several of the interviews, because something didn't add up. A shootout with two dead assassins and no one from Kurgen Real Estate in the office? It didn't make sense. Why there? The last person on the list, that Lila Benoit, once he talked to her, perhaps things would be clearer.

Those questions occupied Rob's thoughts as he slid into a parking spot in a nearby garage. It was half a block to the Bristol Seafood Grill; time to get his head out of murder and into smiling and being debonair. He sighed and reminded himself that dating after ten years alone was more than okay; in fact, it was necessary. He plastered a smile on his face and walked into the restaurant.

Early Morning Call

It wasn't quite six in the morning when the phone rang. Rob had been up for an hour, gone for a run, and eaten a small breakfast. He stared at the number. It was an unfamiliar one, a 518-area code. He answered, "Stone."

"Rob? It's Diana, Milo's ex-wife. Do you remember me?" A familiar voice asked, sounding muted, weary.

"Why, of course I do, Diana. How are you?" The fried egg and half a grapefruit had turned to an unmovable stone in his stomach. Diana calling him could not be good, not at all.

"I'm not good," Diana sighed, a sob escaping. "I'm calling with really bad news, Rob. Milo died two days ago. I know you two must have stayed in contact after you moved; I found Christmas cards from you in Milo's possessions and I just wanted to tell you the news personally."

"God, Diana, what happened?"

"The police said it was a mugging. He was in the wrong place at the wrong time and," she stopped, sniffled, "he fought so hard. There were two attackers and it looks like they were interrupted by a man walking by and they ran off. The good Samaritan got him to a nearby hospital and they life-flighted him to Inova. I thought he would make it. I'm still listed as his emergency contact now that his parents are both gone, and I flew down there the next morning with Gus." She took in a breath and let it out slowly. "He made it out of surgery. He was talking, even joking. But the next day they detected internal bleeding and took him back to surgery. They said he had a bad reaction to the anesthesia and he died on the table." She let out a long breath. "Gus is devastated. They weren't getting along so well. He's fifteen, after all, and he doesn't get along with any adult well right now. But now, he's really hurting, you know?"

Rob felt ill. Had this happened because of his call? Had the Indalo been watching Milo too? Were they making sure there weren't any more loose ends?

"I'm so very sorry, Diana. I just spoke with Milo earlier this week. I'm just... I can't believe he's gone."

"I know, me either. It was so sudden."

"Is there," Rob struggled to find the words, "Is there anything I can do for you, or for Gus?"

Diana sniffled, excused herself, and blew her nose in the background. "No. Jonathon, my husband, he's helping with everything. The funeral arrangements and all the decisions, I just... I just wanted to let you know, Rob. And give you the basic info in case you could make the funeral next Sunday." She rattled off the information, sniffling again. "No matter what happened between Milo and me, I just, God, I'm reeling. He was a good man, and a good father to Gus. Don't be a stranger, Rob. If you are ever in town, look me up, okay?"

"Of course. Thank you, Diana, and thank you for letting me know. I am so sorry." The phone clicked and Rob stood there, in shocked silence.

A mugging. I don't buy it for an instant.

Milo was dead. Steve too. He sat there in the dark, watched the clock slowly click over to 6 a.m. The house was silent; Maddie was still asleep, her plans to stay at Amanda's that night had been changed after Amanda's mother called him in the middle of his date to let him know there had been a family emergency. Maddie had been sound asleep by the time he made it back home.

Outside, he could hear a siren in the distance. Would they come for him next? Would they hurt Maddie? And what would happen to her if he was gone?

His phone chimed, showing there were messages. Rob sighed in frustration; the phone had been acting up, not ringing at times, not showing messages until hours later. He needed to get a new one. It was old, far older than anyone else's. He fought technology, and its built-in obsolescence, obstinately. He had been the last one in his circle of co-workers and friends to get a smartphone, and it had been a used one at that. Now it was outdated and occasionally malfunctioning. A small smile quirked at the edges of his mouth.

Maddie will be overjoyed when I tell her I'm upgrading. She's been at me for months. Hell, maybe I'll spring for a nice one this time, top of the line; it will only be obsolete in a few months.

He reviewed his messages. One from his date from the other night...

Hey, handsome, I had a wonderful time the other day. How about dinner at my place tomorrow night?

Maddie had already added an overnight at her friend Megan's. He would have the evening free.

Who knows, I might even get lucky.

He typed a response back and hit Send. His phone made a whooshing noise.

The other message was from Jack Benton, and it had come in even earlier, around three in the afternoon yesterday.

Jack Benton here. Would like to connect you on a secure line with Lila Benoit. Miss Benoit is currently in a safe location and has engaged the services of Benton Security Services after two attempts on her life.

Two attempts on her life? He had convinced himself that Benoit's friend and co-worker, Kaylee Stromm, was being paranoid, but now this Jack Benton was saying the same thing. *Benton, Benton, where do I know that name from?* He opened up the internet and searched for the name Jack Benton.

His thoughts drifted back to Milo.

Maybe I'm being paranoid. Muggings happen every day. He tried to swallow the paranoia and the fear. He tried to explain it away. But no matter how he tried, he couldn't shake a sense of foreboding.

The search for Jack Benton yielded pages of info, mostly salacious gossip. Rob knew he had recognized the name and now, looking at the first page of results, he knew why. "Jack Benton, playboy billionaire," he read out loud, "Orphaned at age 22, he and his young sister were sole survivors of a plane crash that killed their parents and two other siblings nearly twenty years ago. And the sister was kidnapped and murdered just days after her sixteenth birthday two years later. Huh." He paged through photos of Jack - at his parents' funeral, his young sister at his side. By all accounts, they had been extremely close and Jack had been devastated by her death, even more so than losing his parents. Rob continued to browse the pages, running across a news headline from three years after Allison Benton's death covering the founding of Benton Security Services. Jack Benton was just a decade younger than he was and recent pictures showed gray hairs creeping into the jet black. He had never married and showed no signs of it, although he was one of the more eligible bachelors who wasn't a celebrity.

"According to Celebrity Buzz, you split your time between your California estate and a place in the Hamptons. But I'm guessing you have properties throughout the United States, don't you, Mr. Benton?"

Outside, the sun was beginning to peek above the horizon, the sky a brilliant pink. He stood up from his seat at the kitchen island and walked over to the cabinet and pulled out the herbal tea that Maddie had recently taken a shine to. He smiled at the thought of it, she had wanted him to switch from coffee to herbal tea, citing all kinds of evidence that indicated caffeine at his age was not advisable, and he flatly refused. After nearly three decades of daily, multi-cup infusions of the bitter black brew, he had zero intentions of switching to some hippie-dippy herb-infused cranberry water. It was simply not happening. Maddie, just as obstinate as he was, had continued to drink the herbal frou-frou ever since.

He slid a mug of water into the microwave and pressed the Start button, unwrapping the tea bag from its glossy envelope and setting it on the countertop next to the honey. There was a yawn and creak of the stairs. "Morning, Dad." She rested her head against his shoulder briefly before leaning over and turning on the kitchen light. "Why are you sitting here in the dark?"

"Just thinking." The microwave beeped as it finished. "The water for your tea is hot."

"Thanks, Dad." She yawned again, and Rob heard her jaw pop, "Ugh, I wish I hadn't let Megan rope me into meeting her early to cram for the chemistry test. I really could have used a couple more hours of sleep."

Rob's phone lit up briefly, but when he picked it up and logged in, nothing showed in the messages. "Damn this thing, I swear it is eating my messages. I won't get them right away, sometimes not for hours, I just read two from yesterday afternoon. It's damned annoying." He paged through the list of text messages. "I'll bet I've got another one in the queue, *somewhere*, but where is it?"

He looked over at his daughter, "Well, it's good news for you. I give up, it's time for two new phones."

Her eyes widened, her drowsy demeanor vanishing. "Seriously? Oh, my God, we might actually join this decade?"

"Well, I don't know if I would take it that far." he said, teasing her. "I mean, they still sell flip phones, don't they?" He laughed at her horrified expression. "Don't worry, I wouldn't do that to you. I'm thinking of getting the new Voyage they released last month; how would that be?"

She bounced, her teenage cool shed and the young child she had been trying so hard to eradicate from her demeanor suddenly front and center. "Oh Daddy, that would be so amazing!"

He chuckled as she jumped around the kitchen and then hugged him exuberantly. "I can't wait to tell my friends! When can we go shopping? How about tomorrow after school? Please? Pretty please?"

"Okay, okay, it's a date then."

She twirled, squealing with joy. "I'm so excited!" Maddie stopped suddenly, a serious expression on her face. "But we need to donate the old phones to this guy at the soup kitchen, okay? He collects them and re-distributes them to the women's shelter that helps battered women get back on their feet."

"We will definitely do that, Mads."

She squealed and wiggled. "I have to go tell Megan and everyone else right away! Love you, Daddy!" She kissed him on the cheek and rushed off, leaving her tea steeping on the counter.

Rob had a half-smile on his face as he watched his daughter disappear upstairs. "You would be proud of her, Claire. I know I certainly am."

At the thought of his wife, his smile faded. Ten years of her gone, longer now than the time they were actually together, and he felt as if he was betraying her memory, turning his back on what they had together. Perhaps this whole dating thing was a mistake. What if there had only been one woman for him? One and done, and no one else could come close? Sure, he had enjoyed last night. His date had been beautiful, funny, and they had certainly clicked. But she wasn't Claire. No one had ever touched him like

Claire, not before her, and certainly not after. Sure, there had been fleeting attractions, the flush of desire, but a woman who he wanted to spend his life with? Only Claire had inspired those dreams, and those dreams had died with her, alone, in a car on an icy road.

His thoughts switched to Maddie. She was becoming a young woman. She needed an older woman to guide her, to help her with all the feminine details that left him bewildered and uncertain. Was that why she had been so insistent that he begin to date? Was there some part of her that unconsciously sought that, *needed* that which had been denied her for the past decade? Claire's death hadn't just left a gaping chasm in his life... their daughter had suffered too. He had seen it over the years, in nightmares, her artwork even, and the close relationship that they had. She and Claire had been two peas in a pod, a connection that had seemed magical to him at the time, but one that he had only been a third wheel in. Maddie had been inconsolable when she died, refusing to sleep in her own bed for months, plagued with nightmares, and waking fears of losing him. Their relationship had changed, become closer, and she had clung to him at every leave-taking, terrified that he would not return. But perhaps now she was ready and needed a female influence. He knew that her friends' mothers paid extra attention to her. They had always been quite kind, reaching out to him directly when necessary, but it wasn't the same. They were someone else's mother. Maddie needed someone who would fill Claire's role, at least as much as anyone else *could* fill that role.

It was that realization that made up his mind. "It's time I moved on, Claire." He said it in the silent kitchen, his coffee mug empty, cool in his hand. Maddie needed this, and perhaps he did as well.

Miles away, Lucifer sat red-eyed and sleep-deprived in front of the bank of computer screens, the cell phone clamped in her hand. The phone rang once, twice, and a voice answered, "What is it, Lucifer?"

"We've been shut down on the computers."

"Explain."

"Someone has disabled and removed the keylogger I installed on both of the computers. Well, not *someone*, I know exactly who it was because he sent a text last night and again this morning to Stone."

"I see." That voice, never sounding angry, never changing tone, was far more frightening to Lucifer than anyone else she had ever dealt with in the organization. "And who is it?"

Lucifer fought to keep her voice even, "A Benjamin Carlson; he runs a small spyware store on Independence Avenue. From the text I intercepted, it looks like they have known each other for a number of years. I took the liberty of digging further, and Carlson did some consulting work for the CIA fifteen years ago. I think they met then."

"You said you intercepted a text?"

"Yes, Carlson was alerting Stone of the spyware and then following up with the same message this morning."

"Thank you, Lucifer. I'll handle it from here." The phone clicked and Lucifer sat there, phone in hand, staring at the now-dark screen. Part of her was relieved. She couldn't help wondering what "handling it" meant for this Benjamin Carlson.

She put the phone down. "Really, Luce, I don't think I need to know what that means." There were Indalo, and then there were *Indalo*. Lucifer pulled up World of Warcraft and watched as the game began. She was deep in the Wrath of the Lich King, hanging on by a thread, but still making progress. *That* was what she could lose herself in, not what was going to happen to Ben Carlson. Frankly, it was none of her business.

Riehl answered his phone on the first ring. "Riehl."

"I have another job for you."

"Go ahead."

"A Benjamin Carlson. He runs a spyware store on Independence Avenue. I need you to eliminate him. Burn the building down while you're at it. I don't want a single shred of evidence left. I've texted you the address." The phone chimed in his hand.

"Consider it done." He paused. "Any updates on the woman?"

"We are still trying to track her down. I'll have Lucifer call you when we know more."

Riehl smiled. His balls still hurt, but he was looking forward to dealing with Lila Benoit.

No More Loose Ends

Ben squinted at the business card in his hand and beckoned to Liam. "Take a look at this, will you? Is that number there an eight?"

Liam slid off his seat, walked over, and leaned close. "Which one?"

"That one there." Ben stabbed at the card.

Liam snorted. "You're going blind, old man. That's the fax number; you want this one here." He pointed at the line above it and Ben squinted, moving the card away, trying in vain to focus his eyes.

"Where are your glasses?"

"If I knew that, I wouldn't be asking for your help," Ben replied, exasperated. "Read this damn thing to me, will you?"

"Want me to dial the phone too? I think you might be having a senior moment," Liam teased the older man.

"Why I oughta." Ben swung at the boy, low and slow, and Liam danced out of the way, a grin on his face. "You kids, you just wait until your eyes start failing you."

"I'm pretty sure all of the polar ice caps will have melted by then, don't you think?"

"C'mere boy, I'll show you polar ice caps!"

Liam laughed, swooped in, and grabbed the phone from Ben. "It's okay, old man, I got your back." He dialed the number while Ben grumbled and tried to hide the smile behind more bluster.

The truth of the matter was that he got as much out of caring for Liam as the boy did, possibly more. Before the kid had showed up in his basement, wet, cold, and scared, Ben had been lonely, depressed, and generally miserable. The kid had filled an emptiness, the chasm of grief that had opened at the loss of Angie and little Charlotte in the car crash nearly two decades ago. Now in his late fifties, Ben had lost his parents ten years ago and his only sibling, Frank Jr., two years later of a massive heart attack. He was all alone in the world, until Liam had shown up.

He snatched the phone from the boy after Liam dialed the number and listened, "Oh hell, it's going to voicemail *again*."

Liam grabbed it back out of his hands. "Here, it's quicker to send a text message. What do you want it to say?" His fingers flew as he typed Ben's words and then pressed the button to send it. The phone produced a "whoosh" and Ben stared at it, frowning.

"What the hell was that sound?"

"Just the phone saying the text has been sent," Liam answered, trying to hide a grin and failing.

"Alright then. I hope he gets back to me soon."

"Me too. Both of the computers had keylogger software on them. And it wasn't any I've seen before," Liam said. "This was rather elegant, hidden in lines of code, and it took some work to find it."

"And you're sure that's what it is?" Ben asked, his face showing concern.

"Yeah. Absolutely." Liam's dad was in prison for his hacking skills, many of which he had passed on to his young son.

"Well, Stone will want to know about it. Were you able to get it out?"

"I think so, but there's a couple more tests I want to do. And also, there's the new release, League of Angels III, that I found a copy of that I need to check out down in the basement." The basement was where the internet router was and it had the best reception in the building.

"*Found* it, did you?" Ben gave Liam a sideways stare.

"Don't worry, it won't come back on you. I piggybacked on the porn store's Wi-Fi." Liam replied, grinning.

"It's locked down with a password." Ben stared at the boy. "How the hell did you get around that?"

"Easy, the owner is really into dogs."

"What?"

Liam grinned. "The password is Hundeficker, which means dog fucker."

"Oh Christ, how the hell you find this kind of stuff is beyond me." Ben shook his head. "Well, I'm heading upstairs to fix dinner. I'm guessing you will be running late with this, so I'll just put it in the fridge, and you can heat it up when you come upstairs."

"Will do."

Ben began to walk away, then stopped and turned around. "Homework?"

"Did it in study hall in last period."

"Alright then." He walked a few more feet and stopped again. "Be in bed by ten. I read an article the other day that says teens need at least ten hours of sleep."

"Aye aye, cap'n."

Liam headed down the stairs to the basement. He made his way by feel because the lone lightbulb in the ceiling had burned out last week and finding the ladder and getting it changed out was a hassle. Besides, he would see fine once he booted up his desktop in the far corner. He had lived down here for weeks before Ben had caught him flat-footed one night in early February. It had been colder than a witch's tit, but the dank basement was better than the crack house his mom was staying in and no one tried to jack his stuff here. He had made a nice little nest for himself in a far corner, behind a couple of old doors. It was when he had lit a small fire in the camp stove that the old man had sniffed him out.

Liam made his way to the desk - his feet knew the way - and he felt for the tower and pressed the power button. When the screen came to life, he saw that Ben had added a brand-new space heater, unpacked it and everything, and a note was attached to it. Liam leaned over and read it in the dim light.

"So, you don't get cold while you're killing trolls." The boy smiled. Ben was alright. Hell, the old man was more than alright. He had insisted Liam take a room upstairs on the second floor, even let Liam put a lock on it, and he'd never tried to cross any lines with him, unlike some of the losers his mom had shacked up with since his dad went to prison. Hell, he'd even marched down to the local high school and enrolled him in classes. Just eyeballed the office staff and damned if he wasn't enrolled and attending classes for the first time since last year.

He sat down in the office chair and it creaked in protest. He logged in and pulled up League of Angels, flexing his fingers until they cracked. He checked the time and the clock read 6:26. He had just under four hours; he could complete at least one quest in that time with the cheat codes he'd dug up.

The speakers were set to low volume. Old habits die hard, after all. *People can't sneak up behind you if you got the sound down low.* Besides, there was only so much singing swords and battle cries that one could take. It was the thumps that caught his attention. An out of place sound, completely different from the sounds Ben made as he walked across the floors, or even of something falling. Something hitting the floor, *hard*, and a muffled shout. The building was old, turn of the century brick, two stories high, three if you counted the basement. Ben had owned the building since he moved to Kansas City some twelve years ago, moving into it when the neighborhood was even uglier and more dangerous than it was now. With the shop closed since six, there should be no one in the building except the two of them.

Liam turned the volume to zero and listened longer. Another thump, the sounds of feet on stairs, walking across the shop floor, and the chime of the back door. Liam stood up. What or who had that been? He thought of calling out to Ben and stopped before his mouth could produce sound. Something was wrong. Every instinct in him told him to be silent. He shut off the monitor, removing all light except for the weak light filtering in through one barred window from the street lamp outside.

The building was silent. He moved as quietly as possible to the stairs and walked up them, the occasional creak of a loose riser betraying his presence. He moved silently up the stairs, smelling an odd, nasty smell. It was not unlike the smells from the copper thieves, the ones who burned the plastic off of the copper wires in large barrels, filling the neighborhood with a stench that twisted at your guts and made you breathe shallow, hoping not to suck in the nasty chemicals that hung in the air. *Carcinogens.* That's what Ben had said about them. The smell was stronger on the main floor and he could see little; the security lights were outside and the thick glass blocks that let in light but stopped folks from breaking in allowed only a filtered light inside. There was no one there. Had Ben gone outside? Liam turned to the left as he reached the top step, stopping only at the glint of something dark on the floor to the right. The door to the upstairs, the one that they kept closed when the shop was open, was slightly ajar and there was some dark liquid on the floor.

Liam squatted down, alarm bells ringing in the back of his head. He could hear a strange sound coming from upstairs and this odd liquid on the floor; something was terribly wrong. Behind the door he heard a small sound, almost a gasp, and he slowly pulled the door open, falling backward in shock as he did. It was Ben. A tangle of limbs, blood on the older man's face, from his mouth, his head, and his eyes stared straight at Liam, unblinking.

"Ben!" Liam's voice was hushed, almost a whisper. An overwhelming feeling of fear washed over him. There was no way Ben had fallen down the stairs, no way he had been alone on the second floor. He had heard someone else; he knew he had, and now that the door was open, he could see a glow from above. Fire. Flames spreading fast from the direction of the kitchen.

He reached out and touched the older man, fingers shaking. Ben was warm still, but from the amount of blood, the unseeing eyes, Liam knew what he was looking at. A junkie in one of the crack houses he had lived in with his mom had died one day last year. The same, wide-eyed vacant expression on his face. A mixture of horror and longing, as if he had seen death coming and almost welcomed it. Liam couldn't tell if Ben's face held that same expression, but he knew death when he saw it. Above, the flames crackled and began to build. He could see the century-old wood frame catching fire, the paint smoking, peeling, and blistering.

He had to get out. Before someone saw the fire and called it in. Before they blamed him. Which they would.

Good Samaritan takes in kid off the streets. A kid who broke into his building and squatted in the basement. Good Samaritan ends up dead at the bottom of his stairs and the building on fire.

He was sixteen. Old enough to be tried as an adult if they had a mind to. And with that kind of story, damned if they wouldn't. He had to go. He had to leave Ben behind, possibly to be consumed by the fire. The old man deserved better. He'd told Liam about his wife, his daughter, both killed in a hit and run. The driver had never been found. Ben hadn't deserved that. And he sure as hell didn't deserve this.

Liam steeled himself, reached out, and shut the old man's eyelids. "I'm so sorry, Ben. If I can, I'll find out who did this. I promise you that."

The fire was spreading. He could hear it beginning to roar. There was no time to get any of his belongings, no chance to save the extra clothes Ben had bought him or the Kindle sitting by his bedside. He had to go. *Now.*

Liam stood up, his heart racing, and the noxious fumes drifting down the stairs almost knocked him back down. He coughed, pulled his shirt over his face, and ran not for the back door, but back to the basement stairs. The back exit was well lit, but the street was dark on the east side of the building and there was a window there he could get out of. It was, after all, how he had first entered Ben's building eight months earlier. Down the basement stairs, out through the basement window, and onto the dark street. He could hear sirens now. The second-story windows shone with flames and he could hear the glass popping, exploding. He ran, fast and far, towards the train yard and disappeared into the poorly lit streets beyond it, leaving behind the one person who had given a damn about him since his dad ended up in prison.

It took two fire trucks to put out the fire. Hours later, within the smoldering timbers dripping with water, the firefighters discovered Ben's body at the bottom of the remains of the stairs. "Damn, it looks like the fire started in the kitchen upstairs and the old man tried to run down and out of the building. Probably overcome with smoke and fell down the stairs." They loaded the body up and into the coroner's van.

"Hey, Robbie, did you see this other bedroom here? Looks like it was occupied. We got what looks like high school textbooks, clothes, maybe a teenager?"

"Just the one body. Maybe the kid was out." Robbie shrugged. "Or maybe he started the fire. Tell the captain and I'm guessing the police will want to look into it. It looks like either a grease fire or electrical short, but you never know."

Dominic Riehl stood in the crowd, listening. He tuned out the rant from a slipper and robe-clad overweight neighbor with rollers in her hair who was convinced it had been a clandestine meth lab on the second floor.

"All of the fires around here are from those illegal drug-cooking operations," she announced loudly to anyone who would listen.

A second person living in the building? Why wasn't I told that the old man had someone living there with him? He glanced around at the crowd. There were a handful of kids nearby and he moved slowly towards them.

One of them, a girl, had tears in her eyes. "The skinny kid, Liam, in Miss Forbes class, he was staying here with Ben," Riehl heard her say to the other girl.

"Oh my God, Laney, do you think he's still in there?" the second girl asked.

"I hope not. He was really nice. He helped me prep for the bio quiz last week. He's super smart."

The second girl saw Riehl and tugged at Sarah's elbow, backing away and giving him a sideways look. "C'mon, let's get out of here. That guy is creeping me out."

Riehl didn't follow. He was busy trying to figure out how to deal with the situation. Should he tell his employer? *After fucking up the hit on the woman, and now missing someone who lived in the building? Hell no.* He would deal with this himself. He'd track down this Liam kid and put him in the ground right next to the old man.

He smiled and whistled a cheery little tune as he walked away from the crowd and the smoldering building. All in a day's work.

Alone

Liam watched the eastern sky lighten from black to gray, staring bleakly at the skyline as the sun's rays warmed the horizon. It didn't seem fair, it sure as hell didn't seem right that the sun could rise today. Surely, for just one day, the sun should sit still, the earth should cease to turn, in mourning for a man who had made a difference, and who hadn't deserved to die.

He had cried, sitting there on the roof of the decrepit warehouse near the train tracks, thinking of Ben being consumed by the fire. Had he been dead? For sure? What if he had left him there, conscious, unable to escape the flames?

"Stop it, stop it, you know he was gone." Liam's voice was raspy, damaged from the smoke and the tears. His cheeks were wet again. As much as it felt selfish and self-centered, his thoughts went to the question.

What the hell am I going to do now? Do I find Mom? What do I do?

His books, his homework, it was all back at Ben's and ashes now. Along with his clothes, his computer, everything. He had less than nothing now. He had no home, no belongings, and no one who gave a damn. Except Dad. And Dad was in prison and would be for at least the next five years, maybe longer.

Probably longer. Dad doesn't play well with others.

He shifted, shivering, and noticed the first movements of the city around him. It was coming to life, the traffic beginning to hum along the highway to the south. Headlights still on, the cars coming thicker, slowing and braking. He could see headlights pulling into the parking lot below, the first employees in the metal fabrication company next door arriving for their day's work. He didn't even have a cell phone. The one that Ben had given him had been charging next to his bed and was now nothing more than melted plastic and silicone.

Liam stood up, his legs aching from the cold, and dug into his pockets. A coupon for a free Egg McMuffin and drink from Mickey D's that he had won in English class for having the highest score on the test.

Well, I've got breakfast.

And the rough edge of a card. He dug it out of his right pocket and peered at it. It was the cop's card. The one with the cute daughter, Maddie. Liam smiled, a brief one, immediately feeling guilty at thinking of a girl when Ben was... Ben was...

"Ben's dead. And you aren't. And it fucking sucks." His breath fogged in the cool morning air.

He stared at the card. It listed not only the cell phone number, but also an office phone number. Perhaps that was the number he needed to call. Ben had left messages on the cell phone, but had he tried the office number? His stomach rumbled. He needed to get some food and find a phone to call the cop. Ben deserved that much.

An hour later, the inside of the McDonald's on Independence was almost empty, compared to the long line of cars that snaked around the building, impatiently waiting their turn for coffee and something that could be called food, but was highly suspect. Liam swallowed the last of the greasy breakfast sandwich. The sausage was dry and the eggs rather tasteless, but he choked it down to shut his stomach up. He winced at the bitter, hot coffee and wished he had chosen an orange juice instead.

"Liam? Oh my God, are you okay?" He looked up into a familiar face. Laney, the girl he had helped with a bio test the other day, was standing there, a small gaggle of girls behind her. They stared, one of the shorter ones nudging the other.

"Huh? Oh yeah, I, uh, I was out last night. I got back and uh, well." His voice petered out and he stared down at the remains of his coffee.

Laney set her tray down and slid into the seat across from him, her eyes focused on his. "Where did you go? Do you have somewhere to stay?" She reached out and put a hand on his.

"I, uh." He stopped and looked up at the other girls, before looking away again. "Could I, uh, could I borrow your cell phone? I need to make a call." The other girls tittered and whispered among themselves.

"Um, sure, okay." She pulled a pink phone out of her purse. The case was covered in pink and silver jewels. She slid it over to him.

"I, uh," he stammered and looked back at the girls, "I'm gonna just take this in, uh, the bathroom and make a quick call. It'll be really quick, I promise."

Laney nodded and smiled at him, frowning as her friends continued to whisper and giggle. "Sure, Liam, go ahead."

He slid out of the booth. "Excuse me," he muttered as the other girls parted, moving away from him as if he had a contagious disease.

He walked away, but not before he heard one of them whisper loudly, "Oh my God, Laney. He's probably the one who *set* the fire."

By the time he returned from the bathroom, Laney was sitting alone, her cheeks crimson, her mouth set in an angry, flat line. Her friends were gone, and she was angrily shoving a breakfast sandwich into her mouth.

He slid the phone back towards her. "Thanks."

She managed a small smile. "No problem." The smile slipped away. "I'm really sorry about Tanya. She's a bitch. I know you didn't set the fire." She hesitated, looking at him, at the smudges on his face. "What *did* happen, Liam?"

He shook his head. "He was... Ben was..." Words seemed insufficient. What had the old man been to him? A friend? A mentor? A parent? He'd stepped up, opened up his life, and welcomed Liam into it, with no expectations, no demands, just...

He gave a damn about me. More than anyone in a long time had. He didn't get anything out of it, he was just...

The look on his face must have betrayed his misery. Laney reached out, squeezed his hand. "Liam, it's okay. You don't have to talk about it. I, I understand. Hey, listen, my uncle keeps an old Airstream on our property. It's out of sight of the house. I could give you the keys, and you could stay there for a couple of days. You'd be roughing it a bit, but it's something. At least until you work things out."

"Yeah?"

"Yeah." She pulled her hand back, checked her phone. "Shit, we've got less than ten minutes until the first bell. C'mon."

She stood up, gathering her trash and his, and looked at him expectantly. He shook his head. "I don't think I can."

"Of course, you can. Besides, who did you call? Are you waiting for a call back?"

Shit. I didn't think that one through.

"Uh, well, yeah."

"So, they'll call back this phone number, right?" She wiggled her phone back and forth and he nodded.

She shrugged. "We share the first three periods. If you get a call back before lunch, I'll be able to tell you right away." She said it so confidently, that Liam felt a little less lost. He found himself standing up and following her out of the McDonald's, down the street and into the high school just as the first bell sounded.

Rob Stone walked into the station balancing the coffees. It was his turn to get the jolt of java to keep him and Max going every day. His partner looked up. "Well, look who finally decided to show up. I was about to cave and go get the damn nuclear waste that's eating a hole in the coffeepot down the hall."

"Careful, they made it hot enough to melt the Styrofoam again," Rob warned and Max winced as he took one of the cups.

"Christ, I got no idea how the cups aren't melting into slag." He deposited the cup onto his desk and shoved two Post-its towards Rob. "I pulled two messages off our voicemail. Some kid, name of Lee, Leem..."

"Liam?"

"Yeah, that's it. Also, that Jack Benton guy finally called us back. I was just about to call him, or do you wanna?"

"I'll call Liam, you give Benton a call."

Max saluted him and picked up his desk phone. Rob stared at the message Max had scribbled. He didn't recognize the number, but the only Liam he could think of was the boy from Ben's shop. The one who had stared at Maddie with moon eyes and looked distinctly uncomfortable when he learned that Rob was a cop.

What's he doing calling me?

He picked up his desk phone and dialed the number. It rang three times before a girl answered with a whisper, "Yeah?"

"This is Detective Rob Stone with the KCPD. I'm returning a call from a Liam?"

The girl gave a small gasp. "Um, yeah, hold on." Rob could hear a voice steadily droning in the background, along with a frantic shuffling and incomprehensible whisper of the girl before Liam's voice answered the call.

"Uh, hello?" He was also whispering.

"Liam? This is Detective Rob Stone."

"Uh, yes sir, I..." The boy was interrupted and there was more rustling before a louder, authoritative female voice came on the line.

"I'm sorry, but Mr. Sorenson is in class right now."

"Yes, I imagine he is," Rob said dryly, smothering a smile. "This is Detective Rob Stone of the KCPD and I was returning Mr. Sorenson's call."

"I, uh, one moment." There was a brief pause as the phone was handed back to Liam. "Take that out into the hall, Mr. Sorenson. You too, Laney Miller. I know Mr. Sorenson doesn't own a jewel-bedecked iPhone. Take it to the principal's office and return with an appropriate explanation, if you please." The woman enunciated the last three words in a huff.

A few seconds later and the laughter from the classroom faded with the click of a door and an echoing hallway. "Um, Mr. Stone? I'm back."

"What can I do for you, Liam?"

"Do you know about the fire, sir? The one last night?"

Rob frowned. "No, what fire?"

Max, already off the phone, put his head up. "Oh man, I forgot to tell you. The spy shop burned last night. The one on Independence Blvd in Northeast. They said the owner died in it."

Rob felt ill. "What? What happened, Liam?"

"I was down in the basement. I heard something. Someone. I went upstairs and he was dead. Someone killed him, Mr. Stone. Set the fire."

"Where are you, Liam? What school?" He knew the answer, even as he stood up, the receiver in his hand, reaching for his coat.

"Uh, Northeast, sir."

"You go to the office, wait there for me. I'll be there in five minutes." He slammed the phone down without waiting for an answer.

Liam stared at the now-dark phone and turned to Laney. Her eyes were huge. "You called the cops?" Her face held a mixture of surprise and awe.

"Ben said he was a friend."

"A *cop?*" she asked it again, the look changing to doubt.

"Yeah."

"Okay, look." She slipped the phone into her back pocket and pulled out a pen and her notebook and scribbled onto the notepaper. "This is my address. If you need a place to crash, go in around the back, from the alleyway. It's supposed to be locked, but my uncle lost the padlock, so you can get in through the gate. After school, I'll be home. But don't come to the door." She rolled her eyes. "My mom's weird, y'know? Anyway, just hang out on the back side of the Airstream. I'll unlock it when I get home."

"Thanks, Laney."

"Yeah, no problem." She grinned. "It's all kind of exciting." Her eyes went wide and she covered her mouth in horror. "Oh God, Liam. I'm sorry. I shouldn't have said that. I didn't mean it like that."

"I know. Don't worry about it."

"I'm going back to class. Mrs. Henderson can bitch at me if she wants, but next to you, I'm her best student, so..." She backed away. "I hope I see you soon."

"Yeah. See you, Laney."

Half an hour later, Liam was sitting in a cracked plastic bucket seat at the East Patrol station. It was busy, and Detective Stone hadn't said much in the school office, just flashed his badge and intimidated the hell out of a new secretary and then hustled Liam out of the school and into his car. It hadn't been a patrol car. The detective had gruffly motioned to him to sit in the front seat of the Acura and then instructed Liam to buckle up.

The drive to the station had been a silent affair. That had changed after they arrived at the station. After the second repeat of the events of the night Rob had stepped away to confer with his partner Max. Liam sat there, staring at Rob's desk. There was a note with his name and Laney's phone number on it. There was also a note from a Jack Benton from Benton Security Services. Liam stared at it, wondering what the company did. He pulled the notepaper with Laney's address on it and borrowed a pen to scribble down the name on the other side of the paper.

He listened too. Even as he leaned back and pretended to have dozed off, he listened to the two men talk. They weren't just talking about him, and about Ben. They also talked about this Jack Benton guy who was apparently holding on to someone they wanted to question. Some woman who was under his protection.

The detective had seemed to believe Liam. That had been somewhat of a load off his mind because he had been scared. Scared they would think he had hurt Ben and set the fire. You never knew with cops. They fucked with your head. Liam had seen it plenty of times before. They would pretend to be your buddy, someone you could trust, and then they would haul your ass off to Juvie or jail all the same. They had promised Dad a deal, but then they had taken it away, left him holding the bag and looking at twenty years behind bars all because he didn't finger any of the hackers that they had really wanted. It was such bullshit. So, he listened, because the way it was looking, Detective Stone would probably be talking about handing him over to Social Services next.

Liam knew where that would lead. Nowhere good. He'd been in foster care twice. Once when his dad was arrested five years ago, and again a year later when they realized what a fuck-up his mom was. Apparently, they objected to crack whores and impressionable teenagers growing up in crack houses and getting busted lips from mom's pimp. Hell, it was a toss-up as to which was worse, the shitty digs they had him in where he shared a room with six other boys and ate mac and cheese every day or the rundown, crumbling apartment with peeling lead paint and junkies shooting up in the hallway. Nobody stepped forward and asked for a sixteen-year-old to take care of and love forever. They wanted the cute little babies, the sweet, loving little toddlers.

Ben had been his one shot at a decent life and that had ended with the old man dead at the bottom of the stairs, his body burned to a crisp in the fire. Liam's mind raced. Why had he contacted the detective? Sure, whoever had killed Ben, it was probably connected to Stone. Who the hell else could it be? Ben didn't make enemies; he was a great guy. The only thing that had come down the pike, the only thing out of the ordinary, had been the keylogger software Liam had found. After the second round of the same damn questions, he had gotten frustrated, tired of being asked the same damn things.

"Look, Detective. You aren't asking the right questions."

Rob had looked at him. "Oh, and what should I be asking?"

"You should be asking where those two voicemails Ben left for you on your cell phone went."

The detective had cocked his head, dug into his shirt pocket, and pulled out the phone, searching it thoroughly before answering, "I don't have any messages from Ben."

"But he left them. *Two* of them. A hacker can break an Android phone like yours, easy." Liam snapped his fingers. "You need to be asking yourself who took those messages. Just like you should be asking *who* put the keylogger software on your laptops. Because when you find that person, you will find out who killed Ben."

"My phone has been malfunctioning."

Liam shook his head. "Nope. Whoever's hacked it is getting it to work just fine."

He had folded his arms over his chest and stopped talking.

That had been nearly an hour ago. He practiced breathing deeply and regularly, his eyes closed, his ears straining to hear their muttered conversation. Finally, he heard it, the words he was afraid he would hear...

"I guess we need to make the call to Social Services."

It was definitely time to get the hell out of here. He stretched, yawned, and slowly stood up. "Is there a bathroom around here?"

The partner, Max, nodded and pointed. "Just down the hallway, then turn right and it's the second door on the left."

"Great. I'll be right back. Y'think I could get a sandwich or something soon? I'm getting kind of hungry."

The two men nodded at him, still intent on their conversation. Liam headed down the hallway and turned right. Up ahead he could see the front counter and an exit sign. He kept walking, no hurry, no nervousness.

Just nod and smile if they look at you.

Minutes later he was outside of the station and disappearing into the surrounding streets. He had already memorized Laney's address, but he pulled out the note and double-checked the address. It was written in her flowing, looping script. He cut through an open backyard, past barking dogs and a homeless encampment in an abandoned lot, and skirted the railroad tracks. There was no way he was going back in the system. And no way he was going back to his mom's, even if he could find whatever flophouse she was crashing at now. Somehow, he had to come up with a plan. Because if it was like he thought, if someone had gone out of their way to murder Ben just because of that keylogger software and the bugs Ben said that the detective had found in his house, then they would be looking for him too. They had been upstairs, and it wouldn't take much to put it together that there had been someone else living there with Ben. And if and when they did figure that out, and that he had hacking skills like his dad, then they would come for *him* next.

Quid Pro Quo

Liam slipped in through the back gate. It creaked loudly and he listened for any noise, any indication that he had been heard, before he settled onto a chaise lounge behind the Airstream, out of sight of the house.

The day was warm now that the clouds had cleared. The sleepless night, the grief over losing Ben and the best home he had ever had, it caused his eyes to droop, and he could feel the exhaustion like a weight, carrying him down.

The creak of the Airstream door opening a few feet away was enough to jar him from his dreamless sleep. He sat up abruptly, and the chaise lounge scraped on the wood deck, complaining at his sudden movement. Liam struggled to focus his eyes.

"Sorry, I meant to let you sleep for a little while. You looked like you needed it." Laney's face swam into focus and he relaxed, leaning back and rubbing his eyes.

"S'okay." He yawned then, his jaw cracking. "What time is it?"

"After three, almost four."

He sat up again. "Woah, I slept for three hours?"

Laney grinned at him and shrugged. "I guess. I've only been here for an hour."

"Watching me sleep?" He stared at her. "Creeper much?"

She laughed. "Whatever! Besides, it takes one to know one!" She nodded towards the door. "C'mon, I got the key and opened it up. Come see."

She disappeared inside and Liam followed her, taking in the '50s decor, the cherry red and soft cream paint colors.

"This is really cool," he said as he slowly looked around.

"The stove, refrigerator, and microwave all work. And there's water and gas so you can take a shower." She stared at him; her nose wrinkled. "Believe me, you need it. You smell like burned popcorn."

Liam picked at his shirt, sniffed it, and grimaced. "Yeah, you got a point."

"I think that my uncle left some clothes here." Laney opened a small drawer and pulled out sweat pants and a T-shirt. "My mom's shift started an hour ago, so I could do your clothes in the washer after you take a shower and you can wear these until everything's dry. There's a towel and all that in the bathroom."

"Thanks, Laney." He swallowed past a lump in his throat. "I, um, I really appreciate this."

Laney just nodded and turned towards the door. "You hungry? I'm gonna make a sandwich. I didn't eat lunch and I'm starving."

"Yeah, that would be great." He turned away, pulled off his shirt, and stopped, remembering the name Benton Security Services scribbled on the note in his pants pocket. "Oh hey, Laney? Could you bring your laptop out here too? I gotta try and find someone."

She nodded and shut the door firmly behind her.

A wave of grief came over him as he turned the water on. He had no one now. Dad couldn't help, not from a prison cell, and Mom was too jacked up to help herself, much less anyone else. He couldn't stay here. Laney was cool, and she was risking her mom's wrath to help him, but he couldn't risk her getting hurt. Whoever had killed Ben and set fire to the building, they weren't the kind of people to leave witnesses.

The water poured over him and he closed his eyes, felt the tears slip out and mix with the water. Ben had died because of what they found; he was sure of it. Could he trust the detective? Ben had. But Ben was also dead, thanks to whatever the detective had on his trail. It felt like nowhere was safe. Nowhere and no one.

He finished soaping and rinsing, and his skin no longer smelled of smoke and loss. Instead it held the faint scent of lavender. He reached for a towel and dried off quickly, pulling on the clean clothes Laney had set out for him. Her uncle was shorter than he was, and the pants ended at mid-calf, but the T-shirt fit fine, even a little loose.

He was drying his hair when Laney returned, her laptop slung in a bag over her shoulder and two enormous sandwiches on a plate in her hands. Two soda cans bulged in each of her front pockets.

He opened the door for her and she slid inside, handing him a soda and one of the sandwiches and turning to set her laptop up on the small table before sliding into the one side.

His stomach growled loudly at the sight of food. Liam lifted the sandwich to his mouth and bit down, closing his eyes in relief.

"I kind of included everything because I didn't know what you would like," Laney said, around a mouthful of sandwich. A piece of lettuce fell onto the plate, followed by half of an olive. "I hope it's okay."

"Mmhm, yeah it's..." He stuffed another enormous bite into his mouth and sighed, "the best sandwich I've ever had."

The girl grinned at him, and they said nothing more until every last bite was consumed and their soda cans were empty.

"So, who do you need to look up?" Laney asked as Liam reached for the laptop.

"Benton Security Services," he answered, fingers tapping. "I saw the guy's card in the police station and I'm just hoping, I don't know, I guess I'm hoping they might help me."

"Not the police?"

He snorted. "The detective didn't believe me. I told him his phone had been jacked and he just wanted to call Social Services on me."

Laney frowned, nibbling on her fingernail as she stared at the screen, leaning forward so she could read it at the same time. "Huh, says they provide personal security. So, what, the guy is a bodyguard?"

"His name sounds familiar. Hold on..." Liam tapped at the keys, opening multiple windows. "He's a billionaire... he founded Benton Security Services a few years after his baby sister Allison Benton was kidnapped and murdered. Huh."

"A billionaire who runs a bodyguard company?" Laney asked, intrigued. "So, what are you going to do?"

Liam opened up a web-based email program that Laney had never seen before and typed a short message, pressing Send before Laney could finish reading it.

"I'm sending Jack Benton a message. If anyone can help me, he can."

"What? Like for protection?"

"Sort of," Liam said, glancing up at his friend. "More like, 'Hey, do you want to hire me?'"

Laney gaped at him. "Seriously?"

Liam shrugged. "I'm really good with computers."

"You mean you're good at hacking."

His mouth twitched. "You say toe-may-toe, I say toe-mah-toe."

She giggled. "You're pretty cool, Liam."

"Um, thanks, I think." He felt self-conscious around her, and plenty nervous. Girls felt like an unknown, and unknowable species. Even Laney, who had helped him with a place to stay, food, and clean clothes. What did she want with him?

"Why..." his mouth closed, and he fell silent.

"Why what?" Laney's eyes were locked on his.

"Why are you helping me?"

She shrugged. "You need help. And my friend Tanya was talking trash, saying you started the fire, and that's bullshit. I know you didn't, Liam. I don't care what Tanya says, or anyone else, for that matter; you're a nice guy. My dad, he used to tell me, 'Those who can, should.' And I guess I try to remember that. I knew we had this trailer out here, you needed a place to stay, so I offered."

"Where's your dad now?" he couldn't help but ask.

She hitched her shoulders, looked away. "Car accident. He lived, but he's in a residential care facility now. He doesn't really remember me or mom. Brain damage and all that."

"I'm sorry." The words felt empty, useless.

"What about your mom and dad?"

"My dad's doing a stretch for hacking. He'll be out in five or six years. Mom's high as a kite most days and meaner than hell in between. I haven't seen her since early summer." He looked at her, "But you know most of that."

Laney nodded. "Tanya and some of the others."

"Figures. Why do you hang around girls like that?"

The email program on the computer beeped and Liam's attention was pulled away from Laney.

He pumped his fist in the air and then grabbed the pen and notepad tucked into the lazy Susan on the table and scribbled down an address before returning to the computer and zipping off an email reply.

"What did it say?" Laney asked.

"Quid pro quo."

"What?"

He grinned. "He said 'quid pro quo' - it means a favor in return for something."

"How do you know this guy will even help you? I mean, seriously, how can you trust *anyone* after what has happened?"

"I keep my eyes open and trust my instincts." Liam shrugged, "What choice do I have?"

"You could, I don't know, I mean, you *could* go into foster care. There are good foster families out there, you know."

"I'm not a cute and cuddly little kid, Laney. No one wants a six-foot-tall kid with fucked-up parents." Liam stared out of the window, avoiding her eyes. "Ben was a lightning strike, like winning the friggin' lottery. He woulda..." he stopped, unable to keep his voice even, felt his throat thickening. "It doesn't matter. He's gone. All the wouldas and couldas and shouldas don't matter now. I'm not going into the foster system. I'd rather live on the streets. I'd rather work and just earn my way, y'know?"

Her hand on his shoulder was comforting and kind. "Okay." She ignored the tears that had formed, the ones he brushed away as he stared out of the round streamlined window. "You can trust me, Liam. I'll help you any way I can."

He nodded, sure that his voice would break if he said anything more.

As the sun slipped below the horizon, she brought him his clothes, fresh-smelling and warm from the dryer. "Keep the lights off. My mom comes home late at night and she would notice if there was a light on in here and call the cops."

"Got it."

She stood at the door, uncertain, then leaned over and gave him a quick kiss on the cheek before fleeing out the door. Liam thought about the kiss for a long time as he lay in the dark and listened to raccoons fight somewhere nearby.

Ben would have liked her.

Finish the Job

In the end, it was Lila's fault that Riehl found them. Just two minutes was all it took for Lila to break The Code for the second time and for the GPS tracking to turn on.

Two minutes.

The last thirty-six hours had been anything but fun. Shane had barely spoken to her, hell he wouldn't even *look* at her, which made her embarrassed, pissed, and indignant all at once. He had left twice, saying only that he needed to meet with his boss, or run an errand. To his credit, he *had* brought her pho from the Vietnam Cafe, along with an order of spring rolls and crab Rangoon.

Despite the offering of tasty food from her favorite restaurant, she noticed that Shane Ellis could not, or would not, meet her eyes. They had engaged in mind-blowing sex less than forty-eight ago and ever since he had avoided her as if she carried a contagious disease. Lila gritted her teeth; she knew he had probably gotten his balls busted by his boss thanks to the butt dial, but still, she couldn't help but feel like it was some tawdry experience Ellis would prefer to sweep under the carpet.

Perhaps he got his rocks off like that every day and she was just a cheap thrill. Lila, on the other hand, could close her eyes and still feel his hands on her, the way his tongue felt against her...she gave a small shiver. What she would give for another night like that!

She had even tried to talk to him about it. After eating breakfast alone in the kitchen, she had crossed into his territory, walking down the long hallway to the first bedroom on the left, significantly smaller than her room, and knocked on the door. A small rustle and he had opened the door, pulling a Bluetooth from his ear. He had *not* invited her inside.

"Yes?" He said it while staring slightly to her left, as if addressing a ghost behind her.

"Could we talk about the other night?" Lila asked, a tentative smile on her face.

"I, uh," he said, his mouth closed in a hard line, "That was a mistake and it won't happen again. I took advantage of the situation and forgot my place."

The smile slipped from her lips. "I just, um, I know it wasn't exactly the best situation, especially with the butt dial, but..."

His expression was closed, unreadable. It showed nothing of the passion and attraction they had shared on Wednesday evening. Had she been wrong about him? Had the attraction she felt all been on her end?

"Miss Benoit..."

"I think that now that we've had mind-blowing sex you can call me Lila," she snapped in annoyance.

"Actually, Miss Benoit, I can't," he said, a note of steel creeping into his voice. "I made a mistake and I apologize. Now, if there isn't anything else, I need to call my boss back. He said that a police detective is asking to speak with you, and..."

Lila could feel the hot flush of anger and shame flood up through her pale cheeks. She spun on her heel and marched away from the door. "Right. I'll let you get back to work, then."

I've been a complete idiot. How do I always manage to pick the jerks? Well, at least he didn't ask me to rate his sexual prowess. Although, she thought, wincing, *I went ahead and told him what I thought of it. Mental note for future lovers, never let on that you loved it. If I hear a dull thud it will be that guy's ego exploding!*

She marched to the other side of the house, restlessly pacing through the front entry, the den, kitchen, and formal living room before returning and repeating it. At one point, she unlocked a side door and walked out onto a small balcony off the living room. The wind had picked up, and the temperature had dropped precipitously. It might only be mid-October, but the weather was already clearly heading into colder temperatures. She shut the door and resumed pacing. It was on the third time through, her face still red and flushed, that she noticed the closed door to the office.

Books, it had books in there.

Books, they smoothed out the rough edges of life. Lila turned the knob and opened the heavy wood door. Inside the room were floor to ceiling bookshelves crammed with all manner of reading material. In the center of the room was a large ornate executive's desk, as well as a loveseat that was an obvious match to the massive, button-tufted Chesterfield sofa and armchair in the living room. The books were organized by genre, which wiped the anger off Lila's face and made her smile.

Whoever organized these books is a person after my own heart.

Several shelves held thrillers, another shelf was dedicated to self-help topics, another on DIY topics like gardening and home remedies. There were three shelves dedicated to romance books, another to mystery, and several more for just sci-fi and fantasy.

Lila settled on a book from the last category, a thick paperback written by Charles deLint. She had read several of his earlier books in high school. She settled into the loveseat, placing some of the pillows behind her and draping a fur-covered blanket over her. The temperatures had plunged the night before and Lila had woken up to frost on the windows and a nip in the air. She lost herself in the book, walking into a world where the real world found itself slipping into fairy realms, where magic and cars co-existed. An hour slipped by, then two.

When she uncurled herself from the loveseat, she noticed her phone sitting on the far corner of the desk. She hadn't thought of it in days and immediately Lila's thoughts went to Kaylee. She stood up, walked over to the desk and picked it up. It was new, just under three months, a perk of working for Kurgen Real Estate, and the battery life was phenomenal. When her old phone had crapped out days after her 90-day evaluation period, Blanche had handed her a brand-new phone with a happy smile, reminding Lila that her work in the past three months had been exemplary. And because Lila wasn't one of those people glued to her phone 24/7, the battery usually lasted all week before needing to be recharged. It must have been sitting here since Monday night. She remembered Shane asking for it. She picked it up, and then froze, her finger hovering over the button, an inch from turning it on.

What was it that Shane had said? It was one of the items of that blasted Code he talked about. Let's see, no contact with friends, family, boss. No phone calls or internet access.

She turned the phone on.

I'll just look at the texts and emails. That's it.

There was a long list of texts. One from Kaylee on Monday around seven in the evening, a ton from Blanche pleading for Lila to contact her and tell her she was alright, and two from a Detective Stone asking her to call him. There were also ten texts, growing progressively frantic, from her neighbor George. Lila sighed, regretting ever having given George her phone number.

She turned off the phone and set it down in the middle of the desk. All this waiting, just sitting around and doing nothing, it was maddening. She held herself back from picking up the phone and calling the detective back. She frowned, imagining how Shane would react if she did.

He'd probably go overboard, just like he did when I went for that walk.

From here she could just barely see the horse paddock on the other side of the property. No horses in sight, not that it would matter if there were, because one hundred yards outside of the house was as unacceptable as standing on the back deck was. "Don't go anywhere without me," she said, her voice cranky and petulant even to her own ears. She set the book down on the desk and went to raid the kitchen for cheese and crackers.

Miles away, in her basement studio with blacked-out windows and the bank of computer monitors, a quiet warning beep sounded. Lucifer almost didn't hear it - she had the speaker volume up as she fought an epic battle, the sound of the trolls grunting and the blades singing made her grin as her fingers danced across the keyboard. But the beep was out of place, and seconds later, the game paused, she checked to see what had caused it.

"Yes! I've got you!" Her fingers moved rapidly over the keys, pulling up a map and reaching for her cell phone to press speed dial at the same time.

The phone rang once. "I hope this is good news, Lucifer." No hello, just straight to business.

Lucifer grinned, even though the person on the other end couldn't see. "She just turned on her phone."

The voice's tone changed, sounding pleased, even excited. "When?"

"Just now. It shut back down after two minutes, five seconds, but it doesn't matter. The GPS locater logged the location; I've got the address here for you."

"Excellent work, Lucifer. Go ahead with the address."

Lucifer rattled off the address, a large house surrounded by land on all sides from the looks of it, close to a water treatment plant and the Missouri River in Kansas City, Kansas.

Within seconds, Riehl's phone began to buzz. He had just walked away from the front door of a post-World War II starter home that this area was filled with. The woman who answered the door had been suspicious and threatened to call the police after he asked if she had seen a young teenage boy in the neighborhood. He had posed as a detective before, but this woman wasn't buying it and shooed him away from her door before he could ask to see if the kid was hanging out in the Airstream trailer out back. He was sure he had seen the kid slip in through a gate off the alley as he drove slowly through the neighborhood.

His stop at Northeast High School had been fruitful. He now knew not only Liam's last name, but what the kid looked like, thanks to the rattled young secretary in the front office. The kid being hauled out of there by a KCPD detective had certainly made an impression.

"Riehl here."

"We found her," the caller said, a note of smugness creeping in. "I've texted you the address. She activated her phone a few minutes ago."

"I can be there in a couple of hours, when it's dark," Riehl answered, staring at the small house with the Airstream poking out behind it.

"You'll go *now*. She turned the phone back off. She might be moving to a different location. I want this dealt with. No more screw-ups." The phone beeped and went black. Riehl swore and stuffed the phone in his pocket, then pulled it out again as he walked to his car. Sure enough, there was the address, a good twenty minutes away if he didn't run into traffic. The sun was already sinking into the west. There would be traffic, but it would mean that by the time he got there the sun would have set. That way he could approach under cover of darkness. He reached under his seat and caressed the handgun and extra clip that were attached with Velcro to the underside of the bucket seat.

Time to finish this.

Shane had watched Lila walk away and fantasized about going after her. She was angry, he could see that, but it didn't take away from the lust raging through him.

Angry sex can be fun.

His hand flexed open and closed as he watched her march out of sight down the hallway and around the corner.

If things were different, I'd go find out just how fun it could be.

Shane blew out a breath of frustration. He had never been attracted to a client before, not like he was to Lila. The past two days had been difficult, to say the least. All he wanted to do was reach out, touch her, smell her, and make those lovely sounds come out of her again. She had been so responsive, so hot and wet. Being in the same house, especially the same room, was becoming agonizing. He wanted her; in a way he couldn't remember wanting any woman.

I have a job to do and it doesn't involve fucking the client. And she is a client, damn it.

The look on Jack's face had spoken volumes. He wasn't pleased, and who could blame him? It wasn't done.

He took a chance on me. One hell of a chance. And I've let him down.

Shane closed his eyes and tried not to think of the feel of her bare skin, the musky vanilla scent of her, and the memory of her moans of pleasure as she had climaxed not once, but twice. If his phone hadn't butt dialed his boss, would he have stopped? Shame flooded him.

Not likely.

She was angry. At least he had that. After she had tried to talk to him, touched him, and smiled at him with that sexy little smile.

Christ, I wanted to pick her up, wrap her legs around me and have her right there against the kitchen cabinet.

He had pushed her away. Put distance between them, forced a coldness into his voice. A woman like that deserved better than a man like him anyway. She needed someone who would wine, dine, and romance her, someone who could fly her off to the Bahamas for a mini-vacation on a whim. Shane wasn't that guy. Sure, he made a pretty penny working for Benton. Jack paid his men well. But being gone for days, weeks, and even months at a time? Traveling constantly? He didn't live a life that encouraged something more than a casual affair. And he sure as hell had no place going near a woman like Lila.

Don't shit in your own nest, Ellis.

He needed a shower. Somehow, he had to find a way to put a lid on his desires and focus on the job. He closed his door, stripped off his shirt and pants, and turned on the hot water. It poured out of the showerhead but remained ice cold. "Shit." The water heater was on the fritz, *again*. He pulled his jeans back on. "Maybe it's the pilot light."

In the kitchen, Lila ran the hot water, waiting for it to warm up so she could wash the handful of dishes that sat in the sink. After all, Shane did all the cooking, unless he brought takeout, so the least she could do was wash the dishes. She watched it run and put a finger in it.

Nope. Still cold.

She groaned quietly. That meant she would have to talk to him. Which was like talking to a stone, really. She turned off the water and headed for the opposite side of the house. The door to the basement on the right stood open and the light was on. She paused at the top of the stairs and made her way down the steps, following the muffled sounds at the far end of the basement. There in a dim corner she could see Shane crouching at the base of the water heater, clad only in a pair of black jeans.

Why does he have to looks so damn perfect? Every muscle, not a single ounce of body fat.

Desire warred with resentment. Shane jerked towards her, finally hearing her approach. She could see not just a six-pack, but an eight-pack, the muscles coiled tight, skin smooth on his bare chest, just a thin treasure trail disappearing down into his jeans. Her breath hitched in her throat.

"I came to tell you the hot water wasn't working," she said, struggling to not stare at his chest, "But I'm guessing you already figured that out."

"Yeah, I went to take a shower and it was nothing but cold, so..." He took in the hip-hugging capris and scoop neck tee she had found in the closet that morning, his eyes traveling over her before he shook his head and forced his attention back to the malfunctioning water heater. Her heart fluttered in her chest.

So, he does *still find me attractive.*

A smile lifted the corners of her mouth and she squatted down next to him, one thigh touching his. "How can I help?"

He smacked the side of the machine and it made a dull thump. "The pilot light won't stay lit, so I'll have to give the boss a call." He stood up and extended his hand. "C'mon."

As she slipped her hand into his, Shane pulled her up, his free hand settling on her waist, his mouth inches from hers. This time Lila wasn't taking "no" for an answer. Her soft lips fastened against his mouth, one hand resting on his chest. His desire for her, which had never gone away and had seethed and boiled away inside as he struggled to be professional, pushed its way to the surface and he pulled her close, running his hand along the small of her back, lips parting, tongue darting, drinking each other in. He could feel his jeans tightening, and he drew his left thumb over the firm nub of her breast, felt it respond and harden. Lila gasped as he lifted her against him and walked with her to the far wall. A pile of targets fluttered to the ground as he lifted her onto the countertop of the indoor firing range and buried his face in between her breasts, his mouth searching, nipping, sucking at her nipples through the thin fabric.

The tiny, soft moans she was making were driving him nuts. How could something so wrong feel so good? He slipped a hand up her shirt, gently pinching her nipple until she cried out, and then smothered the cry with his tongue as they locked lips. Her hands caressed him, running along his bare skin, sliding down his back and into his jeans as she wrapped her shapely legs around him. He pulled away, just for a moment, to stare into her eyes.

Her pupils were dilated, black disks with a sliver of green surrounding them. Her skin was moist, a sheen of sweat that smelled of her unique musk and vanilla scent. He wanted her and he didn't give a damn about the consequences.

That is, until he heard the footsteps above.

Walk into My Parlor

It didn't hurt, not at first. More of an ache, maybe a bee sting magnified. But Rob knew it was something far more. Still, he couldn't help but feel confused - was this a dream? He could see the gun in her hand now. Small, innocuous, really. He looked down at the hole in his abdomen, a spot of red blossoming like a rose, petals unfolding, away from the wound, staining his shirt.

That will be a hard stain to get out, he thought as his legs folded, crumpling beneath him, boneless. Hitting the ground hurt worse than the bullet had.

Will you walk into my parlour, said a Spider to a Fly;
'Tis the prettiest little parlor that ever you did spy.
The way into my parlour is up a winding stair,
And I have many pretty things to shew when you get there.

The ground was hard, cold, and his hip ached from a sharp tip of rock or root sticking in it.

"Why did you..." Rob struggled to find the words, his tongue heavy and thick in his mouth, his words slurring. "Why did you do that?"

The evening hadn't started out like this. He didn't normally work late on Fridays if he could help it, and it had been a close one. He had driven with Peisker searching for Liam for nearly two hours before giving up. The kid had vanished on them, said he was going to the bathroom and then rabbited before Social Services had arrived. A bored social worker had shrugged, handed Rob her card and told them to call her if they caught up with him.

"Good luck, Detective. Kids that are Liam's age don't fare well in the system. But if you find him, I can squeeze in a bunk for him at Crittenton or a group home."

As they drove down one street after another, Rob had cursed his luck. Liam was the only link he had to the Indalo, and from what Ben had told him, the kid had talents for hacking that the Indalo would not want him sharing, especially when it concerned their activities. He couldn't help but wonder if the kid had been right. What if his phone had been hacked? He checked it again for messages from Ben. Nothing.

"Oh, no, no! Said the little Fly; to ask me is in vain:
For who goes up that winding stair shall ne'er come down again.
Said the cunning Spider to the Fly, Dear friend, what can I do
To prove the warm affection, I have ever felt tor you?

Breathing was difficult, as if the ground were taking his oxygen and sucking it away into the dirt. His fingers scrabbled, inching towards his belt, his holster, but nothing was there. He lay there and remembered two hours before, Maddie sitting on the side of his bed, watching as he examined his ties and held one after the other against the new shirt, he had bought on the way home.

"No tie, Dad, seriously. She'll think you are old enough to be her dad and not want to go out with you again. And you sure won't get to third base with her either."

"What do you know about getting to third base, young lady? Is it time I started cleaning my shotgun?" he asked her, arching an eyebrow.

Maddie rolled her eyes, "Give me a break, Dad. That joke is so old! You have been saying it since I asked for my first bra!"

"Yes," he said drolly, "Because a lot can change in eighteen months."

"Whatever, Dad."

He reached for his shoulder holster.

"You are not actually going to wear that, are you?"

"What? She knows I'm a cop."

Maddie lay back on the bed and sighed dramatically. "Dad, knowing you are a cop and having it in her face are two different things. Unless you are planning on arresting or shooting her, leave it at home for once. Seriously, Dad, if you don't get with the program, you are going to be old and lonely and probably fat."

Rob laughed. "Thanks for nothing, kid." He set the holster down. "Fine, you win."

I have within my parlour great store of all that's nice:
I'm sure you're very welcome; will you please to take a slice!
Oh, no, no! Said the little Fly; kind sir that cannot be;
For I know what's in your pantry, and I do not wish to see.

Linda's face appeared above him, intersecting his view of the leaves in the trees. The sun was setting, but there was still enough light in the sky to illuminate the rich fall colors of yellow, gold, pink, and red.

She had suggested this park. "A nice walk through the forest after dinner, what do you say?" Her face held no trace of the friendly, happy woman he had spent the past hour with. She was a good cook; she had cooked dinner there in her spacious kitchen, a mix of spicy pepper steak and the sweet freshness of bell peppers, onions and broccoli on a bed of basmati rice. She had winked at him. "Then back here for dessert?"

The way she had said dessert, with a smile and a wink.

Where was that smile now?

Sweet creature, said the Spider, you're witty and you're wise;
How handsome are your gaudy wings, how brilliant are your eyes!
Oh, thank you, gentle sir, she said, for what you're pleased to say,
And wishing you good morning now, I'll call another day.

"Look, the kid will turn up sooner or later," Peisker had said, tired of driving around in circles. "I'll call the school and see if I can get a list of all of his friends, classmates."

"It's three, school's closed and I doubt we will find anyone interested in even answering the office phone this late on a Friday," Rob replied, checking his phone for messages from Ben for the umpteenth time. "Forget it, I'll deal with the kid on Monday."

Max nodded and turned the car around, heading back to the station. "Sounds good, man. Besides, you got a hot date tonight, don't you?" He grinned, wiggling his eyebrows. "Maybe you'll get lucky. If you still remember how to get it up, that is. How long's it been, Stone? You sure that thing still works?"

"Shit, Peisker, just because you want to screw anything that smiles at you." He shut his phone off; it was running low on batteries anyway. "You know, I saw a tranny the other day on Independence that was asking after you."

"Ha, ha, asshole. My wife would cut my balls off if I so much as looked at another woman." They pulled into the station and Rob's phone dinged. Rob squinted at the screen.

"Finally. That Jack Benton guy is getting in touch to set up a meeting with me and that Lila Benoit. Looks like I'll see her tomorrow. You gonna be there?"

"Hell no, I got Simon this weekend. We're gonna drive up to Saint Joe and see my dad."

"Right, I had forgotten about that. Well fine, I'll do all the work myself."

The Spider turn'd him round again, and went into his den,
For well he knew that silly Fly would soon come back again.
And then he wove a tiny web, in a little corner sly,
And set his table ready for to dine upon the Fly;

The life of a CIA analyst is pretty tame, nothing like what others saw on television. Jennifer Garner's character in the television show *Alias* was bullshit, didn't exist, and Rob lay on the ground still trying to process the fact that he had been shot. The why, that was something too. A ball of confusion, mixed with a dull roar in his ears. His blood, pumping out of him, spreading over his hands, his shirt, running in a thick, slow drip down one side, escaping to the ground below.

She hadn't said anything, hadn't answered him, just stood there over him, head cocked to one side, watching him.

This wasn't how it was supposed to go; this can't be happening.

But it was happening. Blindsided, dirt mixing with blood, he could feel his heart slowing, giving irregular thumps every now and then. Cops get shot every day, but he wasn't a beat cop, he never had been. He'd gone straight to detective, and although he carried a service revolver while on duty, he had rarely even taken it out of its holster. And he certainly didn't have it now.

Hell, I spent more time shooting at targets on the range with it than in the line of duty.

He cast around, looking for something, anything, a way to defend himself. But there was nothing. Less than nothing, especially against the tiny, snub-nosed revolver in her hand that had already drilled a hole into him.

And went out to his door again, and merrily did sing,
Come hither, pretty little Fly, with the gold and silver wing.

Alas, alas! how very soon this silly little Fly,
Hearing his wily flattering words, came slowly fluttering by.

Maddie's phone had chimed and she grabbed it, read the message, and quickly typed a response. "Amanda can't wait to see my new phone. I'm going to walk down the block and show her."

"You're abandoning me?" Rob fiddled with one of his buttons. "What if I make a fashion faux pas? Wear leather instead of denim, or vice versa? Do you think she would be offended by a feather boa?"

Maddie giggled. "You are such a dork, Dad, seriously. But brownie point for using 'faux pas' in a sentence. I'm impressed."

"Ah teenagers, start out as whiny brats and turn into snobs." He swung a tie at her and missed as she dodged and giggled.

"You know you love me."

"To the moon..."

"And back. Yeah, I know. I am pretty lovable, after all. So are you." She lay on the bed, silent.

"I thought you were abandoning me for your friend."

"She can wait." She was silent again, then asked, "So what is she like?"

"Who, Linda?"

"No, the desk sergeant." Maddie rolled her eyes and Rob couldn't help wondering if they would get stuck that way. "Yes, Linda."

"She's attractive, successful. She said she's an investment banker."

"Did you do a background check on her?" Maddie asked, rolling onto her belly, her chin cupped in one hand.

"What? No, of course not!"

"Well, you can never be too sure, you know."

Rob stifled a snort of amusement, imagining Maddie in ten years, fresh out of police academy and doing background checks on potential boyfriends. *Huh, that doesn't sound like too bad of an idea, after all.*

"When do I get to meet her?" Maddie's voice held a mixture of anticipation and concern.

"Give it a couple of dates, Mads, before I inundate her with teenage girl hormones."

With humming wings, she hung aloft, then nearer and nearer drew.
Thinking only of her crested head and gold and purple hue:

Thinking only of her brilliant wings, poor silly thing! at last,
Up jump'd the cruel Spider, and firmly held her fast!

Rob felt colder, weaker. His thoughts strayed to Maddie. She had nearly left without kissing him goodbye. He had called her back and she had tossed her head impatiently, reminding him of a young colt full of life and potential. The future was there, his little piece of immortality, and it was ready to run off without a proper kiss and hug. He pulled her close and she snuggled against him, hugged him tightly and said, "Love you, Dad."

Lying there on the ground, the edges of his vision began to tunnel, blackness creeping in, his sight winnowing to tiny faraway points of light at the end of an impossibly long tunnel. "Love you Maddie," he said, his tongue thick and unwieldy in his mouth, "to the moon and…" He felt his heart stop, the blackness close in completely, and then there were no more breaths. He lay still on the ground, his soul and consciousness racing into the void.

"Back," the woman standing above him said, her voice flat, emotionless. She wiped the gun with her blouse and then tossed it from her. It flew in a slow arc before falling with a solid plunk in the lake several yards away. "Love you to the moon and back, Detective."

She turned and walked away.

He dragg'd her up his winding stair, into his dismal den,
Within his little parlour; but she ne'er came down again.
And now, my pretty maidens, who may this story hear,
To silly, idle, flattering words, I pray you ne'er give ear;

Lucifer's phone rang. She stared at the caller ID and clicked the Pause button on the game, muting the growls of the Orcs. "Yeah, boss?"

"It's done. Wipe all records of my presence from Meet Your Match and anything else you need to do - GPS tracking on his phone, whatever, leave nothing."

"I'm on it. I already set up a program to handle it." Lucifer grabbed her mouse, pulled up the tab on her work machine, and clicked a button. "Everything's wiped."

"Excellent. Thank you, Lucifer." The phone clicked and Lucifer stared at the dark screen and the red Indalo etched into the skin on her wrist.

She just killed a cop. And I just helped her cover it up.

Lucifer stood up and Annabelle gave a soft *whoof* from the bed that she was sprawled across. Her huge head lifted to watch her mistress, her tail thumping out a rhythm on the bed.

There was no getting out now. She reached out and gave her dog a scratch behind the ears. Annabelle closed her eyes, stretching and groaning with pleasure. "In for a penny, in for a pound, right, Annabelle?" The dog said nothing, just tilted her head back and forth under Lucifer's fingers. She looked again at her tattoo. She had signed on for this the minute she had let the needle touch her skin; there was no getting out of it now.

Unto an evil counsellor close heart, and ear, and eye,
And learn a lesson from this tale of the Spider and the Fly.

When Seconds Count

The sun had slipped behind a dark, cloudy sky moments before Riehl had arrived at the location his boss had texted him. As he looked around on the road, which dead-ended at the gates of a power plant, he evaluated the possibilities. There were several properties here, nondescript houses of smaller size, and two larger homes set back away from the road. He could see no cameras on the east drive, but the west drive had several, well-hidden, but visible to the discerning eye. The house on the west was up on the hill, perched at the top of a very long drive.

If he wanted privacy and security, he would choose that house. It had a view of anyone coming from any direction, a high fence, security cameras, and isolation. That was the house where he would find Lila Benoit. He was sure of it.

He took his time moving in. Circling along the boundary of the property, in the dark, was not an easy feat. It took time, patience, and he watched the windows of the house for movement as he skirted the perimeter, keeping to the trees. He was dressed in black pants, a black shirt and shoes - perfect for blending into darkness. As he slipped from the tree line to the north of the house, he listened for sound, but the occupants inside were silent. He smiled; that would change when he got his hands on the lovely Lila Benoit. He would take his time and listen to her scream before he killed her. He was looking forward to it.

He circled the house and found a door to a small deck off the living room near the kitchen. He listened for a long while before slipping a thin plastic card in between the frame and the doorknob. He found it fascinating that people forgot the side doors or put less security into them, focusing only on front or back doors while leaving access to a home possible through a flimsy, hollow-core door with a simple lock that a credit card could unlock in seconds. As if because they were so used to coming and going through the front door, so would everyone else. Much of the time, that easily overlooked side door didn't even have a sensor tied into the burglar alarm, *if* a house had a security system at all, which most did not. This side door had a deadbolt, but it hadn't been secured. Within seconds he was inside and had fastened the door behind him, a tiny click as he turned the lock in place.

Riehl moved with silent precision, taking in every detail of the house that he could. He didn't see any signs of life, but it was a large, sprawling structure, and the woman and whoever was protecting her were sure to be nearby. As he stepped out of the sunken den, standing in front of an office filled from floor to ceiling with books on three walls, the floorboard creaked in protest. Riehl's lip curled, and he froze, ears and eyes alert for any sound or sight that would give his prey away. They were here, he was sure of it.

Lila felt Shane stiffen. She opened her eyes. His mouth and tongue, which had been busy sending waves of shudders down her body as he ran them along her neck, was now closed, his eyes fixed on the ceiling above. She nearly asked what was wrong, then the floorboard directly above them creaked.

What room was that? She ran through her mental map of the house above. The office, right next to the den, where the books were and *her phone.*

Oh God. I turned on the phone. I'm a complete idiot!

She locked eyes with Shane, opened her mouth to speak, and he shook his head, a finger to his lips. Then he put his lips to her ear, whispering urgently. He didn't have his handgun in the holster on his jeans, nor his cell phone. Both sat on the dresser upstairs. The basement itself was an armory, so lacking a weapon was not an issue. Not having a phone *was.*

Lila couldn't help but remember the saying, "When seconds count, the police are minutes away." How soon did they have before whoever was upstairs found the open door and decided to come downstairs? They were trapped.

Shane's lips next to Lila's ear explained what she would have to do. She nodded and he opened a closet door near the firing range and guided her inside the dark space. Reaching past her, he pushed a button and a tiny click brought a cool breeze from inside of the closet to ruffle her hair. There was no time; they could hear the creak of the top stair. Whoever was in the house had found the open basement door.

A closet close to the firing range was actually not a closet at all, but a tunnel that led under the front drive and away from the house. He slipped a small, yet surprisingly heavy handgun into one of her hands and handed her a Maglite for the other. "Go to the end of the tunnel, out through the door and wait for me there by the pond." He whispered and gave her a small push into the inky dark of the tunnel, walked out of the closet, and shut the door firmly behind him, sealing her into darkness.

She nearly turned around twice. The ground beneath her sock-clad feet turned from concrete into gravel and then dirt. It was cold and uncomfortable. Behind her she could hear something; she stopped, listening, and heard a tremendous crash, then another, and what sounded like gunshots. She was frozen to the ground in fear... should she listen to Shane and get to the end of the tunnel? Or should she see if she could help him?

I'm armed, after all. What if he needs help? What if he's hurt?

And against her better judgment, against the keen monkey-brained part of her that told her to run away, fast, Lila pivoted and began running back down the tunnel, back to the basement, towards gunshots and danger.

No Proof

Maybe all the hype of "weighted blankets" actually wasn't *all* hype, thought Lila randomly, as she answered the paramedics' questions. The blanket they had draped over her wasn't just warm, it was heavy as well. Perhaps it was one of those tools that remained on the down low, a way to calm the recently traumatized enough to make them easier to handle. If so, it was certainly working. As was the attractive EMT who was asking her questions while a second, equally attractive EMT bandaged her leg.

Why are paramedics and firefighters so damned good-looking?

Despite the heavy blanket and the fact that the assassin sent to kill her was dead on the ground only thirty yards away, shock eventually did set in. Lila began to shiver uncontrollably, even after they added another blanket and closed the door to the ambulance to ward off the blasts of chilled air coming from the river. She had tried to insist on riding with Shane to the hospital, where they would treat his head wound and the arm where the bullet had ricocheted off of the wood and grazed his flesh. Not even the arrival of the silver-haired fox, Shane's boss and her benefactor, Jack Benton, would dissuade her to leave Shane's side.

"You told me never to leave your side. It's part of The Code."

He had stared at her and then guffawed, startling the nurse bandaging his arm. "*Now* you are following The Code?"

"Better late than never." That made him laugh even harder. She laughed too, if only to forget, just for a moment, that she had taken a life tonight.

He must have seen it in her eyes. He reached out with his undamaged hand and took hers, glancing at his boss as he did. Jack Benton watched them both but said nothing.

Shane's boss was older than Shane, possibly by a decade or more, and his jet-black hair was liberally streaked with silver gray. He was handsome and had the look of wealth. Not new wealth either, but lifelong. Jack Benton had never known lack or wondered where his next meal would come from. Despite this, he didn't have the snobbishness or built-in expectations she expected him to have. And he had instantly come to her aid in regard to the police, insisting that any questioning wait for Rob Stone, the detective on the case who they were tracking down now.

It was crowded in the ambulance, but the paramedics allowed Lila and Jack to both accompany Shane. The police officer followed behind in a patrol car. When they arrived at the hospital, however, Jack stepped forward, placing a warm hand on Lila's shoulder.

"Miss Benoit, if you please, they will get Mr. Ellis cleaned up with stitches, and you and I need to speak with the detective when he arrives."

Lila found herself looking at Shane, who nodded at her. She turned back to Jack Benton and walked away from Shane, listening as they wheeled him away to one of the glass-walled rooms in the back of the ER. Jack looked around the large waiting area and found a corner that was empty of others and steered her towards it. The police officer followed, sitting across from them, his eyes watchful as he surveyed the room. His phone rang then, and he stood up and walked away to answer it.

Lila sat, shivering again. "Can I get you some coffee or tea, Miss Benoit?" Jack asked, a small smile on his face.

She shook her head, "I'm not cold... it's nerves, I guess."

"Perfectly understandable." He regarded her for a moment, saying nothing.

The silence was uncomfortable. Lila couldn't stand it any longer. "So, you know Kaylee?"

"I do."

"How?"

He smiled. "That's not my story to tell, Miss Benoit."

Lila grimaced. "Right."

She was saved from having to say anything more to this enigmatic, good-looking man by the police officer who returned from his phone call. "Miss Benoit, I'm going to have to ask you to return with me to the station. You will be speaking with Detective Peisker and he will also take your statement on tonight's events."

"I thought I was going to be speaking to Detective Stone," she said and turned to Jack. "Isn't that the detective that was assigned to the shooting at Kurgen?"

Jack frowned, but before he could speak, the officer answered. "Yes, ma'am, he was, but Detective Peisker is also working that case."

Jack stood up. "Did you say *was,* Officer, as in, no longer *is?*"

The officer looked grim. "I'm really not at liberty to say, Mr. Benton, but I must insist that we go to the station directly. If you wish to accompany Miss Benoit, that is fine, but Peisker will be questioning her at the station."

It was a tense yet short ride to the station, which was just a handful of miles from the hospital. The wait in the interrogation room felt interminable. At one point, Jack Benton turned to Lila and asked, "Miss Benoit, would you by any chance have a dollar that I might have?"

A billionaire was asking her for a dollar?

Lila blinked and handed him the only bill she had on hand, a ten-dollar bill.

"Thank you, Miss Benoit." Jack Benton smiled at her, neatly folded up the bill, and placed it in the breast pocket of his designer jacket just as a tall, heavyset man entered and closed the door. His eyes were red-rimmed, and he tried and failed to smile at Lila. "Miss Benoit, my apologies for keeping you waiting. I'm Detective Peisker."

Jack, who the detective had nodded to but mostly ignored, asked, "Where is Detective Stone?"

Peisker sighed. "Rob Stone has just been found murdered."

Lila gasped, her hand going to her mouth. "Oh, my God."

Jack asked, "Is it possible this is related to your current case?"

"I have no idea, Mr. Benton, but we will be exploring all leads." He rubbed his eyes. "Rob and I worked together for nearly a decade. He was a fine man, a great partner, and a devoted father. Don't worry, the KCPD will not rest until we find out what happened to one of our own. Meanwhile, ma'am, I would like to question you about the events that occurred on Monday night as well as tonight."

"Before I say anything, do you know if Detective Stone was able to find the SD card?" Lila asked, her hands twisting. "The file that I saw, it was on an

SD card and it was there in my laptop. I also copied it onto a flash drive for my boss, Mr. Endon."

Max shook his head. "I'm sorry, Miss Benoit, but there wasn't any SD card in your laptop."

"But..."

"And Mr. Endon handed over the flash drive. It was empty."

"That's," Lila blinked and stammered, "that's not possible." She raised a delicate finger to her mouth, nibbling on an already ragged edge of nail.

"Mr. Endon stated that the flash drive was blank and he had no knowledge of an SD card. I'm sorry, Miss Benoit, but we can't find any trace of these suspicious files you believe you may have found." He stared at her. "So, is there anything you aren't telling me? Anyone you might owe money to? Any crime you may have seen committed or," he paused before continuing, "possibly had a part of committing?"

Lila jumped to her feet. "*What*? You cannot seriously be blaming *me* for this! I've been attacked, not once but three times! I've been shot at! That man I killed tonight; he was the one in the parking garage!" A vein in her neck twitched and Lila could feel heated blood rushing to her cheeks. She began to shake again. Jack Benton reached out and gently put a hand on her shoulder.

Max gave a tired, half smile. "My apologies, Miss Benoit. These are questions I would ask of anyone in your situation. Now, if you could sit down..."

Lila glared at the man and sat down slowly. She closed her eyes and took two deep, slow breaths in and out, remembering the breathing exercises her judo instructor ran his students through each Monday and Wednesday evening at the beginning of class. She needed to calm down and not let this man rile her.

She felt Jack Benton's hand lightly squeeze her shoulder. "Miss Benoit has had some terrifying experiences this past week, Detective."

Max turned to the billionaire and frowned, his mouth settling into a disapproving line. "It is highly irregular to have you here, Mr. Benton. I understand you were communicating with my partner, Detective Stone, but I think it would be advisable for you to wait outside until I have had a chance to speak with Miss Benoit for a few minutes alone."

Jack nodded. "I understand how you might feel that way, but I'm afraid that you misunderstand the situation here. Miss Benoit is a client."

Max snapped. "Yes, Mr. Benton, I'm aware that she has retained Benton Security Services for personal protection, although that worked so well that she had to kill the attacker herself."

Jack smiled. "Actually, Detective, she did not retain my security company's services, those were provided to her at no cost." He reached inside his coat pocket and set down a simple, yet elegant card onto the metal table. "I happen to be an attorney and Lila is my client."

Lila gaped at him and just as quickly shut her mouth before the detective turned her way. *So that was why he had asked for the money!*

Max Peisker did not look pleased. "I see," he said, tapping his fingers on the table. "Miss Benoit, do you wish for your legal counsel to stay here with you while we talk?"

"Yes, thank you."

The detective grimaced, having expected the answer, and began to question her. Some of the more outrageous questions he asked were immediately shot down by Jack, while others he allowed Lila to answer. The hours ticked by as she recounted the incidents of the past week that had led to her shooting the dark-haired assassin that evening. By the second repetition, Lila was having difficulty stringing her words together. It was past midnight and the detective had asked her the same questions worded differently so many times she found herself hunched over, holding her head in her hands. She was exhausted, terrified, and numb.

"Detective, I must insist that we continue this line of questioning after my client has had a chance to rest," Jack said, his hand once again upon her shoulder. "I am assuming she is free to go?"

The detective looked exhausted as well, gray circles beneath his eyes. "At this time, we have no proof of the existence of these suspicious files that Miss Benoit claims to have found, but I think that, until we have discussed this in its entirety, it would be best for her to remain in protective custody. *Not* in a jail cell," he clarified as he saw the look on Jack's face, "but under police protection."

"Fine," Jack said, "But I would like one of my men to be there as well."

"I'm afraid that won't be possible, Mr. Benton," Peisker said, shaking his head. "No civilians."

"Jesse Bardin is one of your own, Detective, a member of the KCPD who has worked part-time for me for the past two years."

Max gritted his teeth. "Fine, Mr. Benton, have it your way." He stood up. "I'll make the necessary arrangements and we will pick this up again in the morning."

"Afternoon."

"What?"

Jack smiled. "I think one in the afternoon will be early enough considering it is *already* morning."

Detective Peisker glared at him and walked out of the room.

Jack gave a low, soft laugh.

"Thank you, Mr. Benton," Lila said as she stood up, weaving slightly from exhaustion. "Have you had any word on Shane?"

"Yes, he's fine and has been released from the hospital. I received a text from him an hour ago. And now, if you will excuse me, I need to contact Jesse and arrange for him to stay with you at the safe house. Frankly, he's the only member of the KCPD I trust with this right now. We will get you some-place safe, Miss Benoit. After you have had some time to rest, we will discuss what happens next. Sound good?"

Lila nodded, weary. More than anything, she just wanted to curl up and go to sleep. She watched Jack knock on the door and wait until they opened it. She sat back down and settled against the cold wall and closed her eyes.

As the door opened, she could hear a young woman's voice clearly. "You aren't listening to me! He was on a date. He met her through Meet Your Match, and..."

"We don't show any matches for your father, Maddie; he didn't meet anyone through the dating service." It was Peisker's voice.

"Yes, he did! Her name was Linda, and..." The door closed, cutting off the voice, sealing Lila into silence with nothing but indeterminate sounds in the distance.

It felt like forever before the door opened again and a man who looked like he was in his late twenties walked in. "Miss Benoit? I'm Jesse Bardin, and I'll be providing protective detail for you."

An hour later, their arrival at the safe house was uneventful. It was a small, decrepit-looking house with a cinder block exterior and bars on all of the windows, a far cry from the sprawling, opulent house where she had spent the last few days. It had a slightly sour smell, one that brought feelings of fear and doubt, but Lila was far too exhausted to care. She said little as Jesse, her new bodyguard, showed her one of the small bedrooms. The door clicked shut behind her and she stepped out of the thin shoes they had found for her and fell into the bed too tired to bother undressing, even if she had felt so inclined. She pulled a thin blanket over her, wrapping it around her like a cocoon, and pulled the cord on the lamp by the bed. Through the thin walls she could hear Jesse speaking quietly to the other guard, a police officer in uniform, before the overriding need for sleep carried her away into oblivion.

Jackpot

L iam stared at Jack Benton. Beside him, Laney folded and re-folded the paper that had encased her straw. She had insisted on accompanying him despite his objections, and he was glad she was there. Her fingernails were bitten to the quick, and her long, thin fingers smoothed the paper out and started again, perfecting each fold with precision before rotating the wrapper and folding it again.

The man sitting across from them was older than he had expected, his hair heavily threaded with gray. His clothes were quality, the kind that spoke wealth in a subtle way.

"I know some good people who could help you; Liam, the foster care system isn't all bad."

Liam shook his head, beginning to wonder if he had made a mistake in contacting Benton. "I want a job, that's all."

"In what capacity?" the older man asked, a half-smile on his face.

"Cyber security, for one; your website could use work as well. And…" Liam paused.

"And?"

"Other things."

"The kind of things that landed your old man in prison?"

Liam hid his surprise in a nonchalant shrug of the shoulders. *So, he's researched me like I researched him.* There was more to Jack Benton than met the eye.

Jack leaned back and studied him. Liam felt his stomach clench in a nervous twinge.

"Where are you staying?"

Liam shrugged. "Around."

Jack looked at Laney, "He's staying at your house?"

"No!" She said it quickly, reflexively, then added, "My mom wouldn't be okay with that. He's staying in the RV, in our backyard."

Liam shrugged again. If this guy had looked him up and knew about Dad, he also knew about Liam's mom, and probably Ben and the fire as well. It wouldn't be a difficult thing to look up the IP address and track his email back to Laney's. *Hell, he probably just knew from looking at us.*

Liam picked at a divot in the Formica tabletop, scraping it with his thumbnail.

"I talked to the police, to a Detective Peisker, about you, Liam. He really wants to talk to you."

Liam rolled his eyes. "Peisker's a tool. Detective Stone's almost as bad."

"Detective Stone is dead, Liam."

Liam shook his head and looked sick. "No, that's not possible. I talked to him *yesterday.*"

"As did I." Jack tapped his fingers on his coffee cup. It had a chip, near the handle, and Liam stared at the crack that ran down one side of the cup and struggled to understand how a man he had just seen living and breathing could be dead. And then he thought of the detective's pretty daughter, Maddie.

I can only imagine how she feels. Losing Ben has been awful, but I knew him less than a year. Maddie has just lost her dad.

All he could see was her face now and he was startled by Laney's hand on his. She squeezed his fingers in hers.

"What happened to the detective, Mr. Benton?"

"It's being investigated as a homicide."

A cold wave of ice washed through Liam. "This is all connected. I'm sure of it."

Jack nodded, his eyes showing admiration. "Yes, I'm beginning to suspect that might be the case. If so, it puts you in the crosshairs as well."

"Me?"

"You said yourself that you found evidence of keylogger software and other tampering. You mentioned that Detective Stone was former CIA, a fact I had my people corroborate. Your guardian died before the fire consumed the building, a fire that is being ruled arson by the way, and now Detective Stone is dead." Jack stared at Liam. "I'm a pretty good judge of character, Liam. Either you are guilty of killing the only man who ever helped you and setting fire to the first decent home you have had in years, or you are in a great deal of danger. At some point they are going to figure out where to find you. Are you willing to let your young friend Laney be hurt like Ben was?"

Liam stole a glance at Laney's face; she looked pale, her mouth a small "oh" of surprise.

"What? No, of course not!"

"Then quid pro quo does seem the best course of action. You come work for me *part-time* and I will make sure you are safe and have a chance to finish your education."

"Finish my education, um, how exactly are we going to do that?"

Benton shrugged. "How do you feel about moving to California? I have a house outside of L.A., a full staff, and you could attend school or take classes online, whichever you prefer."

"I'd prefer not to go to school at all."

"That's not one of the options, Liam," Jack said firmly.

"Take the deal, Liam," Laney whispered. "Seriously."

"How do I know you're on the up and up, huh?" Liam suddenly challenged, trying to shake the older man, "What if you are some perv trying to get me out of state? Away from anyone who could help me?"

Jack smiled. "Look, I know you've done your homework. You researched me before you contacted me. And I'm happy to give you a job, but *on my terms*. You are only sixteen..."

"I'll be seventeen in two weeks," Liam bluffed.

"I can do research too, Liam. You will be *sixteen* in two weeks. You need an education, you need job skills, and you need a place to stay. You will have all of those things here or in California, but I think you would be safer there." He tapped his finger on the chipped Formica, emphasizing each point. Then he reached down and pulled out a laptop from his bag. "I think you're good, really good, so let's say this is a test. Pass it, and you get the job. I'll put 60k a year into a savings fund with your name on it, accessible at age eighteen, give you a stipend of one thousand a month, and you'll have the guest cottage with food and utilities paid, as well as access to a private high school education. That's mandatory, by the way, as is maintaining passing grades." He smiled. "Which shouldn't be a problem, since you are a straight A student."

Liam sat there, reeling as he tried to absorb what was being offered to him. Sixty thousand dollars a year?

I'll be rich! No more scrabbling to survive, living on the streets or those damn crack houses that was all Mom could afford...Mom...shit...

"Get my mom into rehab." he said, "That's part of the deal. And a place to stay when she's better. Take it out of my earnings. A decent apartment and a chance at a job." He stared up at Jack. "You can do that, right?"

Jack nodded; his voice softer. "Yes, Liam, I can do that." He nudged the laptop across the table and Liam opened it and let it boot up. The splash screen showed One Kansas City Place, with Kurgen Real Estate emblazoned across the top of the screen.

"This is someone's work computer," Liam said, and he began to click at the file folders, rummaging through recent documents and file history. "Real estate holding, sales information, et cetera."

"I want you to look for this file and tell me what you see." Jack pushed a business card forward with a file name written on it.

Laney sipped her coffee and watched as Liam's fingers flew over the keys, accessing the file history. "It looks like the file was opened from a different source, possibly a memory stick or SD card, and then copied."

"Copied where?"

"Um, possibly another flash drive? Also, the Cloud."

"Anywhere else?"

"Yeah, a Dropbox folder, a personal one." He looked up. "If the flash drive can't be found, I'd look there."

"Thank you, Liam, that helps." He reached for his wallet, laid a $100 bill on the table, and stood up. "Eat some breakfast. I'll send a car for you at your friend Laney's this afternoon." He turned to go, then stopped. "I'll also get one of my people to work on locating your mom today."

Laney whistled long and slow as they watched Jack Benton drive away in a dark green Jaguar. "Holy shit, Liam!"

Liam nodded and said nothing.

Holy shit, indeed.

Lila had emerged from the bedroom, out of sorts and starving for food. The seductive smell of coffee brewing had crept under the bedroom door and wooed her from sleep. Once she opened the bedroom door, the delicious aroma hit her in a wave, along with something that smelled a lot like eggs and bacon. The man from last night, well, early that morning, really, was at work in the kitchen, his back to her as he stood in front of the stove, the coffeepot steaming next to his right elbow.

What was his name? Justin? No, Jesse.

He looked over before she could open her mouth and nodded, "Good morning, Miss Benoit. Help yourself to some coffee... there is cream in the fridge." He slid half of an omelet onto a plate and placed it at the breakfast bar before handing her an empty mug. "Sugar is there on the table as well."

"Thank you." The words came out as a whisper. She still felt exhausted. "What time is it?"

"Half past ten," came his reply. "Mr. Benton is heading over. He said he had something for you to look at."

"Where's Shane?"

"Ellis?" Jesse shrugged and gave her a smile. "I haven't been read in on that."

Lila blushed then, and Jesse saw it and shook his head. "The boss runs a tight ship, Miss Benoit. I imagine he's been re-assigned."

Lila's face burned even hotter and she looked away, focused on her omelet, and took a bite. She closed her eyes and sighed with pleasure. *Bodyguards who can cook. I've actually died and gone to heaven; there can be no other explanation.*

She opened her eyes to find Jesse staring at her, his eyebrows raised in concern. "Is this like part of Bodyguard 101? You all learn how to cook gourmet meals?"

He laughed and ate a bite. "It's survival; there's only so much microwaveable meals a person can eat."

Outside, the sound of a car pulling into the drive and a door opening and closing had Jesse on his feet. He quickly peered out of the window and strode to the front door to let Jack Benton in. "Hey, Boss. You want some breakfast?"

Jack smiled. "No, but a mug of that fine-smelling coffee would be great. Thanks, Jesse." He clapped the younger man on the shoulder and nodded to Lila. "Miss Benoit, I trust you slept well?"

Lila was suddenly very aware she had not brushed her hair. "Um, yes, like a stone, in fact." Her eyes drifted to the laptop slung over Jack's shoulder. "Is that my..."

"Yes, I managed to get the laptop from the office. Kaylee was kind enough to help me retrieve it."

"I thought you said it didn't have the file on it."

"It doesn't," Jack answered, pulling out the laptop and setting it next to her on the bar. Jesse reached over and retrieved his plate, giving his space to his employer and sliding a cup of coffee in his direction. "But you can access it all the same."

"I don't understand."

"Think back to the day you found the file." Jack said as he opened the laptop. "You said you found it on an SD card, right?"

"Right. And the SD card was in the laptop bag, but it's not there now."

"And you said Morris Endon asked you to save it on a flash drive and give it to him. Is that correct?"

"Yes." Lila looked frustrated. "And he told the police the flash drive was empty, but I'm sure it wasn't."

"Do me a favor. Open up an Excel file, type a line or two, and then save it to this flash drive." He held out a flash drive to her.

Lila suppressed the urge to snap at the man. "Okay, but I really don't see how this is going to help." She pulled the laptop closer, opened the program, typed a few numbers in, and began to do as Jack asked, sliding the flash drive into the port. "Okay, now what?"

"Is the file saved on the flash drive?" he asked, the traces of a smug smile on his face.

"Of course, it is!" She looked back at the directory, stared, and looked away in embarrassment. "I forgot to select the correct drive." She clicked the file again and this time saved it correctly, the flash drive lighting up as the data moved over.

"That happened last time as well, didn't it?" Jack asked softly.

"Yes, yes it did!" Suddenly she remembered. She had been looking at a loan amortization file moments before, one from her Dropbox account. "I had my student loan file open, one that's on my personal Dropbox account. I had been playing with it to see how much interest I could save if I paid an extra one hundred dollars each month on top of my regular loan payment. And then I saw the SD card, put it in, and it saved it to the same folder!"

She turned back to the laptop, searched for the Dropbox folder, and seconds later they were looking at the missing file.

"Jackpot," Jack said, grinning.

Lila felt a sense of vindication surge through her. "Now the police can't say it doesn't exist! Here it is!"

Jack peered at the file, pulling the laptop closer and then clicking on the tabs. His eyes focused on something and he pointed at the screen. "What is that symbol there?"

Lila looked at where Jack's finger rested. It didn't look like any account symbol she had ever seen, more of an ancient pictogram, or rune. "That's weird." It was a simple stick figure with the arms sticking straight out at each side and a half circle above them joining the two ends.

She brought the mouse over the image and it changed from an arrow to a hand with one finger pointed. "It's a link of some kind." She clicked it and the screen flashed as the laptop began to cycle, struggling to open something massive in size.

Five minutes later, Jack let out a low whistle. "This is big, Lila. You realize that, right?"

She nodded mutely, unable to form words. The spreadsheet she had seen, that she had asked Morris Endon about, it had been the tip of the iceberg.

The icon that she had clicked on, that was the real key, the real jackpot. The rabbit hole went deep, far deeper than she could have ever imagined. Her omelet cooled, forgotten at her side, as her eyes raced over the data.

"This is, this is..."

"Corruption. Payoffs," Jack added, "Kurgen Real Estate is a front. A massive, well-engineered front, but a front nonetheless. This is a record of decades of dirty deals, corruption on a level I haven't seen before."

Lila shook her head; everything felt numb, unreal. She took a bite of the omelet, now cold, chewed it mechanically and swallowed. It stuck in her throat.

"This is bigger than what the local police can handle, Lila. These transactions, many of them are across state lines, which makes this a federal issue. We have to take this to the FBI." She stared at him; mouth dry. Her mind raced as she took it all in.

Jack could see it in her eyes, that deer in the headlights look, and the realization that the life she had been living just days ago, was over. There was no going back to normal. Never again.

Witness Protection

The next three weeks moved both quickly and slowly for Lila. There were moments when it felt as if she were on a speeding train, hurtling towards a dark abyss. Meetings with investigators, questions, and moves from one safe house to another.

At other times, there was nothing to do, no one to talk to. She couldn't call Kaylee, or anyone else, and after spending two days being questioned by the FBI, she had been relegated to a small apartment in Chicago, where beefy, grim-faced strangers had guarded her 24 hours a day. They were nothing like Shane, or even Jesse. No shred of humor, for one.

They were polite, but there was no conversation. They didn't even reveal their full names, just last ones, Jenkins this, and Beech that. At one point, desperate for the sound of another person's voice, she had asked Beech about his background. She didn't understand military rank, so it had sounded like a litany of Marine this, that, and the other thing before joining the FBI. She didn't bother asking Jenkins about his background.

Most of the time she spent staring at the television in the hotel room, an endless loop of daytime soaps and reruns from the '70s that had her bored to tears, before finally breaking down and asking for a list of books to keep her occupied. After that, she kept to her room, emerging only to eat meals.

The meals were a depressing array of fried foods served in takeout and fast food bags.

Her guards didn't cook, not at all. Each meal came in a sack or a Styrofoam container and she was pretty sure she was gaining weight from all of the extra calories and lack of exercise.

At least she had her books. A wide variety at that. She had handed Jenkins the list last week and he had blinked at it. "I don't care who you have to ask, or where you have to go, but bring me a stack. If I have to watch anymore daytime TV, Judge Judy or that damned Springer Show, I'll lose my mind."

A smile had ghosted past his lips. "I'll see what I can do, Miss Benoit."

The next morning two stacks of books had been sitting next to her bedroom door in a large plastic bag. The bag was labeled Myopic Books, that listed an address on Milwaukee Avenue. That was the street they were on as well. She wasn't sure of the exact address, and the only stores in view were the UPS Store and a tanning salon across the street, but Lila figured it had to be close. Her two guards stayed in the apartment, leaving only when it was time to fetch meals or run an errand.

It was an eclectic mix of new and used books, which Lila didn't mind at all. One of her joys had been to drift through the stacks at Prospero's on 39th Street. Especially during the last year of school when she desperately needed a break from school and couldn't afford to see a movie or really go out, a trip to the bookstore and a few dollars had given her an escape and entertainment for hours and hours.

She had already read two of the books, but she smiled when she saw them, more than happy to re-visit the stories as one would re-connect with an old friend.

"Thank you, Jenkins, for the books."

He shook his head. "Wasn't me, Miss Benoit. I just passed on the message."

"Oh, well, thank you anyway. And do pass on my thanks to whoever did get them; they found some great titles. A couple I have read, but don't mind reading again, and several I have been meaning to buy and not gotten around to."

He nodded and said nothing, and Lila felt a surge of loneliness return. She missed Kaylee. She missed her life at Kurgen. From what little she had been told, the entire office was closed down and each of the employees questioned. She couldn't help but worry about Kaylee, as well as a handful of the others she had been friends with - Blanche, even if no one else had liked her, Trish at the front desk, and several of the others in the office. Morris Endon had been arrested, but he had refused to talk with the investigators or cooperate in any way. She hadn't seen Shane since that fateful night. Jack Benton had said that he had been re-assigned, his tone had not invited additional inquiries, and it had been several weeks since she had seen the billionaire. These days it was nothing but federal agents, lawyers, and prosecutors.

She sat on her bed, the paperback in her hands forgotten as she stared at the thin folder sitting next to the bed. She hadn't filled out all the paperwork, not yet, and they would be asking for it this afternoon. She had already put them off twice.

It seemed so final - the death of her old world, the start of another. She was free in many ways, no more student loans for one, a whole new identity for another. The locale and background had been crafted for her. She wouldn't even be a data analyst any longer, and she was being sent to an area of the country that was completely unknown to her, a small town in Maine where she would be managing a bookstore. She had even helped choose it, but still, despite this, she delayed signing the agreement, filling out the last of the paperwork - avoiding, if only for a day or two, her new reality. It would be a year at least until there was any trial. The FBI continued to sift through the data they had found, and her part in it was small and insignificant when compared to the massive trail of corruption and dirty deals they had found. Nevertheless, she was in danger from the Indalo. They now had a name for the organization, having found a wealth of information in Detective Stone's home office in the wake of his murder.

"You will be safe in the Witness Protection Program. Frankly, Ms. Benoit, we keep finding more and more levels to this, and you were the one to find it in the first place." One of the agents, a woman with a beak nose and perpetually grim expression, had told her. "That they attempted to murder you, not once but *three* times, it indicates just how vital your part in our case is. I promise you that we will do the best that we can to help you settle into your new life."

Lila had been the one to suggest that she manage a bookstore. If she couldn't dig into data and research market trends, then she could do the thing she loved just as much, if not more: live surrounded by books.

The Bookstore

He shouldn't be here and he knew it. Two girls in their late teens passed by, ogling him, and he could hear them whisper and giggle as soon as they passed by.

The new kid, Liam, had helped, of course. He had struggled to get used to living in the guest cottage there at Benton's home in the hills. Mostly it seemed that he was lonely and missed his life in Kansas City. When Jack had asked Shane to drive Liam out to Los Angeles, they had had a couple of days of driving to bond. The kid had never been out of Kansas City and it had been fun to take a few side trips to see the Grand Canyon as well as a sprawling mountain town, Flagstaff, that Shane had spent a few months in a few years earlier. When he had learned of Liam's serious hacking skills, Shane had sworn the boy to silence and slipped him some cold hard cash, which had quickly disappeared into a pocket.

It had taken him a couple of days, and Shane could only imagine what Jack would say if he knew what the two of them were up to, hacking into the FBI database to find Lila. But here he was, a week and more than three thousand miles later, standing on Pleasant Street in Brunswick, Maine, outside of the bookstore. *Her* bookstore. It was a two-story affair, a creamy-yellow and white turn-of-the-century building with wood floors and red shelves filled with books. On the side of the building was a hand-painted mural, a street scene filled with people, art, even a turquoise Buick on the left. The town was clean, small, and the tourist season was just around the corner. Shane could feel Jack Benton's touch on this. Whether he had funded the purchase of the bookstore, or just known what strings to pull, he had made sure that Lila would be somewhere she could be happy.

He stood back, across the street, half-hidden by a tree, eyes on the building. The wide windows let in plenty of natural light, and the dark green doors were welcoming. For the past two hours he had watched people go in and leave half an hour later with bulging bags of books. Finally, as the sun slipped below the horizon, the foot traffic dwindled and then stopped altogether. The streetlamps flickered on, and the smell of the sea washed through. In the distance he could hear the clickety-clack of a train moving past the railyard and away from the sleepy town.

Would she even want to see him? It had been more than six months after all. Lila Benoit was now Annie Brewer, a bookstore manager who rented a room just blocks away, kept to herself, and led an unexceptional, and rather bookish life. Ever since Morris Endon, Lila's former boss and the president of Kurgen Real Estate had been found hanging in his jail cell, things had been quiet. It had been ruled a suicide, at least by the local papers. There would be no trial, but with Jack's help, the Witness Protection Program still applied. He had pointed out, rather astutely, that they weren't able to prove that Morris had acted alone. In fact, the chances of it were unlikely, especially when you figured in Detective Stone's murder, which was still unsolved.

Jack had made good on his promise. Shane's last assignment had weighed close to four hundred pounds, had two teenagers and a wife that hated him, and guarding the family had meant holing up in a cabin in the desert with majestic views of sagebrush and a sagging wire fence that disappeared into the distance. It was the closest to nature any of them had been in years and had involved endless sniping. Shane was tapped to eradicate the invading vermin, sixteen rats, four scorpions, and too many spiders to count. By the end of it, he had been close to doing for free the job the crime boss in New York was willing to pay seven figures for.

He waited until he saw her approach the front doors, before he crossed the now-deserted street. She froze, in the middle of flipping the sign from Open to Closed, and locked eyes with Shane, a look of shocked surprise filling her face. She smiled then, a slow, sexy smile, and his doubts disappeared. She opened the door and he walked inside, following her as she drew him inside, out of view of the front door and windows. The building didn't have an old-book smell, not at all. Instead, his nose detected citrus, a hint of summer just a couple of months away, a heady, bright smell that promised sunny days and sparkling sandy beaches.

He looked around. The ceiling was high, maybe twelve feet, and there was an airy open feel, despite the number of books crammed onto bookshelves. Half of the bookstore was already in darkness. Lila followed his gaze, a look of pride on her face. "The first thing I did was paint the walls a light color and add more lights. It's slow right now, but the summer draws a lot of crowds and the cafe in the back courtyard will be a great draw. It will serve breakfast and lunch and coffee, of course." She frowned. "I've been forbidden to touch the coffeemaker."

He snorted. "Probably for the best. You nearly killed me with that nuclear waste you made that first night."

Lila laughed. A full-throated, peal of laughter. Shane couldn't help but laugh too. She looked great. Her demeanor was relaxed, not surprising now that she was safe from men trying to kill her. She had shed the smooth, professional look and swapped it out for a more down-to-earth, relaxed look. Her hair was cut short, in a bob, and she was dressed in a jean skirt and a scooped T-shirt that read, "Careful, or you'll end up in my novel."

She noticed his glance and grinned. "I'm writing an erotic thriller."

He stepped closer. "Does it have a good-looking bodyguard in it?"

Her lips curved into a sexy, wicked smile. "Sexy, bad boy, a bit of a controlling jerk at times, but really great in bed."

"As I recall, we never actually made it to a bed."

She laughed, and she looked happy, capable, and sexier than he could have imagined. She grabbed his belt buckle and pulled him against her, "Why start now?"

Her lips met his with a hungry abandon, without hesitation, her delicate fingers warm through his shirt, sliding around his waist, wandering up his spine. She tasted sweet and he breathed in a rush of her musky vanilla scent, and reached out to steady himself, one hand at the small of her back, the other against a pillar. He reached down further, cupped her tight, firm ass in his hand and lifted her up, pinning her between his body and the pillar. She gave a breathless moan, one that grew louder as he broke away from her mouth and moved to her left ear and began to work his way down her neck. Her nipples pushed against the thin fabric of the T-shirt, and he took hold first of one, then the other, leaving the T-shirt wet, his teeth nipping, his tongue licking.

Her legs wrapped around him and she pulled her shirt off, leaving only a lacy bra between them, and slid her hands under his shirt, tugging it out from his waistband, desperate to remove all obstacles between them.

"I was going to ask you out to dinner," he said, pulling back for a moment.

Lila ignored him and slid his shirt off his head. "Dinner sounds wonderful. I know this fantastic Thai restaurant." Her hands were unbuckling his belt and tossing it aside before focusing on his fly. She grinned at him lasciviously. "Help me work up an appetite."

A woman after his own heart. He chuckled, then leaned down to kiss her deeply, tongues entwined, slipping her skirt off, and hooking her panties with one finger. He pushed her against the pillar, his breath warm on her neck, one hand cupping her ass, the thumb of the other hand exploring her wet slickness. She gasped and moaned again. He moved his fingers into her, slipping past the damp panties, teeth nipping at the soft flesh of her earlobe, feeling her body tremble in his hands.

"Come for me."

She shook her head, her breaths coming in gasps. "Not until you are inside of me."

Shane didn't have to be told twice. He let her guide his way, her hands warm, urgent, as they stroked up and down his shaft, pushing, pulling, and then wrapping her legs around him as he thrust into her. She arched her back, one hand on his chest, the other on the pillar behind her holding on, alternately tightening and relaxing the muscles, until he was sure he would go insane. He thrust, again and again and again, and her cries of pleasure as she met each thrust were intoxicating. He could feel the waves of orgasm coming towards them, a tsunami of impulses and bliss rushing his way. Lila moaned louder, faster, and he slid in and out, desperate to bring her with him.

The bra straps had slid down, as had the fabric, and he leaned in, taking her left nipple in his mouth, thrusting as he sucked, nipping with the next thrust, staving off the rush of orgasm, waiting for her moans to come closer together.

Seconds and centuries, there was no difference. Not in the moment that the wave came crashing down and the multicolored bombs exploded behind his eyelids. A rush of orgasm unlike anything he had ever experienced scorched his neurons and Shane felt it through every inch of his body. A second later, Lila let out a cry, shuddering in his arms, her eyes closed and mouth open in ecstasy.

They slid to the floor, still entwined, a slow descent to the wood floor and the clothes they had scattered there. She lay against his bare chest, skin moist, a strand of her hair tickling his lips.

Shane groaned. "Oh, my God."

Her soft, breathless giggle tickled the skin on his chest. "I'm strongly considering chaining you up in my office in the back. I could visit you every day, multiple times in a day if you like."

He snorted. "Chain me up? Hell, if it is like that every time, you couldn't get rid of me if you tried."

She sat up, straddling him; one small breast had escaped from the bra and he found himself staring at it, mesmerized. And despite having had the most satisfying orgasm ever just moments before, his dick was waking up, hardening again, eager for an encore.

Lila leaned closer, smiled, her lips slowly curving up. "I'm ready for you to take me out for dinner." On cue her stomach rumbled and they both laughed. "After that," she said as she reached down and caressed his chest, "I expect dessert."

Hours later, after dinner and a walk back through the quiet town, they finally used a bed. As Shane lay there, sweat beading his skin from an encore that proved even better than sex in a bookstore, Lila laughed quietly.

"I actually had a dream about you last night. The first in months that didn't include being shot at by assassins. I can't help but think that some part of me knew you were coming." Her finger drew lazy circles on his chest.

Shane couldn't help but notice how well she fit against him, as if she were made for him. The curve of her hips, her body molded to his.

"You're going to give me a swelled head."

"Really?" She reached down and stroked him. "And here I was worrying that it might be all worn out."

A laugh rumbled from his chest. "Give me a minute to recover and I'll show you different."

"I don't doubt you would." Lila propped herself up on her elbow and stared at him. The lightning lit up her face and he could see she looked serious. "I have a good life here, Shane. It's simple, no frills, but I love it, even more than I thought I would."

"I can tell." Shane waited for her to say it, knew it was coming.

"I guess that, in a way, this life is better than my old one. I miss Kaylee, and a few friends from my old life, but I love this town and running the bookstore. After six months, I feel at home, more than I ever did in Kansas City. At least, not since I lost my mom." She paused, broke eye contact, stared at her fingers. "Thank you for coming to see me," she said, grinning, "and for some mind-blowing sex, but..."

Shane reached up, tucked her tousled black hair behind one ear, and finished it for her, "But where is this going?"

One tear glistened in her eye. "Yeah. Just so I know where I stand with you."

Shane kissed her softly on the lips, "I'd like to stay, if you'll have me. Fair warning, though, Jack will call, probably sooner than we are both ready for, and I'll be off on assignment."

"Protecting some other sexy woman in a rambling safe house? Lila asked, a touch of jealousy in her voice.

Shane laughed, "Are you kidding me? Jack has made it his mission to give me all of the assignments involving three-hundred-pound ex-gangsters with bitter wives and entitled offspring. It's been hell."

Lila giggled, "I like Jack more and more every day."

Shane heard the low buzz of his cell phone and sighed. He had hoped for a longer break than this. He had to wonder if Jack knew exactly where he was.

He pulled out his phone, thumbed it off silent, and logged in. There was a text from Jack.

Maine is stormy this time of year. Your next assignment is waiting.

"Shit." At this rate he was going to be on the top of Benton's shit list for the next decade. It was worth it, though. *She* was worth it. He typed a reply to Jack.

I'll be in L.A. tomorrow on a red-eye.

The response was immediate. *Nope. Tonight. Private jet waiting at airport. Sending Uber now.*

"Shit."

Lila's smile dropped. "You have to go."

"Yeah. But I'll be back. That is, if you want me to."

She nodded, "You'd better." She kissed him deeply, hungry for more time and they sat there in the darkness until he heard a car pull up in the drive and a moment later a door slam. It was time to go.

Headlights lit up the front door as he opened it. "Hey, did you call for an Uber?" The kid was young, acne covering his face. He stood there impatiently on the doorstep.

"Yeah, that's me." He turned back to Lila who had followed him, wrapped in a white robe. "I'll see you soon."

She stood up on her tiptoes and kissed him deeply as the teenager gawked at them. "You will come back, Shane Ellis, or else I'll have to come and find you and drag you back."

Shane didn't want to walk away. In that moment, all he wanted to do was stay, right here, with this mesmerizing woman. Lila made up his mind for him. She gave him a push, "Go on. Off with you. I have to work in the morning."

He walked away, conflicted, and got into the Uber. It was time to go to work, but all he could think of was Lila. He groaned as he thought about Lila, alone in the bed, waiting. He only hoped that this assignment would go by quickly. He would count the days until he returned.

Author's Note

Thank you for reading this book. *Hired Gun* is my first foray into romantic thrillers, but it won't be my last. Next on the list is *Steel and Smoke*, a book centering on Jack Benton, a billionaire and the founder of Benton Security Services. An excerpt is included on the next page.

I hope you will now take a moment to write a review on Amazon. As an indie author, I can tell you, reviews are essential to my success! They don't have to be in-depth, just 2-4 sentences about the story and what you thought of it can really make a difference. Potential readers will be able to read your input and decide whether the book is worth their time. Besides, while writing a book tends to be a lonely endeavor, reviews help buoy my spirit and encourage me to continue to improve my craft. Your opinions matter!

Learn more about Shane Ellis and how he became a bodyguard and began working for Jack Benton by reading *Better Choices*. It was the most unlikely of beginnings! You will also receive updates when new books are released. I send out a monthly newsletter that summarizes all my work - with non-fiction organizing tips, short stories, news on upcoming sales/free book giveaways, and so much more.

Join my subscriber list by going to:

https://mailchi.mp/c05ceb84e66a/subscribe-me and receive *Better Choices* for free!

Note: Your email address is always kept private and never shared!

Now, turn the page to read the excerpt for *Smoke and Steel...*

A Voice from the Past

Present Day...

"**I** love you, Jack." The feel of her body nestled in the crook of his arm; her soft lips captured in his. The ratchet of a nail gun in the distance jarred him from his sleep. His dream evaporated, leaving behind an emptiness that compressed his heart. It had been more than five years, and a dream brought her back as if it were yesterday.

The sun barely lit the horizon, creating a hazy indistinct glow through the large picture window on the far side of the room. The latest wildfire, now contained, had trapped pockets of haze in the valley. A decent wind and heavy rain would deal with that, but Mother Nature seemed loathe to cooperate. The air quality remained poor, and Jack had been forced to limit his daily run to the treadmill inside of the house, where the air filters cleaned the quality of the air and smoke didn't burn his throat or redden his eyes.

He sighed, stretched, and glanced over at the other side of the bed. He didn't miss Tiana and he certainly wasn't dreaming about *her*. A few months of fun, but not worth the pettiness or bullshit mind games. He wanted something more than just a pretty body by his side. He rubbed his hand through his hair, thinking of Kaylee. The softness of her skin, how she had felt in his arms, it hung in the air.

Maybe I want too much.

In all of his life, only one had captured his heart. And she was half a continent away and likely had forgotten all about him.

Jack sat up, tossed the covers off and stood. The haze was driving him nuts, the people in L.A. were driving him nuts, with few exceptions, and he thought about going somewhere, anywhere, to get away for a while. A thought that was quickly discarded as more basic needs made themselves known.

In the opulent marble bathroom filled with stark colors of black, white and gray, he stood in front of the mirror, critically examining his reflection. His hair was no longer black streaked with just a little gray. It was now predominantly gray, streaked with black. His father had been the same, as he recalled, the color gone by the age of forty, even if his face had remained youthful. He wondered briefly how Dad would have looked today, some twenty years older.

Jack ran his hand over his stubble and then slipped on his running shorts. He'd get in a run, then shower and shave before Azule showed up. He shook his head thinking about his assistant, she had been worrying over some investments that had tanked, and wanted to talk to him first thing about Benton Security Services. Azule's mind was a formidable weapon, one she wielded on a daily basis. He wasn't sure what she was going to say, but he knew something was bothering her, it had been for weeks, and he dreaded the conversation they would have in a few hours.

He left his suite and made his way down the curving staircase to the main level. He pressed a panel in the wall and walked through it to another set of stairs leading down to the basement. The door closed soft and silent behind him. The basement was comprised of a completely self-sufficient living space which included three bedrooms, each with their own bathroom, a kitchenette, and a large living area. One of the bedrooms had been converted into a workout room. There were no windows, nothing to even indicate that the house above *had* a basement. And it had served its purpose well a time or two in the past. It was quite literally a panic *suite*, rather than a panic *room*.

Malcolm was still asleep, not that he expected anything different, his baby brother never varied from his routine and that meant that he had at least an hour before Malcolm would emerge from the furthest bedroom and head upstairs. Plenty of time for him to get a workout in.

Jack stretched first. He could feel the muscles tighten around the scar that ran along his abdomen, a curve of white, silvery flesh that wrapped around from the left of his belly button into a long, upwards curve towards his back. No matter how many years had passed, or how much he had continued to work his muscles, tone his body, the scar tissue still gave him twinges. It was a permanent reminder of his failure to keep those he loved safe.

As he reached for the weights and ran through his reps, toning each muscle, slow and steady, he could think of nothing else. It was the dream that had started it. It had certainly set the tone for his morning.

Jack shook his head, hoping to physically shake out his thoughts of her. It did no good to think about it, no good to miss her.

He stepped onto one of the two treadmills and pressed the preset for a punishing five-mile trek, his feet stretching as the treadmill rose in height. It wasn't the same as being outdoors, pounding down one of the trails outside, but he also wouldn't be gasping like an asthmatic in less than ten minutes. The air quality remained poor, thanks to the wildfires and haze that filled the air.

Two hours later, Jack sat in his office across from Azule and wished he had followed that brief, waking desire to flee Los Angeles.

"Benton Security Services is over-budget by nearly one hundred thousand in the past six months," the large, buxom woman declared, her full lips pressed tight, disapproval written all over her face. "It doesn't make good business sense."

Jack leaned back, folded his arms against his chest, unconsciously mimicking the woman across from him. "I understand that, Az, but..."

"But nothing, Boss. You can't run things at a loss, not in this economy, and not if you want to stay rich. Benton Security Services is hemorrhaging money and your other investments aren't keeping up."

Jack hid a smile. Azule was a financial wizard, among other business savvy talents, but she was rather one-minded at times. To her, if the money wasn't growing, then it was in danger of heading the other way. As it was, he could overspend twice as much, for the rest of his life, and still never see a significant decrease in his overall worth. No one, not even Azule, was privy to all of his financial dealings. The fact that it bothered her, however, was exactly the reason he kept her on.

"This is a project I'm willing to take a loss on."

Azule scowled at him, her rich dark skin showing frown lines around the eyes as she contemplated what to say next, whether to argue further, before shaking her head and rolling her eyes. Was she appealing to the heavens to save her from the clutches of a mad white man with far too much money and not enough sense? Jack wasn't sure, but he couldn't help but grin when she threw her hands up in disgust.

"Have it your way, Jack." Her eyes narrowed, "Where's the mantiquer? I haven't seen her in days."

"Mantiquer?" Jack asked, laughing.

"You know who I'm talking about."

"Tiana?"

"Right, her."

Jack couldn't stop laughing, "Why did you call her a mantiquer?"

Azule sighed, rolling her eyes so hard he saw the color disappear into white, "Women like that don't want you, they just want your bank account. Guaranteed she was with a couple more on the side. Hope you wore your pelvic poncho when you were tapping that."

Jack threw back his head and guffawed, the sound filled the room as he rolled the words around in his head.

Guaranteed, "pelvic poncho" is a term I won't be forgetting anytime soon.

The phone rang then. Not the one on the desk that Azule insisted on answering, but his private cell, which only a handful of people knew of. Jack reached into his pocket and pulled it out, his eyebrows rising as he saw the 816-area code. He didn't recognize the number, but there was only one person he could think of that lived in flyover country, and he was the one who had helped get her there.

He pictured her face as he stared at the phone. It rang again, insistent.

Azule looked at him curiously, but said nothing, her eyebrows raised.

How long had it been? Four years? Going on five? Not a single call, no emails, nothing. The silence had been complete. It had felt like a death. It still did.

The phone rang a third time and he pressed the green button, bringing it up to his ear, "Jack speaking."

"Hi Jack." Her voice was the same, unmistakable, and one that he couldn't forget. His heart beat faster, and he could feel a warmth spreading through him. It was as if she were here, standing next to him, and her unique scent, of honey and vanilla, filled his nose.

"Kaylee." He breathed her name out, his mind a whirlwind of emotion, and Azule's eyes crinkled around a smile, one that looked almost victorious. She nodded at Jack, and then stood, stepping out of the room and closing the door firmly behind her.

"I'm sorry to call you like this, but," there was silence and he could picture her nibbling on her lower lip, a habit she had tried hard to eradicate but one that was intrinsic to who she was. "I need your help, Jack. It's for a friend."

"Five years." The words escaped his lips, "It's been five years."

"I know." She sighed then. He could see her face, imagine just how she looked. Eyes closed, her face a mixture of sadness and regret. "I thought it would be best. For both of us. For Malcolm. I just wanted to forget my life from before and concentrate on starting over again."

Jack wanted to be angry. He had been. But now? He knew how afraid she had been, that the shadow of the Oladni Corporation, and of the darker force of the Indalo behind it, two forces that seemed too large, too overwhelming for them to fight. It was, after all, why she had been in danger in the first place. The Indalo had taken everything from her, and it had nearly broken her. She had watched everyone she loved die as a result. She had done it to protect him, even if he hadn't needed protection. If he didn't handle it right, she would rabbit again, and Jack wasn't ready for that.

"I understand." Saying those words felt like he was chewing on sharp glass. It was a lie. He didn't understand, couldn't.

"I'm calling for a friend," she continued. "Someone in need of protection. I think her life is in danger."

How long had he hoped for her call? And even if it wasn't to have her return to him, he couldn't help but take this small opportunity and run with it.

"Tell me more," he said, his voice all business. "I'll be happy to help."

Jack listened as she described the situation. Her voice sounded stronger, more self-assured, and he had so many questions. But they would wait. He listed off the main phone number, the one that would route through Azule and set a bodyguard detail into motion. The property there in Kansas City, Kansas would do as a safe house. It was well-stocked and prepared. He had made sure of that when he knew that Kaylee would end up living in the area. From the sound of it, Kaylee's friend was in dire need of it.

"Don't worry, I'll make sure she's safe." He promised.

The relief in her voice was unmistakable, "Thank you, Jack." She paused, then said softly, "For everything."

There was a click, the rapid triple pulse that indicated the caller had hung up on the end, and then nothing. Jack stared at the dark screen. *That was it?*

Azule was waiting for him to re-emerge, her long, ornate fingernails tapping away at the computer. She looked up, gave him an assessing stare, and stopped typing.

"Well?"

"Benton Security Services will be receiving a call from a Lila Benoit in Kansas City," he said, "Put Shane Ellis on it."

Azule nodded, scribbling the details onto a notepad. Then she stared back at him expectantly.

He shrugged, turned on his heel and returned to his office. As the door closed behind him, his steps slowed and he stared out at the thicket of trees outside his window. Like the rest of the L.A. hills they looked dry, desiccated by too much heat and not enough rain. El Nino was in full force.

Five years.

Just hearing her voice had brought it all back. His entire body was reacting. Even after all of this time, all that Jack wanted was to wrap his arms around her, press his nose into her hair, and feel her body against his. He was shocked by his reaction, but the thrill of connecting with her again helped him realize that there was a reason why no other woman had stayed in his life longer than a few months. This time, he was going to do something about it. *This time? I'm not going to just stand there and watch her walk away.*

Interested in reading more?

Book Two of Benton Security Services, Smoke and Steel *is coming in Spring 2021. To be notified of its release date as well as information on my other published books, subscribe to my newsletter by clicking:*

https://mailchi.mp/c05ceb84e66a/subscribe-me.

Acknowledgements

I couldn't have written this book (or any of my other books) without the faith and love of my family. Thanks to my wonderful husband, Dave, my daughter Em, our lovely foster daughter Little Miss, and of course, my parents and mother and father-in-law.

I was also lucky enough to go to an outstanding private high school that allowed me to pursue my love of writing instead of suffering through creativity-killing grammatical exercises – thanks to Dori, Rachel, and Kate for that – you saved me and allowed me to fly.

A shout-out to my friend and copyeditor, Kerrie, fellow homeschooling mom and awesome human being.

To my many friends and neighbors and supporters on Facebook, you keep me going (and often laughing) when I'm sure I can't write another word.

To my ARC readers, for your astute and timely feedback. Thank you so much!

And to everyone else, you know who you are. You are extra-special, in a good way!

About the Author

Fueled by homemade coffee ice cream, a lifelong love of words, and armed with strong female (and male) characters I cross genres like the Ghostbusters crossed the streams in pursuit of the question.

"What is the question?" you ask.

The question is simple. It asks, "What would you do, if..."

What would you do if you were fifteen years old and the world as you knew it fell apart? Would you run? Would you fight? Would you survive? – Meet Jess and her brother Chris in War's End[1].

What would you do if you had a chance to live your life over? Not just once, but twice? – Meet Dean Edmonds in Fate's Highway[2].

What would you do if everyone you loved was lost to a terrible virus and you faced the real possibility of the extinction of the human race in the dark void of space? – Meet Daniel Medry in G581: The Departure[3]

What would you do if hitmen were after you and you had no idea why? – Meet Lila and Shane in Hired Gun[4]

If I don't keep you turning pages late into the night, desperate to know what happens next, then I have failed at my job. I'm a Taurus and born in Missouri. That makes me bull-headed and stubborn to boot. I don't believe in failure or mistakes, only learning opportunities and clever conversation. There's not much I won't do to make you burn the midnight oil reading my words while you suffer sleep-deprivation the following day. It's my secret superpower.

---

1. https://books2read.com/u/bwYNpY

2. https://books2read.com/u/bPJG5Y

3. https://books2read.com/u/4jDgPl

4. https://books2read.com/u/bP0dOj

Born in flyover country, I've also lived in Arizona and northern California. I am an eclectic mix of snark and oddball humor. My colorful metaphors would make a fishwife blush. I'm an incompetent gardener, a dreamer and doer, in love with old houses and shooting pool, and chief organizer of all thing's household and financial. Feed me tiramisu and I'm yours forever.

Join my Facebook group at General Malcontent's Grumbles and Scribbles: http://bit.ly/3jo0MVU

You can also find the latest updates on my writing adventures at: http://christineshuck.com

Sign up for my newsletter at: https://mailchi.mp/c05ceb84e66a/subscribe-me

Follow me at:

Twitter: @christineshuck

Facebook: Christine.D.Shuck

Instagram: christinedshuck

All Published Works

Christine writes cross-genre and her books can be found in e-book and in paperback through most book distributors.

Non-Fiction:

Get Organized, Stay Organized – 2008

The War on Drugs: An Old Wives Tale – 2012

Fiction Series:

War's End

The Storm

A Brave New World

Tales of the Collapse

Gliese 581g

G581: The Departure

G581: Mars

G581: Earth (Summer 2021)

G581: Zarmina's World (Spring 2022)

Chronicles of Liv Rowan

Fate's Highway a.k.a. Schicksal Turnpike

Benton Security Services

Hired Gun

Smoke and Steel (Spring 2021)

Broken Code (Fall 2021)

Don't miss out!

Visit the website below and you can sign up to receive emails whenever Christine D. Shuck publishes a new book. There's no charge and no obligation.

https://books2read.com/r/B-A-BOLF-ABGY

BOOKS 2 READ

Connecting independent readers to independent writers.